For The LOVE Of STRANGERS

BRENDA NISKALA

For The LOVE *Of* STRANGERS

COTEAU BOOKS

www.coteaubooks.com

Edited by J. Jill Robinson
Cover designed by Jamie Olson
Printed and bound in Canada at Friesens

Library and Archives Canada Cataloguing in Publication

Niskala, Brenda, 1955-
For the love of strangers / Brenda Niskala.

Short stories.
ISBN 978-1-55050-425-5

I. Title.

PS8577.I75F67 2010 C813'.6 C2010-902575-X

10 9 8 7 6 5 4 3 2 1

Mixed Sources
Cert no. SW-COC-001271
© 1996 FSC
FSC

COTEAU BOOKS

2517 Victoria Avenue
Regina, Saskatchewan
Canada S4P 0T2

AVAILABLE IN CANADA FROM:
Publishers Group Canada
9050 Shaughnessy Street
Vancouver, BC, Canada V6P 6E5

Coteau Books gratefully acknowledges the financial support of its publishing program by: the Saskatchewan Arts Board, the Canada Council for the Arts, the Government of Canada through the Canada Book Fund, the Government of Saskatchewan through the Creative Economy Entrepreneurial Fund, the Association for the Export of Canadian Books and the City of Regina Arts Commission.

Saskatchewan Arts Board
Canada Council for the Arts | Conseil des Arts du Canada
Canada
Government of Saskatchewan
Regina
City of Regina

This book is dedicated to my mother
who may think she recognizes some of the people,
places and events in this book.
It's fiction, Mom.
I love you.

CONTENTS

Looking for Adventure

At 79 in the year 2042

YOU DON'T JUST DRIVE THROUGH A WALL OF fire, Kathy thinks, braking her GreenCar to a noiseless halt at the smoke line. Prairie fire flickers on both sides of the highway, the wind just enough to stretch the walls, to dwarf the workmen silhouetted on the edges.

How beautiful, this flame against the glory of the sunset, the living orange and scarlet shooting life into the sedate azure and crimson. Between sun and fire, the smoky black hole invites her to drive in, to drive through the flames. A form of vertigo, she had long ago determined, her troublesome draw to leap from balconies, to dive into waterfalls, to crash into the grilles of loaded semi-trucks. The big splash. Tempting, but no.

Joy and Andy, her daughter and son-in-law, will be frantic with worry at this delay. That could be relied upon, with the certainty of winter. Already Kathy hears the whispered conversations about her, the plans for her future that will, no doubt, one day reduce her to a simpering dependent begging for the chance to sit outside in the garden, for Christ's sake. But she is determined to drive to the last possible moment, although on days like today, her vision already smoky with the buds of cataracts, that thought is not appealing. And the delay will take her into nightfall, when her vision fades to almost non-existent.

So. So what? She taps out a quick text message: "I've been delayed," then programs a set of soothing flute music into the player, leans back into her contoured seat and prepares to spend the night entertained by the spectacular flames, the dancing sky to the north and west.

The smoke is pleasant, not overwhelming. It reminds her of grass-burning, the spring cleaning of the yard, and of the rich green undergrowth thickening after the burn. She remembers, too, the smokehouse where her father used to hang strips of meat or, after a summer at the lake near Deer Run, jackfish, trout, and whitefish, such a delicacy even now. But never as wonderful as jackfish fresh from the water.

Sixty years ago. A beach, a cast iron pan, fish sputtering in lard, a log rolled close by, where Kathy half-crouched near the flames of another, much smaller fire and Ron lounged beside her, his right thigh close to her left, his eyes on the fire, reflecting that light as he turned to her, kissed her neck just below the chin.

"Umm, nice," Kathy said.

"Very nice," Ron said, reaching over until they tumbled into the sand.

"Hey, the fish!" Kathy struggled to get up.

"Is cooking nicely," he murmured, his lips on her ear.

"I could stay here forever," she said, staring at the stars fringed by spruce on the shore.

"Nothing's forever," Ron said. "But when we're old we'll come back here and roll in the sand again."

Kathy pushed her hands beneath his t-shirt, stroking his smooth stomach, tickling the lovely valley of his pelvic bones. "When we're old, we'll need help getting up."

"Not me," he said.

The fish had burned to a cinder on one side but was wonderful, the best she'd ever tasted.

JOY AND ANDY HAD SERVED JACKFISH AT THE luncheon after Ron's funeral.

When she got the call, she had been in the midst of packing up her husband, Kevin's, things, having placed his ashes on the mantle over the fireplace only a month before.

"Mom," Joy had said, her voice breaking, "Dad's dead."

Strange. She didn't need to know how or why or when. Only that it was so. Ron hadn't been her only love, but he was her first, so sweet. Now that young, fierce and foolish part of her lived in her memory alone.

Kathy had breathed in and out slowly. "When's the funeral?"

And so Joy and Andy had accompanied her to the funeral, and now, six months later, they were to meet her at a place by the lake at Deer Run where the sand holds the ash of many fires. They planned to sit on a charred log, watch the sun carve a golden path in the calm face of the water, and sprinkle the contents of two urns – her first lover and her last – into the sunset.

She knows she will hug her daughter fiercely, and with only a little help, scramble up the bank to the clearing, leaving Joy and Andy to enjoy the evening and the sweet sand. She will insist on some time alone, and she will walk to the edge of the meadow, the place where a stone keeps the warmth of the day, where a person can lean, rest and remember, and perhaps, if she holds still long enough, the deer will come out for their twilight feeding.

She'd insisted on driving the four hours north to Deer Run alone. Well, not quite alone. She pats the urn of Kevin's ashes on the passenger seat. Joy and Andy will bring Ron's remains. If only they didn't worry and fuss so much. This could prove to be her last great road trip. Her last adventure.

Kathy watches as well as she can from the rearview mirror while the efficiency expert in the car behind her marches to the fire line. Not long ago that woman would have been her, doing the right thing, always keeping busy, never stopping long enough to appreciate the beauty of the world around her, to notice the loneliness of her own life. Kathy remembers how important it was when she was forty-something, to be in control. The marching woman is a mother. The shape of a woman betrays motherhood, no matter how many hours in the gym, no matter how long since the children have left home. The marching woman is trying to catch up, to make up for all the time she thinks she has lost, just when her mind and body are demanding gentler treatment.

Kathy no longer needs to control, assess or challenge danger. She has lived long past the awkward transition between lonely and happily alone, resistance and acceptance. She recognizes herself as a bloom, like the golden gaillardia, the purple prairie aster, the burning smell of ditch weeds, sweet and slightly astringent.

Her face is warm. She closes her eyes to the smoke, meditates on her vertebra, a yoga exercise to keep the pain away. Her focus is just above the lumbar when she hears a whoosh, the echo of old time rock and roll, and opens her eyes to see herself as a young woman, driving fearlessly toward the flames.

At 47 in the year 2010

CRUISING TO A SMOOTH STOP, SECOND CAR in from the prairie fire, Kathy slid out from the driver's seat of her sensible VW to see what could be done. The smoke would be difficult for kids or the elderly to tolerate. She made a mental note to tap on the window of the car ahead, where the granny leaned on the head rest, rather close to the billowing sulfurous clouds.

Right now Kathy was able-bodied and available to help, so she abandoned her car and strode to the fire line, her steps slowing a few feet from the men digging earth and throwing it on the creeping burn. Rakes and shovels, that's all. No fire boss, no cell phones, no helicopters, and no pumps for slough water.

The man closest to her grunted in effort.

God, it was hot.

He said, "Back off. If you have a shovel, bring it. Otherwise, stay out of the frigging way."

She never traveled without a shovel from November to April. It being September, she stepped back, focused on the profile of the workers, the contrast, the expressions of exertion, or was that exasperation? At forty-seven, she was well accustomed to people not taking her seriously, but she was also used to being in charge.

God knows she had to be. No one else will do it for you. She had raised Joy by herself, had pushed and clawed up the food chain, from farm kid to house painter, to university prof, for heaven's sake, although she'd abandoned that, in the end – too much bullshit – to work with the teenage kids at the alternate school.

The alternate school. Now there was an exercise in classroom management, in empathetic psychology. Her students were the outcasts of the education system. Life had thrown them a few rough curves, and often they'd had too little structure and not enough love in their lives. Some were rediscovering their culture, from Cree and Métis families lost in the urban shuffle. Borderline kids.

Kathy's job was to draw them out, and she wasn't afraid to ask for help. When her friend Anna entered the room for her weekly class visit, the air changed, became thick and almost smoky. They would all settle cross-legged in a talking circle, and the ones who wouldn't look up or answer a question or even respond to their names would raise their heads, their hands, then their voices. Anna, Kathy's workmate on the painting crew, Joy's reluctant godmother, childless herself, had become the kokum, the grandmother, the Cree elder with street cred to this rag-tag group of teenage poets, artists, dancers and actors. For that is what they were, each and every one, so connected to the fire of creation that they did not fit into the analytical classroom, the math and science kingdom.

The ones who knew roughness best learned to care for the rats in the corner cage, the classroom cat, then the younger children, the weaker among them. The bullies became breakdancers, freestylers and drummers. The victims became singers, flute players and poets. Kathy's main job was to get them to breathe, to push them on the path from fear to joy.

Oh, she had failures, their eyes hardening beyond her reach, their despair an unlit tunnel to self-destruction. But she was able to catch a few, and turn them gently into fighters, into lovers. Fighting for themselves. Loving themselves.

She was heading back to teach, after a wonderful summer with Kevin, her new man, who lived and breathed his work in the oil patch but could afford to take a couple months off to just be with her. It was like playing house, with none of the complications relationships had in the past, with none of the urgency of making a family or a home. Joy and

Kevin's twins, children from their other partners, were all grown up and on their own. Kevin and Kathy each had homes. They had each other. And their work.

A whoosh of flames where a clump of tall grasses suddenly caught made Kathy step back in spite of herself. Kevin had told her about wild fires, how a single spark could explode in an oil well, as if the earth shot liquid flames into the sky. Adrenalin rushed through her, a hot flash, and she made a mental note to call Kevin from the next town. Whenever she was able to drive on. Damn this delay.

She was eager to get back to work. September was tough. Always new kids, new problems. There would be a few familiar faces, those who had been with her last year, who knew the routine, to form a core out of the chaos. In fact, she missed them. And she missed Anna.

On the last day of school before this summer's break, Anna had joined Kathy and twenty students for a class party wiener roast in the park.

"You know, our ancestors believed that fire was a living thing," Anna had said as she squirted a generous swirl of ketchup over a crisp hot dog. "And a powerful friend. In Cree culture, fire is part of ceremonial life."

Two of the boys, Roger and Sam, nodded vigorously. They had been fire keepers at a wake and considered themselves experts. Roger pulled a knife from his pocket and cleaned the bark from a green poplar twig, sharpening the point carefully. "When we kept the fire, we had to stay awake all night. They told us to make sure it didn't go out. It was our job to keep the spirits from the doorway where the wake was going on." Where their mother's body was laid out. "Around midnight it was kind of scary."

One girl muffled a giggle. Kathy smiled too. It was difficult to imagine the street fighter frightened.

Sam squinted up at Anna from the fireside where he roasted yet another hot dog, and said "When we helped at the sun dance, we had to keep the fire going outside the lodge for four days. It was hard work, too. And we got to watch the elders' helpers prepare the smudges – sweetgrass, sage, all sorts of stuff."

Kathy backed away from the small group around the fire, allowing them to talk more privately with Anna, and waved another of the boys over to her car, parked beneath the spreading aspen on the park trail. "Would you help me with this, please?" she said.

He helped her pull a three foot, hollowed log from her trunk and they carried it to where the students gathered. The bark circumference of the log was zig-zagged right through in random patterns.

Sitting down beside it, Sam followed the patterns on the log with his fingers. "What's this?" His brown eyes met Kathy's blue.

"In Finland, where my father came from, on the longest day of the year some people light a fire in a log like this and burn it all night long," Kathy told them.

"You going to do that tonight?" Sam asked.

"Of course," Kathy said.

Anna glared at Kathy, one of her old warnings. Kathy knew what it meant: are you asking for trouble? "So now, if you see a strange flame at my house tonight, you'll know why."

"And if you see an out of control fire at her house tonight, you'll know why," Anna said.

"I guess it's my turn to be a fire keeper," Kathy said.

"You'll have to be, I think," Anna said. "I think we all have other plans."

So that night Kathy lit her first midsummer's log. She had simply wished to show her students a bit about herself, about other cultures, but maybe Anna was right. Perhaps she should expect trouble. Kathy tried to keep lookout all night through the front window of her bungalow, while she sipped wine, read a thick paperback, and enjoyed the beginning of summer holidays. The log pulsed eerily at the end of her walkway, a humble glow by midnight, mere embers by morning. When she went out to check it at six a.m. she found a small turquoise pendant shaped like an arrowhead at the base of the log, and three cigarettes. When she wasn't looking, her students had been by.

On the dash of her car, just above the CD player, Kathy kept the photo she'd taken last June, the twenty smiling faces, glowing a bit by the dusky light of the fire. Anna waved shyly at the camera, like a child. How many of them had made it through the summer? It wasn't a question of returning to school, it was a question of survival. How many of her students would she see again?

Kathy fanned thick smoke from her face and marched back to her car. She would stay out of the frigging way, but she would record this fire too, damn it, for posterity. Her digital camera captured the whoosh of the growing walls and the highway, their dark centre. She made another mental note: obtain email addresses and send copies of the photos to the granny, the mother in the compact car behind her – God, it wasn't that long ago she was there – and even the blonde in the old powder blue bomb, but no, that would be difficult, as it looks like she's going to pull out of the line and pass. Kathy committed the plate number to memory as the blue car virtually flew into the turmoil of smoke and flames that represented the rest of the road north on #11 tonight. Would there be uncertain travelers waiting on the other side?

At 23 in the year 1986

FLAMES, DUSK AND NO WAY TO CALL HOME. This is the kind of situation a mother always fears. Kathy twists from the driver's seat of her Toyota, to check on her baby. Joy's sound asleep, but she would wake up soon, would need to eat and would sense her mom's fear. Kathy pops in a cassette of soothing lullabies, adjusts the volume and hums along, an attempt to soothe herself. She hates this delay on the road to her childhood home, but she hates fire more.

She remembers her father's firm instructions from the top of the Cockshutt combine as shoots of orange arced into the floor boards of the old Fargo one-ton:

"Run home. Now. As fast as you can. Run," he yelled. He almost never yelled. Eight years old and tall for her age, she could run. She tore down the field, her breath aching in her chest, muscles pinching in her sides. Every few yards she'd stop to catch her breath and check behind her. The fire had spread in the dry stubble. Dad had a shovel and his jacket, and was flailing one moment, scooping the next. He needed help.

She burst into the farmhouse kitchen. "Fire!"

Mom had already seen the smoke and was on the phone.

"Fire truck's coming and the neighbours too," Mom said. "Thank goodness you're not out there. You stay right here with me."

But the waiting, not knowing, was much worse than being out there. Kathy helped her mother make a loaf of salmon sandwiches and coffee with cream and sugar. They dug the peanut butter cookies out of the freezer and warmed them up. Everyone in the district turned out, the older women and youngest children dropped off at the house. Everyone else drove on to the fire, where Kathy could see them pull water jugs and spades from their half tons and race to where flames licked the machines and the tinder-dry wheat stubble. One of the neighbours rolled through the yard with his International 1066 and a twenty-two foot cultivator.

They had the fire guard in place and the flames stamped out before the fire truck arrived from town. "You'll have to pay for them coming way out here anyway," one of the neighbour ladies said. Everyone nodded sadly, realizing that it would likely cost the year's harvest.

"At least it didn't get away on them," another lady said. "If it had sparked the pasture, there would be no stopping it for a hundred miles." They all sighed dramatically, and exclaimed over their good fortune.

When the fire-fighting neighbours straggled back to the house, all blackened and dusty, Dad had Kathy go down into the basement and bring up a case of beer.

Now, as a mother herself, Kathy understands the urgency and relief in their voices. Gas tanks, grain dust, fire and children. Hello.

KATHY SWIVELS TO CHECK ON JOY AGAIN, THEN back to the flames.

Here on the main highway they don't have the manpower to put up roadblocks yet. They surely don't expect people to drive on through that smoke. Besides, there were already two cars stopped ahead: a sleek ultra-modern two-door and an imported compact, both gleaming in the reflection of the sunset, of the fire. No doubt the lady in the VW would soon find out more. She acted like one of those investigative reporters, pushing her nose right into the workers' faces and bugging them. Taking their pictures, for God's sake.

And the old lady in the two-door at the front of the line, right in the smoke, is she having an asthma attack or something? What if she's dying in there? Kathy will have to leave the car and check on the elder soon, but her first responsibility is her child. She turns to Joy, snuggled on the car seat in the double dusk, and spots a fourth car zooming up behind hers on this lonely stretch. A wild-haired blonde at the wheel of a pristine powder-blue Duster. Rock and roll booms into her child's sleep, but Kathy does not curse. Instead her lips move into a soft grin. Her eyes water, as they are prone to when she is sentimental, or overstressed or sleep deprived. That could have been her. Not that she'd do a thing differently. The kid's the most important person in her life. She has never loved anyone more. Perhaps she will never love that much again. There's nothing to be sad about. The wave of sadness intensifies as she watches the blue car disappear into the flames.

At 19 in the year 1982

Eight-track blaring, windows open, long hair streaming. Left foot on the dash, right foot pushing pedal to the metal. Hand-rolled cigarette burning, both hands beating, *looking for adventure.* Pushing this baby fast as she'll go. Five dollars in the gas tank, going 85 in a 60 zone, passing everything in sight.

It's the long weekend and she's still got a few hours of divided highway before the two-way traffic, then the washboard single lane winding through spruce on the road to the cabin at Deer Run.

She's packed for good times, going to meet Ron, her main squeeze, her love-love-lover. She's got tobacco, two cases of beer, coffee, a loaf of bread, condoms, and a couple of cans of beans. A sleeping bag and a cabin key.

She'd phoned him after work. He wasn't around. Never mind, he'll be there. He has to be. Looking forward to this hot weekend, just the two of them.

Work in small town Saskatchewan is kind of a drag. Oh sure, the job's great. The painting crew Kathy and her good bud Anna contracted with, doing this big project, means four months of excellent coin. It's so cool seeing new paint brighten the grey of Main Street nowhere, making it look like somewhere.

Anna, for the first time since Kathy had met her, in training at Women in Trades, is content, relaxed, has stopped looking over her shoulder every few minutes, scanning every room and parking lot, as if danger itself lurked, ready to knife her or club her or – it was like Anna says, you don't come off the streets and go white bread straight without a bit of adjustment. Anna is thirty-five, has survived twenty years of selling her body, and is strong enough now to want something different.

Kathy's hungry, so hungry to make more and more money this summer, *and* to live life to the fullest, after a whole year of university. Already she's strong from hefting bales over her head, hauling five-gallon pails of feed, although she struggles with the painting: stroke after stroke, perched on a ladder or scaffold, not stepping back or off. Wow, she's feeling it, while Anna, with her finely muscled brown arms, thrives.

Anna chooses to stay in small town nowhere for the weekends. "There are a few more coulees I want to explore," she tells Kathy, pointing with her lips to the open prairie, where glaciers gashed deep ravines into the table top. Kathy knows the terrain: places where creeks, even rivers and lakes, glisten beneath willows, where poplar leaves tremble, where deer startle from the buck brush, from the sweet green meadows, until they decide you are no threat, holding a stare, brown eyes reflecting a world of peace.

Part of Kathy wants to stay too, but she wants to see Ron more, is losing touch with Ron. After a week of painting and a fast drive back to the city she would often arrive at the rental house she and Ron shared, their home, to find the usual crowd still there. Had they left at all since the last Sunday? That's why this trip to the cabin, just the two of them, would be so brilliant.

Oh, their friends were good people. Creative, intelligent, interesting. Kathy knows if she were still going to university, she'd be partying it up with the best of them. It was just that now, when she has only two nights a week with Ron, she wants all of him. To herself.

Last weekend, Kathy met Ron's old friend Rosie on the steps as she lugged her backpack from the car to the house.

"They're all out there," Rosie said, tilting her head to the back of the house. Ron had built a fireplace where a dozen or so people could lean back on lawn chairs and watch the flames. Kathy groaned.

Rosie squinted her eyes at Kathy, her version of a smile. "We're talking politics, Blondie. Something you might as well get interested in, since you're sleeping with an Indian." Rosie is an eagle feather politician, and never lets Kathy forget their differences. She is probably good for Ron, as he rediscovers the culture he was ripped from as a child. Part of the scoop, he'd been jostled from foster home to foster home until he ended up in Deer Run, a safe place.

Rosie's a lot better for Ron than the likes of his former crew. Kathy met them too, briefly, and she suspects they'd been at the house once or twice when she wasn't there. Bad actors. Chuck, who claimed to be Ron's half-brother, had the empty eyes of a predator. Chuck let Ron take the rap for some B&Es up north, and since then Ron has had the sense to keep him at arm's length. Chuck's girlfriend, Sushi, has the street eyes of Anna, but with a speculative, conniving edge. Kathy shivers thinking about them.

Kathy inched past Rosie and into the house. The music was way too loud for early evening, even in the kitchen; cases of beer were stacked behind the door, a half-full bottle of rye stuck to the counter top, and the air was sweet with dope smoke. Which was fine for the student life. But. "Party politics, Rosie?"

Rosie grinned at her. "Face it, Blondie. If you're going to hang with this crew, you have to learn to go with the flow. Or fight," Rosie said.

"I'm not a fighter, I'm a lover," Kathy replied, and slung her backpack into the bedroom. She poured herself a drink of rye, a water for Rosie, who does not drink, and they headed for the back yard.

"Fight for yourself, girl. If you love, you're already fighting." Rosie pointed at Ron, oblivious, on the other side of the fire. "These men just love to fight." Rosie laughed. "Anyway, you're here just in time to clean up."

When she came around to hug his shoulders, it was all Ron could do to nod at Kathy through the smoke, to acknowledge her arrival.

Kathy hated being the bitch, but a girl's gotta do what a girl's gotta do. She walked over to the stereo and pushed the power button. "'Bye, everyone. I need some time with my man," she announced.

Ron gave her that blank *what the?* look as if she were somehow intruding. A stranger in her own home.

"Yeah, Kathy," he'd said finally. "I need to pass out for a while anyway."

Kathy knew the tough indifference act was for his guy friends, who would not approve of her being bossy, of his being pussy-whipped. And for Rosie. Rosie did expect Ron to be a fighter. But Kathy had to – well, someone had to be practical. Someone had to pay the bills. So she was working and paying the rent, and maybe he didn't like that either.

Kathy's eyes are watering now too. *What the?*

Harvest dust hangs heavy in the air. The sun, already huge and low, glows neon orange and pink in the striated sky. Smoke. No, not her Drum rollie. Over the rise, the flames vibrate, a red wall as intense as the sunset, the men on the ground dark silhouettes before the grass fire.

The men are trying to hold the line along the train tracks, which follows the highway on this stretch for at least fifty miles. The fire has jumped the road, creating a tunnel of flames.

"Shit! Oh wow." She tamps her cigarette on the ash tray, and eases her foot from the gas pedal. The smoke coming in from the ditches burns her nose, stings her eyes even this far away.

Three cars line the side of the road, as if there is a roadblock or an accident. She passes a Toyota wagon with a *Baby on Board* sign swinging in the back window. The mother on board has the overhead light on in the dusk and has turned around to meet her baby's gaze in that white glare. Through the window Kathy can see worry lines etch between the mother's eyebrows in the eerie light.

Kathy touches the brakes as the driver of the next vehicle, a forty-ish exec-type woman, marches toward the fire, camera in hand.

"God, I wish I'd thought of that." Kathy had left her Instamatic at the apartment. The roll of film from Christmas still had a few exposures left. This prairie fire would have been worth a snap or two.

An elderly woman seems to be asleep at the wheel of the two-door closest to the fire. Her white hair reflects the yellow-orange flames, a mad halo. Her face looks perfectly composed, perhaps a bit too much at peace. Kathy slows the Duster almost to a stop. That's how she wants to look when she gets old.

Whatever. They can wait out the fire, the three of them. Or follow her. Her right foot hovers over the brake for the time it takes to sail past and into the smoke. Her heart beating as loud as the bass, she tosses the end of her cigarette into the larger fire and grips the steering wheel with both hands. *Whatever comes our way.* She enters the tunnel of flames. Drives through the wall of fire. Nothing stops her. What the hell.

Stag Line

KATHY CAN HEAR THE VESPER BELLS RINGING from the safety of her room in St. Scholastica. Vespers service, the singing of the monks; side to side; answer to answer, was designed to soothe, to inspire.

The church windows illuminate the faces of the men, grace their dark robes with a patchwork of colour. At Vespers, monks intone well-worn, age-old answers, and in her head, only questions: what can she say to protect her girl? Can she trust her girl's father to respect and care for their teenage daughter? How can she live without Joy? Kathy walks past the snowy gardens, the steamy barns, towards the cemetery.

Snow blows in from the south, the last cold blast of the winter, bitter, invigorating, blinding in the expanse of prairie surrounding St Peter's Abbey. She'd made it to this safe place before the storm. The sparse and orderly convent rooms, opened by the brothers for people like her, were a luxury she'd sought out before, in distress, but now they shelter her contemplation. Her girl, Joy, was about to leave home, wanted to live with her dad, and the prospect of the sudden absence after fifteen years of just the two of them, was gnawing on Kathy's peace of mind. Could she trust her girl to make the right decisions? This was her last chance to help Joy negotiate the rocky ledge between group intelligence and her own good sense, between what Mom (or Dad) says and what she knows. Between what is natural and what is overprotected. Between what is natural and what is dangerous.

The girl is determined to live with her dad, but Kathy wants her home to remain a safe place for her daughter to come back to, a place for nurturing. Like St Pete's is for her.

Spruce sentinels line the road to the monastery graveyard. They sway with lodged frost. Between the rows, chickadees flit demurely. Kathy digs into her jacket pocket, among the clumps of dried tobacco, for a few sunflower seeds.

"Come here, my chirpy ones, come on." The small flock of birds swoop by, one by one. Then, as if they'd made a decision by committee, three vie for the privilege of perching their strong, achingly delicate feet on the edge of her palm. At first they each seize one seed quickly, then flee to the safety of the upper branches. Each eager landing and clicking as seeds are opened creates puffy blizzards, weather fronts in miniature. The chickadees elect now as a group to take turns pausing on her fingers, examining her with one bright eye, then the other, heads cocked thoughtfully. They dare to pick up two seeds. "Ah, you're getting greedy." She keeps her voice smooth and low, the voice she uses for all birds, animals, young children. They don't startle, would have made less than a handful of grey feathers had she decided to close, to capture. Less than a mouthful for her cat, which did not accompany her on this retreat, but would not have hesitated a moment in betraying their trust.

Would she have been able to forgive him? For only doing what was in his nature?

When there is something unnatural about chickadees coming to roost on a human hand; about the way these trees grow, little soldiers; about thirty men living in close quarters, peacefully, and without a woman's touch.

As if to argue the point, the branches nearby part, and one by one, a train of deer cross the road, trooping to the cattle barns, where a scoop of grain and bundle of hay is spread for them. Something unnatural, something wrong with deer being fed, when the winter should be killing off the weakest of them. Should be strengthening the herd.

A lovely stag pauses to study her, as if she were another tree, a large bird, a possible food source. She regards him as if he were a talisman, a message from the gods, a possible trophy. "Shoo, go on, don't you know people are dangerous?"

In nature the stags battle for ascendancy. One wins. The rest go off and hang out, practise fighting, look for new herds to conquer. Some go to monasteries.

As part of the herd, after a short rutting season, the females must nurture themselves, deliver fawns, nurture them, do all the laundry. Then, when they're totally worn out, they can lie down in the snow of the season's last blizzard, a grey cloud on the horizon; they can lie there and just not get up again. Or find someplace where they're fed. Where they're given a warm place to stay and are not expected to talk to anyone.

When Joy flies away, and begins a life making decisions without her or in spite of her, who will the kid trust when she's lonely? When she's found love? Every instinct in Kathy's body prompts her to tie Joy up in a sheltered place so she doesn't have to get hurt.

Before Joy leaves home, Kathy will tell her daughter how wild her mother was in her youth, naturally crazy and impulsive. Of course that's not really how it was. It couldn't be; wildness was not allowed. Her favourite question had been "Why not?," which was answered most often by one of her parents with "Because we said so." She would not do that to her daughter. No.

Kathy is hoping this weekend's contemplation will help her sort out her fears for her daughter, what to say to her. But it is also a chance to remember about being alone again. She hopes Joy will also benefit from some guidance from Ron. Does he tell Joy the same stories she does? About being young, about being in love, about knowing, trusting, believing, regardless of how the adults around you may or may not approve?

Every summer, after spending the rest of the year almost completely in charge of making the meals, maintaining the house and supervising her younger siblings while her mother helped out with the seeding, harvesting, the feeding of the animals, Kathy was sent to work at her grandmother's up north at Deer Run. Population six, except in the summer when the lake front exploded with action.

"To help out," Kathy's folks said. Working for Grandma, cooking for her and Uncle Merv, washing the walls, hanging out clothes, and hoeing the long rows of potatoes were the interlude, the lull between weekends when her cousin Diane could get away too.

Grandma did not approve of the use of make-up and provocative clothing on her grandchildren, but when cousin Diane was old enough to drive, what happened after her clunker Heavy Chevy left the farm yard was no longer under Grandma's influence.

The summer she turned fifteen and Diane got her driver's license was the hottest one ever. Wahoo! Even at fifteen, Kathy thought teenage girls sure did a lot of squealing when they got together, and she and Diane were no exception. The sounds they made matched the feeling in the throat, in the gut, that tingling mix of bravado and fear, a tentative battle cry in a dangerous world. After the very solemn walk to the car, after assuring Grandma they'd be back by 9:30 and careful near the water, they made a break for it, screaming and howling their way to the lake-shore, where they walked the firm tan and icing-sugar sand all the delicious evening, hoping guys would drive by.

"What'd you wear?" Diane asked, twisting around, her back against the car door.

"My t-shirt, what'd you think?" Kathy smiled smugly.

"No, dammit, what'd you really wear?" Diane insisted.

Kathy lifted her t-shirt to reveal a patch of bright pink bikini.

"Ooooh, shit. That'll burn their eyes, eh?" Diane said, suitably impressed.

"Wait till you see it. What about you?" Kathy asked.

Diane handed Kathy the wheel while she wrenched the neck of her sweater over her head. She wore a modest denim swimsuit top beneath.

"Man, I hope those guys in the van are there today. That dude with the long hair will sure want to get to know you," Kathy said. She wouldn't mind getting to know him either.

"So, maybe I'm not interested in those guys in the van," Diane said, having perfected the mysterious, aloof look.

"You sure were interested last weekend." Kathy's half-formed hopes of pursuing that flirtation flickered.

"That was before I met Victor," Diane said.

Man, Kathy hated being out of the loop. A lot had happened since last weekend. "Who's Victor?"

"He's not my *boyfriend*. We're just friends. We have a *mature* relationship," Carol said, trying way too hard.

"Sounds pretty boring." Kathy had never had a boyfriend, let alone a mature relationship.

"You can meet him at the dance, Saturday," Diane said.

"There's a dance? At the lake? Yeah, as if I could get out of the house." Kathy had never been to a dance with her cousin. "My folks would never let me go."

"Yeah, well, your folks aren't around. I'll cover for you, promise. Besides, there'll be all sorts of relatives there. It's god damn near impossible to say hello to a guy around here without everybody knowing," Diane said.

"So does everybody know about *Victor?"* Kathy asked. The level of restrained excitement exploded into a flurry of high-pitched squeals.

Diane led the way once the car rolled to a stop by the public beach. The two mile stroll, from one resort confectionery to the other, ran the gamut of lake-side delights from docks and bobbing boats, swimming spots and kitschy cabins, to a narrow tongue of undeveloped Indian reserve land and a fish plant, prickly with sawdust. Although it was early evening, the sand was warm between their toes.

"This looks like a good spot." Diane laid down her towel.

Kathy checked the area carefully. A bunch of little kids splashed in the shallows, but otherwise this stretch of the beach was deserted. "Okay, coast is clear," Kathy declared.

Sweaters and slacks were yanked off, in favour of revealing bikini-tops and barely-there shorts. They shared the tiny lipstick case mirror, applying and reapplying just the right amount of eye-liner, bronzer, and gloss. It was not easy to do without getting sand in the face.

There was a certain amount of magic to the ritual. From experience the girls knew if they simply walked the beach, nothing would happen. No one would appear. If they stopped, undressed, applied make-up, within five minutes of the snap of the compact, someone interesting would materialize. It had not failed once all that summer.

This time the van pulled up almost immediately. Four guys emerged, whooping as they dashed right by Kathy and Diane and into the water. They didn't even pause long enough for the girls to ignore them.

Diane came to her senses first. "Come on. Let's go for a walk."

For one gut-tingling moment, Kathy thought the long haired guy, who really was quite handsome, was waving at them. But no, he was splashing his buddies. "Let's go," she said.

They were almost fifty yards down the old lake shore road when a car slowed down alongside them; an old red bomb with a tangle of feathers on a roach clip dangling from the dash. A guy leaned out the passenger side window: longish fluffy jet-black hair, amazing cheekbones, blinding white T-shirt, the sleeve pulled over a pack of Players on a well-muscled arm. His eyes hid beneath black mirror shades. "Hello girls." His blazing smile was directed at Kathy.

Kathy knew nothing about pheromones, those lovely bursts of certainty, of chemistry, but she was hit hard. Although the girls marched away quickly, with only the faintest "Hi," her heart beat with the slap of her flip flops. She knew she would see him at the dance. He would dance with her.

It astonished Kathy how little resistance she and Diane met with from their grandma when they brought up the subject of the dance. They were careful to explain how they wouldn't be in until late, maybe after midnight. Grandma believed them, trusted them. Besides, Kathy realizes now, Grandma knew the hall would be full of relatives. She used to go to those dances too. These many years later, Kathy sees the likelihood of a besieged grandmother, way out of her depth. Until her own daughter's hormones clicked in, however, Kathy believed she had experienced some sort of sympathetic magic. Surely both things could be true.

Kathy and Diane changed their clothes several times in preparation for the dance. It was Kathy's first time selecting trapping gear for a specific person. Almost superstitiously, she didn't share her hopes with her cousin, in the event the guy with the mirror shades did not rematerialize. She didn't want to look too young, too loose, too uptight, and finally settled on a T-shirt pulled snugly, just thick enough to hide her nipples, and frayed jeans skin tight to the knees, deer hide purse slung across her breasts, fringes at her right hip, where she could knot the soft strings with her fingers.

She had to ask several times if she looked all right. Diane laughed. She had chosen her going-to-dances shirt, a Chinese-silk top that opened perfectly from the throat to just above the cleavage.

"This is just a weekend dance. It's not like it's our grad or something."

Kathy knew then, and she knows now that after that night, everything would be different. There's not much she would have or could have done differently, either.

The hall at the south end was never a ballroom, more often a location for farm auctions, but that night the dance floor was sprinkled with so much wax you had to watch how you walked. There was a slight haze across the room from the dust that rose through the cracks in the wooden floor, and from burning cigarettes. All the lights seemed to have haloes. No one turned the lights down, not even for the waltzes.

Kathy and Diane stayed at the back and watched the first few self-conscious couples move to the music. In the first set, the band played old time polkas and two-steps. Kathy wouldn't have known the movements even if he did show up. As if he'd dance to that kind of music anyway. Diane assured her that the beats would change.

The band, a local family and friends, wore shiny turquoise shirts crossed with white fake leather fringes. Their clothing matched the colours on the drum, which bore the name of the group: The Rythymeers. They knew their crowd, and soon every person in the hall over the age of twenty-one was out there gliding and hopping in mismatched couples. Some were dancing with children, as Kathy's parents once had done with her.

The girls hugged the back wall, becoming part of the solid stag line of teenagers. When asked to dance, Diane and Kathy consulted, and frequently invitations were declined. They were saving themselves for the right guys. And the right music.

The music changed from country to rock.

Victor walked across the hall and asked Diane for a dance. Kathy appreciated their bravery; the first teen couple up, moving stiffly, grinning, mouthing the words to *Bad Moon on the Rise.* The next tune was a slow one and Victor escorted Diane back to their spot at the wall. He was thin and tall, and spoke with a bit of a lisp, and Kathy caught herself mimicking Victor as soon as Diane introduced them. He quickly excused himself, and joined the guys outside.

"Oops, sorry about that," Kathy said. "I think I hurt his feelings. Didn't mean to."

"Nah, forget it. He's boring anyway," Diane said.

Kathy was beginning to wonder if her intuition had failed her. Her prospects of dancing with anyone but an uncle or an older cousin seemed pretty dim at this point, and was she that desperate? Most of the stag line had moved outside for tokes and beers. And then, well into the band's interpretation of "Smoke on the Water," just like in the movies, the wind seemed to burst the doors open and *he* was there.

He didn't wear his shades. His eyes were brown and wide, like a deer's. He hadn't seen her yet. On his arm, a blonde, easily a year older than Kathy, made her grand entrance, very comfortable with the many greetings she received.

"There's Judy, and that's Ron. Ron's that new guy, the one in the red car, Kathy, remember?" Diane said and moved towards the blonde, leaving Kathy alone against the wall. Kathy could not look any more, leaned back, clasped her hands together tightly so they would not visibly shake, and saw nothing but the floor for several minutes, fighting tears. He was with someone else.

Kathy sensed him before she saw him, then: the heart fluttering scent of patchouli, stale smoke, maybe whiskey, and the warmth of his body leaning on the wall beside her. She knew it was him without looking up.

Whenever her dad was getting ready to go out Kathy loved the firm thrum of leather soles on the lino, the buzzing of the electric razor, the scent of the splash from the small brown bottle with the deer's head on it. Dad's aftershave, always mixed with the sweet sharpness of the snort. It was a clean, exciting smell.

This was different. Ron's scent was more of a musky drift. It carried the thrill of something secret, forbidden. Something wild.

"Hi. You're Kathy," he said, leaning in close to her, speaking over the music.

Kathy tried to find something to say. "I saw you earlier this week, didn't I?" Great, how gorpy. Haven't I seen you somewhere before?

"I know. I was just cruising around, looking for babes," Ron said.

For babes? Was she a babe? Kathy wasn't sure whether to be pleased or insulted. She couldn't meet his eyes for more than seconds, stared instead at the blonde across the hall, seated now amongst a half dozen laughing people. *She'd* know what to say.

"And you're Ron," Kathy said, giving up trying to be witty. She was still staring like some dolt across the hall, partly because she wondered if she'd get killed up here, stealing someone else's guy, and partly because she couldn't look too long at him. He was soooo good to look at.

"Do you know Judy?" Ron asked, pushed himself from the wall and began to walk across the dance floor, but paused a third of the way. "Come on." He held out his hand. His hand was as soft as Grandma's, with a tough aliveness to it, as if it could as easily become a fist. He didn't let go, even when they were right in front of the blonde Judy, who by now had seen them holding hands, and was no longer laughing.

"Judy, this is Kathy," Ron said. Kathy studied the floor in embarrassment, and only then did she see the cast under the slit-open denim of Judy's left leg. Of course. He was just helping her up the steps.

"So what'd you do to your leg?" Kathy asked, and Judy let go that easy laugh of hers, so that Kathy thought she'd like to be her friend one day, and launched into a detailed account. Kathy wasn't really focusing on the story, though, as Ron's hand tightened on hers. Then Judy said, "Has anyone seen Richard?" She turned away from Kathy and Ron.

And then Ron and Kathy were dancing, a slow one. Touching. Kathy's arms around his neck, right there in front of all those people, in front of her cousin. It felt so right. The blood was high in Kathy's ears.

But Diane called her off the dance floor. She grabbed her by the arm, dragged her into the bathroom, helped her with her makeup, and warned her, sort of. Kathy felt like what boxers must feel like, head in a daze, focus deep in the body, being given a staccato of crucial advice: Ron was older, over seventeen, and had a bad reputation.

"What kind of reputation?" she asked, checking her hair in the tiny, cracked mirror.

"You know, with girls."

"Well, so what? I'm a girl, and he seems really good to me."

"Never mind that. Victor's invited the gang to a cabin party! You and Ron can come too." The girls shrieked. "Party!!!"

The cabin was just a few hundred yards down the beach, but everyone else drove. Diane jumped into Victor's car. "See you guys there!"

"Would you like to go for a walk by the lake?" Ron asked, and slung his arm around her waist. They walked as one animal. Every once in a while his lips would brush her ear, her neck. Every few steps they'd pause to kiss: soft, wet butterflies.

Booze and smokes, a dozen kids crowded around the kitchen table of the two-room lakeside cottage, a few more outside passing tokes. Victor had pulled some beer. Even before her first drink, Kathy knew where she wanted to end up: in the currently empty bedroom. She just wanted to be alone with Ron. Ron wanted to be alone with her too.

While everyone else was reaching for their second or third beer, and the conversation had set firmly in the rut of telling jokes, teasing, burps, and farts, Ron grabbed her hand. "Let's go somewhere to talk."

She and Ron drifted as one into the bedroom, she lay down beside him, and Ron rested his head on her belly where her t-shirt had pulled up, kissed her there. And they talked. Even that was too much. She drew fingertip brush circles on the satin skin of the inside of his arms. When his lips touched hers, when his whispering tongue was on her ear, she wanted to lunge at him with an energy she'd never before experienced, her body wanting to fit him like a piece of clay, to be part of him like a rib. Even through their blue jeans.

"You're really lucky, you know," Ron said, leaning on one elbow, his free hand feathering Kathy's cheekbones, her forehead. "Having so many relatives around, people who care."

Kathy stroked his hair back from his face. Hair soft as an angel's. "They're pretty cool," she said.

"Your cousin Diane stood up for me when I came to live here. This isn't an easy place to move to, you know. Strangers are only supposed to stay on the lakeshore, leave September first," Ron said.

"I've never lived here. My mother did. Right over there." Kathy pointed arbitrarily towards one of the cabin walls.

"I hardly knew my mother," Ron said. "When I

moved up here, I met my sister, but we don't really know each other."

"So you're alone?" Kathy spoke softly, thoughtfully. How could this be? Ron didn't speak for a while, and she pulled him down to her, hugged him.

"I'd really like a family someday." He spoke into her T-shirt. "More than anything else."

Kathy's breathing became heavy when his lips caressed her neck. "More than anything else, I want to leave the farm and go to university some day," Kathy said.

"I've never been able to talk to anyone like this before," he murmured, as she slung her leg over his waist, and pulled him to her.

Just then, Diane, a bit embarrassed and quite a bit drunk, appeared at the bedroom door. "Kathy, we'd better go home now, or else. S'late!"

"Have one more drink," Ron suggested, but Diane was not moving, stood in the doorway until they disentangled and stood up.

"Come on, cuz, we're already in deep shit!" Diane pulled Kathy behind her. Some people at the party stared when Ron and Kathy followed Diane out of the bedroom. One girl giggled. One of the guys said, "Another one bites the dust, eh Ron?"

Kathy's cheeks were hot, her hair tangled and a bruise from Ron's lips on her neck may already have been visible even in that dark room. At the car door, kissing each other's faces like puppies, Kathy started to feel the loss, the less than wholeness she would live with from that moment on. Diane started the car, and

Ron took a half step away. "I'll see you around."

Kathy climbed into the front seat with her cousin, waved a casual farewell.

"Well," Diane said, "What happened?"

"Not much. We talked."

"Yeah, talked. That's not what it looked like to me! But isn't Victor sweet? He invited everyone over, and bought us all beer, and –"

"So he's not that boring after all?"

"No, he's really funny! Do you know what he said tonight?" Kathy only half listened to Diane's recap of the night's adventures as the girls finished the last of their beer. Once or twice she glanced at Kathy sideways, half smiling, and half winking. Kathy listened quietly. This was the most luscious night ever, she thought.

They were almost at Grandma's when Kathy saw a deer, lit by the moon gleaming through a break in the trees. Antlers ablaze in the white light.

"Look! Look at that deer." As it turned, it flashed its tail, a sign of danger.

Diane turned to where she pointed, and then to Kathy, shrugging. She had not seen a thing.

So maybe it was a ghost deer. Nothing natural about it. Kathy always trusted her gut instincts, always believed in things she didn't have words for.

"I think my folks have come early to take me home," she said. She didn't think, she knew, just as strongly as she'd been drawn to Ron.

When they turned the corner into Grandma's yard, her parents' car was parked in front. The house was in darkness, but had that breathless feeling to it. As the girls stumbled in, smothering giggles, the ominous air of the waiting house sobered them. The chesterfield was opened and made into a bed. After taking turns in the bathroom, they rested like sardines on the narrow mattress.

Later that night, unable to sleep, Kathy struggled with the questions: Did he really mean every word he said? Is this love? Because they talked, did they now have a mature relationship? Over time, Kathy thought she had answers to each of these, but was still as unsure as she'd been that night.

Diane shook Kathy urgently. "Wake up. Quickly, goddammit. Before your folks get out of bed!" she said.

Kathy had only just fallen asleep, and was not cooperative until Diane hissed in her ear. "You'd better hide that hickey or the shit will really hit the fan."

Kathy's eyes were open, her hands immediately at her neck. "Is it that obvious?"

"Do bears shit in the woods? It practically glows in the dark," Diane said. By now, the girls were giggling. Kathy's dad cleared his throat from the nearby bedroom.

"Get into the bathroom, right now. I'll try to find some make-up."

"Or a turtle-neck sweater?" Kathy suggested, as she rose, headed for the empty bathroom.

"That'll look real natural. It's already at least seventy degrees in here," Diane said.

Of course Kathy failed in hiding the hickey.

Nothing hid hickeys. But at least there was only one visible. She breathed deeply and went into the kitchen to face the music. She was the last one to sit at the round, oilcloth-covered table.

All conversation stopped. All eyes swiveled to Kathy. "So, what time did you girls make it in last night?" Dad asked. Neither of them had been wearing a watch, could only guess. Everyone else knew to the minute. Diane busied herself, spooning out porridge.

"We kind of lost track of time," Diane, the bravest, said.

"And who the hell were you girls out there with? Don't try to tell us you were at the dance," Kathy's mom said, getting warmed up. "You girls were not raised to go partying around the countryside until all hours of the morning."

Some relative had seen them slip out of the hall, had made it their business to fill the folks in. Great.

"Pass the brown sugar, Mom?" Kathy said. She couldn't stand the suspense.

"What is that on your neck, young woman?" her mom asked.

"I, uh, got hit by a branch, out berry picking?"

"Don't you lie to me. I know exactly what you've been up to," Mom said.

Kathy blushed and lowered her head.

"And what about your reputation? What are people going to think of you, now, huh? How could you? Going on with that half-breed like a sex-crazed slut. Our family comes from this town, Kathy."

"You're not to go near him again, under any

circumstances," her father said. Often the arbitrator of disputes, this time there was no charming him.

"I don't know what you think was going on last night, but I didn't do anything wrong. And I had a wonderful time," she said. Her voice shook in defiance.

"Huh," Grandma said, and that was the last word spoken. Diane met her eyes once, gave a tiny smile, then lowered her head, too.

The rest of the meal was eaten in silence. No amount of sugar would make Kathy's porridge palatable. Finally, Diane excused herself from the table.

"You'll be hearing a few words from your parents on this too, Diane!" Kathy's mother said.

"Take me with you," Kathy whispered to Diane as she pushed away from the table.

"Are you kidding? We're already in big trouble," Diane said.

Kathy stood up and followed Diane to the door. "Diane?" Kathy called to her as she slipped out to the yard and her Chevy.

"See you next summer, Kath."

Kathy was taken home in shame, the entire three-hour trip a tight fist of anger, punctuated by tirades of rebuke and bouts of denial. Through it all, to the growing horror of her parents, Kathy was elated, firm in the opinion that what she had experienced was good, was natural, was somehow holy.

When Kathy tells her fifteen-year old daughter the story about how she met her father, she'll tell Joy she loved Ron from the first moment, wanted him, and that sometimes a girl has to trust herself, even if every adult around her is saying she's done something wrong. Sometimes the wildest thing a woman can do is believe in herself, in what she feels. Sometimes she may even, thank heavens, get a sign or two along the way to let her know she's on the right track.

The bells begin to ring at the Abbey. Not Vespers this time, but dinner. As she walks towards the dining hall, it occurs to Kathy that her daughter ought to come out here, to feed the birds. They will show Joy what Kathy is saying, free as they are to fly out where they wish, which can be tough; to come home, the one safe place, if only for a sunflower seed or two once in a while. She will be that safe place for her girl, will trust her girl's wish to know her father better, will be all right alone.

The snow feels like styrofoam beneath Kathy's feet, sounds like it too, brittle with a crisp, deliciously juicy rip.

When she opens the door to the dining hall, to her own silent table, the festival aroma of roast chicken, potatoes and gravy sends her on a spiral of happiness. Kathy has found a place of comfort, where no one is called down, doubted, judged. Here is her answer. Even the wildest person by nature could get used to this much respect once in a while, could come to trust it.

The Grass Dance

CHUCK'S LAST VISIT HAD TURNED OUT badly. Ron was still paying for the missing stereo, and the neighbours would remember the car that crunched their fence. Chuck always brought along his creepy girlfriend, Sushi, and Muddd, the driver and the muscle. Chuck always brought trouble. Ron would likely have to cover for them again.

"It's just a boring village, a sleepy hamlet, dammit." Ron had to raise his voice over the crackly connection, but he'd already let it slip that he had the house to himself.

"I'll be there in five hours, Goofball," Chuck said from the phone booth just out of the city. "Don't give me that boring shit. The ice is out of the lake and Deer Run is going to roar."

Ron couldn't argue with him about that. Some of the cabins along the shore were already lit up all night.

Okay, so maybe this one night wouldn't kill him, Ron thought. So much for his new start. God, it was hard enough being practically the only brown skin in town, without being the one to bring the trailer trash in. But it might be good times. Besides, Ron still owed Chuck.

So when the dirty red Mustang Muddd was driving this time skidded around the corner and paused in a cloud of dust in front of Ron's new home, he hopped into the back seat and leaned forward to slap hands with Chuck and Muddd in greeting. Sushi was curled under Chuck's left arm and didn't even acknowledge Ron.

"Brewskie time," Chuck announced. "Only one guy inside?"

Ron nodded and directed them to the local beer parlour, on the only block of Deer Run's Main Street. Shit, Kathy was there.

Muddd nosed the old Ford into the open stretch of gravel right in front of the bar. Ron rolled down the back window and half-waved at Kathy, where she leaned against the wall under the Licensed Beverage Room sign. Exotic in the pink glow of the neon, she did not look cheap. Just hanging out. Damn, sixteen and she knew the right way to lean against walls. He wouldn't have to wade through the usual pack of giggling girls to get to her. When he had to take off, she'd be cool, there would be no big scene, no last minute case of the clingies.

Ron's first impulse was to leap out of the back seat, run to Kathy, and hang with her. Then, remembering what was about to take place, he wished she'd just take off. Ron didn't want her to see this part of his life. He'd have to warn her.

Chuck dropped his arm from Sushi's shoulder and twisted his head slightly to follow Ron's gaze. "Your current squeeze? Listen, Moon Face, we're going to need you nice and alert out here. Don't fuck up or I'll cut your nuts off myself."

"Not to worry, Chuck. I'm with you."

Muddd yanked the keys from the ignition and tossed them. Ron caught the key-ring mid-air and opened the car door, his eyes focused on the swirl of dirty-blonde hair, the legs in frayed denim cut-offs. Kathy, the only girl in this resort town he'd like to date, lived a world away from Chuck's gang. Not that she was innocent, just clear of complications.

"Listen, if she's that good, why don't you bring her along?" Chuck didn't pass out invitations loosely.

"Yeah, so we could all try her out," Muddd said. Muddd laughed every time he opened his mouth, so you never knew when he was serious.

"Nah, Muddd, you're not good enough to eat her shit," Ron said, and slammed the door, mentally kicking himself. You don't talk to Chuck's right-hand man like that. Suicidal idiot.

But then he heard Chuck grunt, his version of laughter. "Just be ready and have the car in gear, Shit Stick. You've got about thirty seconds."

"Yeah, I hear you," Ron said. He caught Kathy's eye and she smiled at him.

Ron sauntered over, his heart pounding. "Hi, whatcha doing?" he asked, slung his hip against the wall and glanced towards the doorway as Chuck swaggered into the bar. Muddd and Sushi followed a deliberate several heartbeats later. It would be obvious to anyone watching that he and Kathy were too young to enter the premises.

"Waiting for my cousin," Kathy said. "You going to the dance at the north end tonight?" She whispered the words, as if she were too shy to talk. Her right hand caught a lock of her hair, the colour of dried prairie grasses, and she twirled it round and round her finger. Ron had a clear image of pulling that finger to his mouth, kissing her fingertip. He had to look away.

The getaway car gleamed hellfire red in the neon glow. Kathy was blushing. Maybe they could just go for a ride together. He had the keys.

"I'm not sure what's happening tonight," Ron started to say. "Do you want to –"

The bar door burst open, and they could hear a jumble of breaking glass and yelling from inside. Chuck, carrying four cases with some difficulty, ran straight to the car, calling, "Let's get out of here, Rat Face."

"See you later," Ron said to Kathy, touched her cheek, and leaped into the driver's seat. He wrenched his denim jacket from the back and threw it at her. "Here." As he pulled out, hailing stones at the front of the building, he imagined Kathy shielding herself with the jacket, her hand over the spot where his hand had touched her.

Chuck slugged him hard on the shoulder. "Around to the back, the back," he yelled.

Ron obeyed, his gut churning as if he'd just left a safe dock in stormy weather.

"No worries, man. They were so busy watching our floor show they aren't even going to miss these babies until next time they count bottles," Chuck said, stashing the beer flat on the car floor and covering it with the remaining jackets.

They pulled up just shy of the back door of the bar. Muddd and Sushi tumbled out the fire exit, Muddd pulling a handful of Sushi's white-blonde hair. Sushi had her nails firmly entwined around a hank of Muddd's mane, dangerously close to his face. Sushi was a distraction anytime, but she almost smiled as they completed their bar room brawl production. As the door swung shut, they disentwined and ran for the car, just out of the sightline of the bar keeper.

"Jesus fucking Christ, Muddd, try to be a little more convincing," Sushi said as she hopped into the back seat. "How many did you manage to get, Chuckie?"

"I ordered but neglected to pay for forty eight bottles of beer, free gratis, and courtesy of your friendly neighbourhood beverage room," Chuck said.

"Woof-woo," Muddd howled.

"That guy will remember you next time," Ron said.

"Easy now," Chuck commanded. "Let's get out of here." The car glided down the back alley to Ron's place.

It wasn't really Ron's place, of course. Ron had never had a place. He lived in seven different foster "homes" over the last fourteen years. He hadn't run away from this one.

His sister even went to Deer Run school, but she really didn't remember him from before, when they were a family here. At least he could be protection, would be there for her. "They think we look like Indians," she'd said to him once.

"Yeah, half." What else could he say? Kokum was gone and they didn't belong there on the res anymore, so they both avoided the reserve kids who came to school in town.

Chuck was as close to a brother as Ron ever had, a foster brother. Ron had new friends now, people like Kathy. In the city Chuck moved in a totally different circle from anyone in or around Deer Run. Chuck was the man. He had the connections, the ideas, and the drive to control the lives of others.

It was Chuck, flung into the basement bedroom they had once shared, who had helped Ron get away the last time. Chuck was a white kid in trouble with the law and Ron had a reputation for running, so the foster parents had taken special precautions – bolted the doors, barred the basement windows, locked away the shoes and boots every night. The bathroom was off limits after 10:00 pm., so they were given a pail for night events. Chuck had leaned over that pail, throwing up in dry-heaving, gut-wrenching sobs. When he stood up, Ron could see Chuck's lips were bruised and raw, and the sides of his mouth were torn.

"What happened to you, man?" Ron asked.

"You don't want to know."

"Shit, I'm going to call the cops on those bastards," Ron whispered, his effort at comfort.

Chuck shook his head slowly, and gestured towards the noise of men laughing upstairs. The party had been going on for hours, the regular Friday night crew. This week the foster mom wasn't home, and the old man had dragged Chuck up there. "Those *are* the cops," he said thickly. "I'm getting out, tonight." Then he grabbed Ron by the shoulder and yanked him out of bed. "You're coming too, kid. If I'm not here, it'll be your turn to play." He spat in the pail once more. "Let's go." They had nothing to pack. No shoes. The door had been carelessly left unlocked.

Chuck and Ron were old hands at running. The parking lot of the neighbourhood confectionery swarmed with kids who had nothing to do but hang out. Susan, as she was before Chuck named her Sushi, slouched under the Open 24 Hours sign, smoking cigarettes and scaring little kids with her vampire hiss.

Chuck made like he was going to go inside, then caught her eye. "Hey," he said.

"Hey, yourself," Susan said, swung her head away and then back at him. "Haven't seen you around for a few days. You been in a fight?"

"Yeah," Chuck said, moving to slouch beside her.

"Lost your shoes, huh." Susan blew smoke through her nose, a single exhale of a laugh. "Who's the kid?" She pointed at Ron with the burning ember of her Player's.

"My, umm, brother," Chuck improvised. "You got a smoke?" They had a cigarette together, watching the sad parade of late night shoppers.

Ron sat down on the edge of the sidewalk, brushing the gravel from his feet.

"We're looking for a place to crash tonight," Chuck said finally.

Susan stared at him hard, then glanced at Ron. "You can stay at my place. My parents have an old couch in the basement."

"Perfect," Chuck said, and they followed Susan home. Susan led them down the alley, through the junk-covered back yard of a tired-looking bungalow. The door was unlocked. She fed them some instant noodles and found some old shoes from her brother's closet. Ron slept on the couch that night, and Chuck slept with Susan.

Susan's parents came home late from the bar and slept in the next morning. They shrugged when their daughter came out of her bedroom with Chuck, but when Ron climbed out of the basement, they looked at each other, and Ron knew he was caught. He was too young to be inconspicuous, too brown to be acceptable in their home. Ron the runaway was still tying up his runners when the worker arrived. They were at their wits' end, she told Susan's parents.

Social services put him on a bus to Deer Run, where he'd come from as a child in the first place, twelve years before. Five hours from everything and everyone he knew. Placed in the care of two tough but caring old-timers who'd given him a home. That was two years ago.

Ron had arrived in the late fall. His new home was simple, almost humble. He liked how quiet the place was. A few pieces of furniture from the '50s were the most decadent part of the accommodation, his single bed at least a couple decades older. Calendars from various years decorated the walls. His new foster parents were seasoned, had had a few tough cases, and to his own surprise, he found himself working to earn their respect.

Tonight, the foster parents had left him in charge of the house. Chuck had stopped by with Sushi and Muddd to visit Ron here before, but now they had the run of the place. They could sit around the living room, guzzle a few cool ones, pass around a hoot or two, get primed for the night's festivities. Chuck sprawled on the only couch, pointing lazily with his buck knife at a stereo near Ron.

"How about a little music, Scuz Bag?" Chuck never used real names. Muddd was easy: mud in 3-d, the original primitive man, alive and in person. The name suited him. Susan, now Sushi, had black-ringed eyes and tight pale lips that emphasized an anger she seemed to thrive on, like a black hole, a negative in leather scowling from beneath Chuck's arm. Chuck complained about what a cold fish she was.

"Yeah, going down on her is kinda like eating sushi," Muddd said once, sucking in abrupt gulps of laughter.

"How the hell would you know?" Chuck had demanded in mock fury, striking his much larger, hairier buddy hard on the back. Chuck smiled then, and the name Sushi stuck. But Chuck never seemed to be able to settle on a name for Ron.

"Let's feel these floor boards vibrate, Ice Brain. After all, this stereo's part mine. If you blow a speaker I'll just have to see that it's replaced." Chuck grinned benevolently, licking the blade of his knife before replacing it in its sheath, which he almost always tucked into his boot or the back of his jeans. He must have copied the move from some movie actor. It always gave Ron the shivers.

Ron slugged back a bit of liquid comfort. "Come on, Chuck. This sound system is all the old geezers can afford. Give it a break."

"Yeah, your folks sure have poor taste, man. They replaced the one we liberated with this shit?" Muddd spoke quickly, holding in a toke, then exhaled, coughing.

"That old insurance scam only works if they have coverage, which they didn't, still don't, so lay off," Ron said, treading a thin line between loyalties. Chuck was glaring at him already.

Muddd was oblivious. "Maybe we should shop around for a better unit for them, huh Chuck."

"Fucking good idea." Chuck held the sliver of paper containing the last burning ember delicately between thumb and forefinger, breathing in through his teeth.

"Oh shit, Chuck. I wanted to go to the dance," Sushi whined, then added quickly, while Chuck held a lungful of smoke, "I suppose this means I won't get any time at the beach tomorrow either. Shit." She rubbed the full length of another toke across her lips, passed it to Muddd and, carefully folding the plastic baggie around the Zig Zag papers and the remaining joints, slipped them into her purse.

"Cops would never search a woman's purse," Chuck said. "Especially a chick like Sushi." Sushi looked at him disdainfully. "They're liable to get bit. Or hit," he added when Sushi swung her Mexican leather bag at him.

"Never mind the fucking beach. All those fat cat southerners, man. Their cabins must be full of goodies. While they're at the dance we'll have to check that out. Yeah, I think we'll do a little midnight shopping, Muddd."

"Screw this noise, I'm going back to town," Sushi said. She grabbed her leather jacket from the couch and the pack of Players from the coffee table, slung her purse over her shoulder and headed for the door. "See you next time, Ron."

"Wait!" Chuck said. He looked at Ron and Muddd in mock amazement, then tugged at his belt as he stood and strolled over to Sushi.

She waited obediently at the door, her entire body slouched in an overt expression of sarcasm. "What's this, you going to kiss me goodnight, Chuckie?"

For as long as Ron had known Chuck, he'd never seen him show affection to a woman. Sushi was a complete mystery to him, too: what she put up with and why. In this one respect, though, Sushi was like Kathy: she didn't need anyone, not even Chuck. There was nothing even vaguely clingy about Sushi. Guys like Ron and Chuck didn't want to have anyone needy around.

"You know what I want," Chuck said to her.

Sushi reluctantly opened her handbag and pulled out their stash. Everyone saw her palm a couple and slide them into the inside pocket of her purse before handing the baggie back to Chuck. "Mine. For the road." It would be a long, lonesome night out there with her thumb out.

"She's on probation," Chuck explained, as if she needed a reason for not being there. "If she gets nailed on a B and E –" he finished the sentence with a flourish of finger slashing over throat, and a small clicking sound. Then he turned to swat Sushi's backside but she was already out the door, her heels hitting the gritty sidewalk. It could have been the light but Ron thought Chuck looked disappointed, just for a flash.

MUDDD'S CAR ROLLED NOISELESSLY DOWN THE tree-lined lake front trail across the bay from Deer Run. It wasn't a good night for sneaking around. They could see each other's faces clearly. Dogs and kids played under the spruce, even though it was within an hour of midnight. But Chuck and Muddd were feeling no pain, Ron realized, and neither was he. They'd finished three of the four dozen beer and Muddd was passing Chuck another joint in the front seat. Ron was finishing up the last of his beer in the back. A thrilling mixture of terror and anticipation clutched Ron's gut. He wanted to crow, to bay at the almost full moon.

"OK, we grab the booze and cigarettes, so they blame it on the Indians, but we're really after wallets, purses, the big stuff." Chuck glanced back in time to see Ron duck. "What's bugging you, Shit Face?"

A woman walked the short path between her outhouse and cabin, her face clear for a moment in the break in the trees, and then in the reflection of moonlight from the lake when she stopped to watch their car drive by. She had squinty eyes, and one arm half raised. In the other hand she carried a pail. Ron recognized her from Deer Run. If he could see her that clearly, she might have recognized him. Chuck had chosen a line of modest cottages for starters. No security systems, cheap locks, easy pickings. They were going to be hitting people Ron knew.

"No problem, Chuck, just being cautious," Ron said. "By the way, I do have a name. Try saying it just once, Chuckie."

"Toughen up, Little Fart. Don't act suspicious. Never look guilty." Then, with a fierce sidelong glare at Ron, he said, "and don't abandon your post. Even if the girl of your wet dreams is spread-eagle on the sidewalk. If you're with us, no more of that taking-off shit. Got it, *Ron?"*

Chuck paused, then launched into one of his lectures, preaching as if he was Jesus or something, and they were his disciples. Maybe it was the beer talking, but Chuck's voice seemed just a bit edgy tonight, not as certain as usual. "You're never going to be anything until you can buy your way out of trouble. How many rich people you see in jail? It ain't because they're more honest. And man, with your report card and mine, we'll never be rich any other way. Besides, you love it, right? This is fun, man."

And it was. Ron found his half-formed idea of being an electrician or plumber, one of those men other people really do need, too simple and silly when he was with Chuck. Chuck wasn't talking a bungalow in the burbs. He already had the right contacts for sales and services of all sorts. He chose his people carefully.

"I figure if a guy is a good man, I mean a really good man, he'll keep his mouth shut, even take a fall for you, no problem," Chuck said. "And if he won't he's out."

Muddd cut the headlights and steered the Ford into the driveway of an A-frame, all in darkness, just off the trail. Chuck and Muddd were already working on the glass French doors when Ron, in a bit of a daze, tried the cabin door. It opened. He walked in quietly, and swung the window wide open from the inside.

"Come on in. Make yourselves at home," Ron said.

"Holy shit, don't you ever fucking do that again," Chuck whispered furiously, the anger barely hiding the astonishment he'd let slip for a moment.

Ron and Muddd turned away from him, snickering.

Ron did a slow wave with the flashlight over the interior. "Not much here."

"I don't get it. How do people afford a cabin like this, and then there's nothing inside," Muddd said from the kitchen as he rummaged through the cupboards. "No booze, no food, well, a few cans of meat and some macaroni. Shit, man, these guys haven't been here yet this year. Let's try another one."

Chuck said, "Just a minute. I want to leave my mark." He opened up the bed, cozy with quilts and woolen blankets, and pulled down his fly.

Ron ignored Chuck. "No TV no radio, nothing. Just a minute, there's a box under here." Ron pulled a cardboard apple box from the floor of a curtained closet. Inside he found toys: a sand pail, a bright plastic shovel and a worn stuffed bear. Muddd and Chuck were arcing spurts on the windows, the cupboards, the sinks. "Gonna piss on these too, boys?" Ron asked.

Ron felt a little stoned and quite drunk, but not in a good way. This wasn't fun anymore. Muddd and Chuck looked like little kids: sad, bad ones. Ron backed away from them and turned to the cabin's lakeside window. The water's edge was marked by a ring of lanterns and the odd square of interior-yellow light through patio doors all along the shoreline.

The neon sign above the dance hall was just visible across the bay. That's the place to be, Ron thought. He dropped the flashlight and was already out the door and half way to the dock when he heard Chuck call in a hoarse whisper. "Wellson, where the hell are you going?" He didn't answer.

If Ron could swim straight across the bay, he'd be at the dance before midnight. Kathy would be there. The pier was spongy underfoot, almost rotten, but he ran to the end of it and leapt off, flat-bellied to avoid the slippery rocks he knew replaced the sand here. The splash his body made sounded defiant, louder than any noise coming from shore.

Chuck's voice carried over the water, directionless but farther and farther away." What's that stupid half-breed doing? Go get him. Is he trying to kill himself or something?" Chuck was drunk enough, angry enough, not to care who heard him.

God, the water was so cold it was sharp. Ron flopped and flailed in the calm lake, then lifted his head up and kicked towards the golden moon trail across the water, the glimmer stone road.

"Stupid fucker! Stupid shit!" Chuck yelled, sounding genuinely sad. His voice echoed over the water.

Stupid fucker yourself, Ron thought. Those guys are so going to get busted, would be by now if there was a detachment within fifty miles.

After a few moments the water felt warm. It was good just to let go and float, kick a little. It was too far to swim. His shoes were going to drag him down. He would probably drown. Easy. Easier than all that other stuff he'd had to do. Like how was he supposed to keep Chuck *and* Kathy? Did he even want to keep Chuck? Or Kathy? Ah, he'd probably just lost both of them. Especially since he's been spotted in the company of suspicious strangers, linking him to the break-ins. All he could think of for a closing line was a stupid song. *Freedom's just another word for nothing left to lose.*

His breathing grew ragged and he gasped a couple times, big shaky sobs, his heart like a drumbeat in his head. He kicked a bit harder and headed to where he thought the sand bar began; he wasn't going to drown even if he was too beat to swim. He'd made it across the bay, which was still about five miles out of town.

When his feet finally touched earth, it was rock covered, that thin slice of wild shoreline: the reserve land. Every other inch of lake property on this end was lit with plastic lanterns cabin owners had strung on their beachfront decks, the water's edge carved up by wooden piers, boat ropes, canoes and fishing boats turned over, at rest on the white sand. Here, the trees and weeds were thick. Even if he were trespassing, no one would care; there was nothing here to protect from teenaged marauders.

There was only a single thin dark line; the path leading away from the shore.

He'd been down that path once, long ago. It wasn't used often. This landing for explorers, adventurers and survivors was the right place for him tonight. Even the branches of raspberry, wild rose and scrub poplar tearing at his pant legs and t-shirt seemed animated. His runners squished with every step. He was breathing hard, like some bog critter.

He could sure use a cigarette. Someone at the hall would have a dry one. It was kind of eerie out here in the dark, but sometimes Chuck was just too much. "I'd rather take my chances with the wildlife," Ron muttered, in case he wasn't already making enough noise to scare off any lurking bears.

The bush got thicker for a few hundred yards, just before a hay meadow. Across the meadow lived the family that drove the horse-drawn wagon. When he reached the open field the moonlight sparkled on fishnets hanging outside the tiny neat house. It was so much like his first home, the only home he'd had before moving back to Deer Run. Inside, it would be simple: one room, a table, bed, a couple of benches – maybe quilt-covered.

Ron was sober now, but he kept seeing things in the shadows: a pair of gleaming red eyes, a narrow face. Maybe he should sit down and take a breather. A large rock at the fork in the path still held some of the day's warmth where he leaned against it. There was something pounding in his head. *Pounding, like a drum beat. And powwow singing, high pitched, wailing it out.* Oh man, he was hearing things not real. The powwow grounds were over on the south side of the reserve. Only a few people lived quietly on this little spit by the lake. The sounds would not go away. *The grass dance prepares the ground for the rest,* Nokum had said. *It pushes the standing grass aside and down. It is the first dance.*

On a school trip years ago, while the other students ran to the activities room, Ron happened to glance at a painting and found he couldn't move away, he felt so good just looking at it. In it a kokum sat on the dirt floor of her single room log cabin, sewing a star blanket quilt. The open door let in the light, and a child stood at the entrance, looking away. There was something about that, the child looking away, something he wanted to remember: a place of no fear. No fear of being caught doing something wrong. No fear of not doing what you should.

You should was not part of being free of fear.

Ron stared at the painting with the kokum and

child until he started to feel dizzy. He had to go outside. As he left the building and cut across the grass, the pounding, the music and singing started in his head. An Indian guy with long braids, a fine black hat and fancy shirt passed him, heading into the building. When the door closed behind that guy, the singing stopped, with three sharp taps to the edge of the drum. Ron had turned around to follow the man, but when he got back inside the gallery, people surrounded the painter. The man's face looked open, innocent somehow; he was not attentive except in the most distant way to the pushy people around him. The music did not follow Ron and the painter there.

Another time, when Ron was on the run, cutting through back alleys in the old part of the city, he passed an elderly lady pushing a grocery cart from garbage bin to garbage bin. She wore a long printed skirt, a kerchief over her hair and a navy wind breaker. Her skin was bark brown and deeply wrinkled. He ran by quickly, always embarrassed by people like her. An insistent beat burst in his head, the drums moving fast as they did for the grass dance at the Deer Run powwow when Nokum took him there. He stopped, swung around. The old woman was smiling. She looked beautiful standing there with her cart. Then a car drove by. They both turned towards it and as they did, the music stopped.

There was no one around now. The house in the clearing stood in darkness, although the moon made the nets hanging in front glisten, magical star blankets. There, in the hay meadow between him and the house, a six-point white tail tossed its head, its brown eyes catching the mystic light. If only he had a gun. The buck didn't move. It knew he was there; it watched Ron.

Ron had learned to do this from Nokum long ago: he pulled the package of soggy Players from his shirt pocket, peeled the paper off one of the cigarettes and sprinkled a clump of tobacco on the light sandy earth at the edge of the path.

Instead of snorting and charging into the bush, the deer put its head down, sniffed the grass across the clearing, as if it knew a gift was being left, as if it too could hear the drummers.

He never made it to the dance hall. When he woke up, his back still leaned against the rock and his feet were numb. A mist hung over the clearing. He stood up, breathed in the sweet, pungent smell of dew on wild hay. Kids' voices echoed from the yard across the field, and he decided he'd better get moving. Those people wouldn't appreciate him sleeping in their meadow.

His legs found the rhythm of a song his grandma had sung to him; he began the long walk back to the main road, back to Deer Run: *Hey Hey HmmHmm Heya Hmmmm.* He remembered her, his kokum, sitting on a quilt-covered bench, hunched over a basket, braiding lengths of sweet marsh grasses.

"What a strong and brave boy you are," she had said, and something about being alone. His sister was gone, that's right, and Ron hadn't been strong enough to keep her and grandma too. They took his sister to the residential school. He was afraid he would never see her again. His chest hurt. Although he wasn't more than five, his kokum let him light a match and burn a little of the sweetgrass, while she sang, *Hey Hey, HmmHmm Heya Hmmmm.* He couldn't understand the words. He understood Nokum would be gone pretty soon too.

Now, as he walked, he felt something very big inside, as if pieces of his heart had scattered to many different places, to his sister, his long-dead mother, his now deceased kokum. As if part of him was part of everything else, *Hey HmmHmm Heya Hmmmm.* Ron stopped walking, stood by the roadside, a place as good as any, not part of the reserve, not part of Deer Run either.

He wanted to do something he hadn't done since he was a kid. He kneeled, crouched over, touching the sandy earth with both hands, then pushed himself, and rolled down the steep grassy incline, right to the bottom, to the ditch. There, flat on his stomach, he breathed deeply, peeking like a deer through the brush. Quack grass, dandelions, dock and reed grass covered him. Moss was soft beneath him and each pebble of gravel seemed to have a colour, shape and beauty of its own. He was not only part of this place, but part of all places, and all people too, even the dead, like Nokum. Another part of him was Chuck and Kathy and even Muddd, and he couldn't lose them now unless he forgot and lost himself. He had to remember always that he wasn't alone: his heart beat slowly, steadily; all around him the sweet meadow grasses, the smudge of earth.

Ron was still lying in the ditch at mid-morning, startled out of sleep by Chuck's voice.

"Hey you stupid fucker, where the hell you been?" Chuck growled from the open car window. "Get up and get in, before someone finds you and beats you up. You don't go sleeping in the ditches around here, man."

Ron felt as though someone else's feet walked up the graded ridge of gravel. He watched his body slide into the back seat. The car reeked of alcohol, stale smoke. "Care for a good morning toke, Tail Rot?" Chuck asked, waving a skinny joint in his direction.

"Not up to it Chuck," Ron said.

"So you sure missed some fine action last night. I tell you, those stupid pigs were so cheesed off." Chuck paused to light the joint. "And this animal, what he did at the dance, man you should have been there."

Muddd giggled.

To his surprise, Ron did not find Chuck and Muddd clever or tough or even reckless and daring at this moment. For sure, not threatening. Ron felt sad for them. "Holy shit." Ron exhaled. "I'm frigging cold."

"Here, man, the shirt off my back." Chuck pulled off his worn denim jacket with obvious effort and threw it. Ron pulled it over himself, and tilted his head towards the rear window.

"How about some music, Chuck?" Ron said.

"Sure thing, anything you say, Pond Scum. You don't run out on me again, you hear," Chuck said, the mixture of affection and malice in Chuck's voice exactly the same as always. It just didn't go down so well today.

"Shut up, Chuck," Ron said. " I got some thinking to do. How about a ride home?"

"Shut up, Chuck?" Chuck said. He shook his head in mock amazement. "And now he's thinking, Muddd. Thinking with waterlogged brain cells, yet. Listen, Shit Face, we'll give you a ride *home,* all right, but we're kind of on our way out of town for now. We've been cruising this loser resort all night, and things are likely to be a bit toasty here for a while."

Ron looked out the window. Chuck had the instincts of a fox. He'd never stay in one place long enough to get caught. "Just drop me off at the foster parents' house, okay. Chuck, you're like my brother, man."

"Right, but a brother doesn't run out on the man, man." Chuck pointed his joint at Ron to emphasize each word.

"I don't think it's a good idea for you to come up here anymore, Chuck," Ron said.

"Not a problem. You're not going to be here much longer anyway," Chuck said. "There's nothing in this wad hole worth staying for. Even your little girlie."

"Kathy?" Now he had Ron's full attention.

"Yeah, she didn't want to play with us either," Chuck said.

She'd ignored them, most likely. Or they'd left her alone. That was as close to respect as Ron could expect from these guys. "Things aren't like they used to be for me, Chuck. I've got nothing to run from anymore," Ron said. "I think I'll hang in here and see what happens. But don't you worry, buddy, nothing you've done can fuck it up."

Ron wasn't a bit surprised when the cops showed up at his foster parents' door that evening. Chuck and Muddd were long gone, and he didn't know where they were heading. Didn't want to know. He'd already cleared up the mess from last night's party, showered and left a note for the folks on the table: 'Some old friends came into town. We got into some trouble. I have been arrested. Don't worry. I'm sorry.'

At the signature rap on the door, he grabbed his jacket and stepped outside. The patrol car gleamed red in the glow of the sunset. Two officers, tense and watchful, stood on either side of him as he clicked the lock and pulled shut the door of his home.

"Ron Wellson?"

Ron nodded.

"We're here in regard to a number of events that occurred last evening across the bay and in the resort village of Deer Run. You have been identified as a passenger in a red Ford Mustang which was involved in several infractions. You are being charged under the Criminal Code with the offenses of Break, Enter and Theft, Mischief in a Public Place, and Causing a Disturbance. We must warn you, you have the right to call a lawyer, you are under no obligation...no promise..."

Ron didn't try to understand what they were saying and made no effort to respond. He walked to the cruiser, and stood silently by the rear door. He held out his hands for the cuffs, but the older officer shook his head quickly. The younger cop pushed Ron's head down and nudged him into the back seat. The patrol car door slammed.

They'd never catch up to Chuck and Muddd. The getaway car was stolen, Ron guessed, and abandoned somewhere between here and the city. And he had nothing to say. Taking the rap was his last gift to Chuck, a squaring up of an old debt. Now he was free.

His pulse beat was loud and rhythmic in his eardrums, and he could hear the singers, the high pitched wails. He pressed his face to his sleeve to wipe away some moisture, and caught the whiff of meadow grasses.

Between the Ditches

SHE HOPES THE BUCK BRUSH WILL STOP THE drifting, catch the snow, so thick now she can't see the intermittent yellow line that fades to black in most spots anyway. Glossy Buckthorn, alternating with Silver Buffalo Berry, forms shadowy stripes on the hills on either side of the highway, where introduced species invade the drifts of native weeds. Kathy knows the roadsides on the way to her home but today the narrow broken blacktop and its shoulderless ditches are changed by storm; eerie fingers reaching out, flurried bouquets of wet flakes blinding her as if all the elements have united to push her and her baby away from her parents' farm. As if accepting Mother's invitation required yet another test.

Even the short clipped grass marking the border between the oiled road and the ditch is obscured. She has to stop in this whiteness, wait it out, hoping no fool is zooming up behind her or looming out of it on the wrong side. She can't drive to the next field or farm approach, can't make it another hundred yards, she is so seasick in the white blanket of motion, in the wind that rocks the car. It's been over a year since she's driven these roads, the longest time she's been away since she left for university. The longest time she's ever been away. But it is crazy to be out here with a child. She tries not to remember the horror stories, the blue children, too weak to suckle, toes and fingers bleeding from the cold, the result of foolish parenting. Mother made an art form of reciting tragedies, and these come back to haunt Kathy now that she is a mother too.

The last time she was home, the family relaxed around the kitchen table, like they always did when she went for a visit, drinking coffee. Father and her brother had a deck of cards and a cribbage board out at one corner. Behind a pile of catalogues, Little Sis was writing out yet another order that would not be sent until next year's crop was in. Mother was glancing through the weekly paper. The supper dishes were done, and Kathy had to go back to the city tomorrow, back to classes. University. They'd been so proud.

It was now or never. Everyone was there, talking, half paying attention to whatever was in front of them. Kathy was twisting her coffee cup round and round on the perfectly clean arborite. "I'm going to have a baby," she'd said, and immediately took a lukewarm gulp.

The moment expanded like an intake of breath, as if someone had put a stop-motion hidden camera behind her eyes, as if her father's *fifteen two and the rest won't do* would never be pegged, his hand suspended over the cribbage board. The paper slid through

Mother's hands to the floor, and Kathy's brother breathed out heavily. "Oh boy," he'd said for all of them.

"Are you crazy?" Mother said.

"No, pregnant."

"My God, what have we raised here? Just when you were doing so well. You haven't told anyone, have you?" Mother asked, pausing to look around the table. No one else seemed prepared to speak. "And who's the father, that Indian I suppose?"

"Ron and I aren't together anymore." Kathy's voice was soft and calm, a perfect camouflage for the blinding flurries within. "I'll be a single parent, I guess."

"A single parent! Do you know what that means? Do you know what any of this means?" Mother brought her fist down on the table.

There was more: everyone had their say. Kathy watched their lips, knowing they were asking questions, and when she didn't respond, asking each other. The voices around her seemed to rise and fall, *what will you do? ...she support a baby?...neither black nor white and belonging nowhere...* and Kathy was in a shelter of some sort, where she could see them, but couldn't quite hear, wasn't quite able to feel, couldn't react.

THE MOVEMENT OF THE CAR, THE LOW VIBRATION of the wheels and the hum of the motor lulled her little girl to sleep as soon as they hit the road, but now, pulled over to the ditch side, they're pummeled by bursts of wind. The heater fan screeches. She'll have to get that fixed. It's a sound she usually can't hear on the road for the wind coming through the crack in the broken side window. Her eyes are burning but she continues to stare, mesmerized by the swirling snowfall.

She's hit the ditch on this road more than once. The first time, she was a bit drunk and watching the freezing slush slide wetly across her windshield, following it until her wheels lost their grip. She'd been there until the morning when visibility cleared, and another car stopped, the driver mercifully checking inside, where she was huddled, her legs and arms like cardboard, no longer part of her body.

Another time, when she was speeding down these back roads on the way home, she heard, no kidding, heard someone from the back seat yell *Hit the brakes. Now!* She did, and over that dip, she skidded in front of a dead end sign, over one of those steep-edged coulees with the deep slough at the bottom of the drop, like a buffalo pound. That time no one else was in the car.

And then there was the time she hit the ditch deliberately.

But she didn't do that to herself anymore, lose control like that.

She and Ron were out at the campground, where they spent the summer nights, under the stars. It should have been a romantic evening, but she was late, and Ron had already had a few beers, belligerent in the face of her tardiness. He was leaning over his truck box, pulling out the axe for firewood when she pulled up.

"Hey," Kathy said.

"You took your time getting here." He didn't turn his head or acknowledge her arrival; he was completely focused on the stack of wood on the ground by his feet as he set up the first log and swung back.

"I was at the doc's," she said, leaning on her car nervously, wishing she could orchestrate this better.

Thwack! The axe split the birch cleanly. "Mmmhmm." Another log set up. Thwack!

Kathy caught him between axe swings, held his arm firmly. "I'm going to have your baby, Ron!"

Ron's eyes widened in alarm. He pulled his arm back. Thwack. "Sure it's mine?"

Kathy doesn't remember getting back into her car, skidding out of the park and onto the access road, deliberately aiming the fishtailing car past the edge of the road, into the steep drop-off to the valley below. The thud of the front tires indicated the car had been airborne. Miraculously she did not roll it, but steered into the incline, the automatic pilot of the experienced driver. When she braked, gritty clouds flew in front of the car and caused her to cough through her weeping.

Ron's truck was right behind her. He ran to her window. "Are you all right? Are you crazy?"

Kathy rolled the window down a crack. "Yes." She pulled away from him.

Yes, she was exhausted, and yes, he was half cut, but Ron's reaction to her pregnancy betrayed everything Kathy believed about a lover – that he would be loyal, that he would not be blaming, that he would be ready to adapt to change and survive. That he would be as thrilled about new life as she was.

Kathy frowns, bites her upper lip, and glances at Joy in the car seat. Her baby, her Joy; even when she causes pain, to look into that perfect face, those lips pouting now in some suckling dream, is a fierce pleasure.

When Joy was born, Kathy mailed her folks a birth announcement and a tiny photograph, the one they take in the hospital. Still no response from home. Hell, even Ron had been there for the birth of their daughter.

The labour was complicated. Kathy was enmeshed in a grotesque octopus of cords and belts and clips and monitors, all indicating distress. Baby had been in the birth canal way too long. Kathy leaned over a kidney dish, twisting awkwardly, dragging a half-dozen tubes and beeping instruments with her as she heaved to her side, puking up the last bitter drop of fluid in her system. Now the doctor and nurses were consulting with each other – they'd given up talking to her hours ago – but she could hear words like anesthetic and caesarean. She'd been on the drip, chemical inducement that stimulated crushing contractions in her abdomen, for sixteen hours.

"Is there someone we can talk to? Do you have any family nearby?" a nurse asked, leaning over her, simultaneously conducting a tug-of-war with the kidney dish. Kathy knew she wasn't done with it. The nurse knew it was in the way.

There was no one to call. No one they could talk to. "Does it have to be family? I guess you could try the father." And that's how Ron came to be in the delivery room, taking charge even as he was gowning up.

"How can she do her work with your electrical toys everywhere, even inside her!" Ron said, and to Kathy's amazement, she was quickly freed of the internal and external monitors, the intravenous, the hated belt. Ron placed his warm hands on her stomach. "You're going to be fine, Kathy. I'm going to make you some tea, and then we're going for a walk."

Minutes after the tea, after a few short steps around the delivery room, Joy was ready to arrive.

Perfect, except where the internal monitor had pinched her head. Kathy had immediately fallen in love with her daughter's sweet-smelling skin, her eyes so black the pupil and iris were one. Her fine black hair whorled to a peak on her round skull. Skin the smooth tan of her father. She looked exactly like Ron.

Ron stayed long enough to watch Kathy try the first feeding. "That wasn't so bad, was it?"

"Bad? They called you in to sign for me, Ron. They'd decided I was not capable of consent to my own surgery. They wanted to slice me open!"

"But they didn't. And here you are. Isn't she a joy?"

"Sometime you're going to have to tell me how you knew what to do back there. Thanks for coming to help."

Ron's eyes were locked on the baby. "Can I hold her?"

"Sure, of course." Kathy pulled the nuzzling lips from her breast and set their baby in his outstretched hands.

Ron cradled Joy in the crook of his arm. "She sure smells good." Ron's eyes shone. Kathy could almost swear there were tears there.

She touched his sleeve. "So. Any questions?"

Ron passed the tightly wrapped bundle back to Kathy. "No," he said stubbornly, reluctant. "No questions at all." He slumped out of her room. He hasn't seen Joy since. Or her.

The moment she even thinks about feeding Joy her breasts became bricks attached to her chest, and she can feel the drip of milk, wet and cooling in ever larger circles, staining the layers of T-shirts and sweaters she wears to ward off the cold. Never get your breasts cold. It only has to happen once; you bite your lips in agony as the sweet needy mouth pulls at the nipple. Think about something else.

She'd finished her classes, found child care for Joy, trained at Women in Trades for the skills that might pay enough to put herself through the rest of her degree, managed. Alone.

And now, finally, Mother has phoned. "I guess we should have a look at that baby of yours," she said. No apology, no questions like how have you been getting along? How have you been supporting yourself the last twelve months? How was your labour and how is the baby? Just a catch in her voice, as if she was trying to remain friendly, reasonable. "Come on out, we'd be glad to have you for a visit." Not to stay long, of course. Not to run into any neighbours, or advertise the fact that her child had a kid out of wedlock, that her daughter gave birth to a mixed-race child, that her girl is a university drop out.

The wind howls. How can Joy sleep through this? God, she looks like Ron; the short straight eyelashes, the delicate curve of the upper lid. She will learn about her father as she grows up. Kathy will pass on everything she can remember about him.

Only once had she taken Ron to her family's farm. She should have called first; she usually did, but she knew how it put Mother into a dither whenever she brought anyone along, and this time, she had just wanted everyone to be natural. There was no way to prepare them for Ron, but she picked her time, on a day both she and Ron had free of classes and work, and at mid-day, when Father would be in from the fields and her brother and sister still in school.

"Mother, Father, this is Ron. He used to live in Deer Run."

Father stepped forward to shake Ron's hand.

Mother stood a few feet back, with a dishtowel twisting in her fists. "Yes, we've *heard* about you." As if some terrible rumour had been going around. "You're from the Deer Run reserve, aren't you?"

"No, from town," Ron said.

"Oh," Mother said, and bent over to scrub a spot on the cupboard.

Was that good or bad? Kathy worried, watching Mother's face.

"Come on, sit down," Kathy said. She tugged at

Ron's arm and pulled out the chair *company* always sat in, at the head of the kitchen table, close to the door. Ron pushed his back flat against the chair back, his hands resting on the red vinyl between his knees.

"You're living in the city now, then?" Father asked.

Ron nodded at Father.

"So, what are you doing with yourself there?" Father was halfway to the stove. "Say, would you like a coffee?" Coffee was always on in case a neighbor dropped by on the way to or from town.

"No thanks," Ron said.

Oh no, Ron, please take the coffee, Kathy thought. You don't refuse coffee.

"Tea, if you have it," Ron said. "I'm taking sciences, working my way through university."

Good. Sciences. They'd understand that.

"Tea," Mother said, abruptly.

"Here, I'll make it." Kathy leapt up to fill the kettle.

"They must be pretty pleased on the reserve, you getting educated and all," Father said, as he took his usual chair at the table.

"He's not Treaty, Father," Kathy said.

"My father was white," Ron said.

"From around there?" Mother asked, too eagerly. She wouldn't sit down.

"I don't know." Ron seemed undisturbed as the inquisition took an awkward break.

"We have a cabin up at the lake," Father said, pushing his coffee cup towards Mother.

"That's where my family homesteaded." Mother managed to get an edge of defensiveness into even this simple statement, as she filled Father's cup, "But we never had much to do with the reserve."

"Where's the tea, Mother?" Kathy knew it would help if her mother kept busy.

Mother moved to the counter, deftly lifted a tin box from the lower cupboard. "Will you have something to eat?"

"We haven't had a thing since breakfast," Kathy said.

Mother automatically reached for the fridge door.

"You know, I was in the city the other day, and there was this Indian family in the store. They seemed so clean and well behaved. Not drunk or nothing." Father said, taking a sip of his coffee.

Ron glanced at Kathy, who winced.

"Well, isn't that good to see." Mother's voice had a righteous ring to it as she sliced a roast of beef. She was looking for an argument, and she was just getting warmed up. "Welfare putting you through, then?"

"Pardon me?" Ron almost choked.

"Is welfare putting you through university?" Mother asked, a bit louder.

"Mother, he already told you, he's working his way through." Kathy took a chair close to Ron.

"So where you working?" Father asked.

"Carpenter's helper." Ron said. "Interior renovations mostly."

Kathy could see Father melting. Nothing wrong with a man who works with wood, with his hands.

"In this day and age, you need an education," Mother said, pouring herself a coffee in the chipped cup on the counter.

"Ron is getting an education. Want to pour some of that, Mother?" Kathy leapt up and grabbed two cups from the cupboard, sliding them towards the teapot. Her mother poured almost reluctantly. Kathy grinned at Ron and set a cup on the table near his elbow.

"If I graduate, I'll be a geologist." Ron pronounced the word slowly, so the folks would understand. They understood.

"Bush work." Mother was rolling just-warmed doughnuts in sugar. "You'll never be around to see your family."

"I have no family," he said.

"And I hope you never do, with work like that." Mother's lips were pushed together tightly, her voice quavering slightly.

"Well, Kathy, so how are your classes going?" Father asked, turning away from Mother.

Mother didn't say another word through lunch. Neither did Ron.

"I want to show Ron the coulee before we head back to the city," Kathy announced as soon as she decently could.

"Your mother always like that?" Ron asked when they'd walked far enough away from the house, on the trail that led to the pasture ravine.

"Like what?" Kathy asked.

"You know, kind of mad," he said.

"Yeah, she's always like that." Kathy grinned at Ron. "Especially with my boyfriends."

"It's like she's brittle, or something, like she's ready

to snap." Ron reached down to pat the dog, which had followed them into the hills.

"I don't know what's bugging her, but it's not just you," Kathy said. "Although they didn't handle the Indian thing very well, did they?"

"Too bad I left my tomahawk at home." Ron half-laughed, and they didn't talk for a while. Kathy reached for his hand.

The pasture sliced a quarter section of the glacier-cut hills, the Coteau Range, high lands. Too rough to cultivate. This was where Kathy had played as a child, escaped as a teenager, gone for comfort as a new woman. Aside from a few cattle, the horses, (yes, the deer and the antelope) and the ever-present dog, it was a place where you could be alone, could really howl at the moon if you wanted to. And sometimes get answers from the coyotes.

Kathy paused at a badger hole, which had been undergoing renovations since her last visit.

"Wow, I don't remember seeing any of these around home." Ron almost poked his head in before Kathy could pull him away.

"Badgers aren't friendly to surprise company," she said.

"Like your mother?" Ron asked. They laughed, easy with each other again.

It was harder walking past the dugout, and they had to go single file, following the cow paths cut into the hillsides. She felt compelled to pick grasses and other plants, roots and all, as they walked, something she'd always done, as if by taking these with her, she could keep part of this wild place. She meant to transplant them, and sometimes did get them back into soil, although they almost never survived, certainly never thrived in the clay of her backyard in the city.

"Sometimes we see cougars out here, and eagles," Kathy said. "Used to be pheasants before the American hunters." A flock of ducks sounded an alarm from the dugout.

"Are we going to see anything?" Ron lowered his voice.

"Sure, but we'll have to walk quiet," she said.

"No bears though?"

"No bears, no wolves. Fox. If we're lucky, maybe a coyote," Kathy said, remembering them, like big dogs, trotting on the rise, always a bit torn between curiosity and fear, and the farm dog fretting; should she chase them or run away?

Kathy left the path, skidded down the steep cut to a trail barely visible in the tangle of willow. "Yeah, the cows have tougher hides than we do. This is my favourite spot," she said, taking two quick steps and leaping over a yard of cattle-trampled mud to a huge rock, which at the height of spring run-off was in the centre, and now rose from the side of a thin stream meandering lazy and green. Across the flowing water was a meadow as lush as any fertilized lawn. "Come on, there's room." She dangled her feet in the water, and patted the sun-warmed monolith.

"What's this?" Ron asked, crouching on the lichen-covered granite and pulling at the branches, twigs, the picked flowers she was sorting.

"I want to grow these," she said.

"They *were* growing. You know, before your family, the farmers, came here, it was like this all over. These ones you've taken, they're the fighters." He plucked a pale limp frond from her hand and pinched it a bit, breathing in the fragrance. "I like this one. It's always been here. The male sage. See, it's the tall one. Sticks out, like this rock. Female sage grows in clumps. It's better for you, Kathy, to clean the air, clear your spirit." Ron waved the plant in a circle in front of them. "I don't think you'll get either of them to grow in a pot."

Wild things, Kathy thought sadly, as he returned it to the clump of plant life and earth she'd collected. "That's what Mother always tells me too." Maybe Mother knew, but she expressed it as a hunch, a premonition. Mother had dreams so real she'd sometimes phone Kathy in the middle of the night. "Are you all right? I just had the most horrible feeling." Mother dreamed car accidents, thefts, always danger. Never things that had really happened, but things that could happen later: a baby out in a snowstorm, Kathy running after a deer.

Ron swung his arm around her shoulders. Kathy's face was shadowed by the overhanging willows, then by his face. "You know, I think there *is* room for both of us on this rock," he said. They were sheltered from a rising wind.

THE WIND HAS A SHRILL VOICE. THE GUSTS buffet the car, some so hard she fears the cracked windshield will burst. She turns on the radio, a low drone to cover the shrieking.

What was Mother like before the growth of new bodies in hers, before those seeds became part of her inner landscape, lush, invasive? She could have been a school teacher, a learned woman, but at twenty-two, she chose marriage, caved in to the avalanche of diapers soaking in steaming tubs, a career made up of the cast iron fry pan and simmering pot of peeled potatoes, the onslaught of dirty surfaces which she bleached religiously, daily, until her hands peeled and bled. Her world was the square box of a house on a farmyard, forty years of hard labour. A labour of love?

Mother has difficulty expressing love. So do I, Kathy realizes, tapping the steering wheel nervously, praying baby Joy won't have to be unstrapped, unwrapped, fed out here.

Joy's eyes are open, her pouting lips stretching to a baby's yawn. The road is visible in blips now. Kathy pushes the car into low gear and edges a bit farther down the highway. The tires catch on an icy patch, the spinning like the growl of an angry animal. There is a roadside service station just a few kilometres away, its tables stained with spilled coffee and embedded grease, where she can stop for a rest, warm up with a coffee, maybe clean up the toilet seat enough to sit there a while and feed her baby. The things she goes through just because her mother finally decides to call. Mother has never had to drive alone through blizzards. For all her frustrations, she's had a pretty safe life. Maybe that was the problem. Mother could have, should have had a few more challenges. Maybe she would have thrived on a bit of adventure.

Kathy still can't see well enough to drive safely. Low beam, high beam, it doesn't matter, the tunnel the lights make caves in on itself in the ebb and flow of the snow. She pulls over once again, judging her distance to the ditch by the crunch of gravel and brittle grasses at the roadside as she stops and slides the car into neutral. The constant movement of the snow mesmerizes her. She is so very tired.

Like a moving picture backdrop to a live play, she imagines her mother, radiant, walking out of the blustery white, wearing something flowing and flattering. Her face is smoother, youthful. It is almost real.

Mother, what are you doing out here?

Waiting for you. Come on out and see what I've been doing.

Ah, look, I've got my baby in here, and it's too cold, so how about you show me from right here, Okay?

Look, here's my latest; it's very unusual. I've been working for years trying to get just that colour.

Mother holds an African violet close to the window until the whole windshield is a huge white flower, with a vivid purple border. The yellow stamens and pistils brush against the glass, the leaves ruffled and scented.

And look, this amaryllis, I've finally developed one that's hardy. See how it blooms even at these temperatures.

Amaryllis, Mother, isn't that the one that's almost extinct in Afghanistan? That's where it's from. That's its home.

Look, the California poppies!

And yellow and orange nodding blooms surround Mother. The roadside is a warm tunnel of green.

This is where I belong.

Mother spreads her arms in two directions, calming the storm.

It's my greenhouse, full of exotics. Remember that apple tree?

A huge branch of fragrant blossoms sweeps the car front, making it shudder.

I'm good at this. I'm really good at this. And I'm so happy.

Kathy closes her eyes, bends her head to the steering wheel. She's never seen her mother like this. So powerful. When she lifts her head once again, the vision is gone.

Here she is, out in a flipping blizzard, with a baby, because her mother has finally found the nerve to call. Hope is a traitorous impulse – that everything will be okay, that her parents could be as ready to adapt to change as she is. She is really thirsty. Her lips hurt from biting them, and Joy must be hungry. If she could just push on a bit farther, get to the gas station café. She edges the car onto what she hopes is her side of the road. Once, she would have had more faith, would have just booted it, trusting in the instinct that had served her so well in the past.

After twenty minutes of struggling to see, to stay between the ditches, she reaches the T-junction and the turnoff to the roadside garage, Halfway House. Its red neon glares, just up ahead. Yellow fog lights glance off the polished pavement, marking the intersection where she needs to turn west. She can see well enough to pull into the parking lot.

Her shaking legs brace the car door, pushing it open, until it suddenly flings on its hinges in the wind. She stands against the wind, stretches, forces the driver's door closed and struggles with the back door. Leaning over the car seat, she fumbles with the baby seat clips, her fingers numb. She unzips her jacket, pulls Joy inside, and stumbles into the café, which is strangely quiet after the noise of the blizzard. Inside, it is storm dark in the middle of the day, as if they haven't figured they need the lights, even though the air is so dense it's grey out there. But that makes Kathy decide it is safe to feed Joy at the corner table. Which is clean and private enough. And allows her to keep an eye on the weather as well.

"A coffee, please," she says to the woman behind the counter.

"Nasty one," the woman says, nodding at the Plexiglas windows that seems to ripple against the wind. "How are the roads?"

"Fine, if you can see them." Kathy's hands shake as she tries to hold her baby's head and open the plastic container of real cream for her coffee.

A half-ton looms out of the storm, stopping a few feet from the front window. A man in a ball cap advertising some sort of irrigation system pulls the door open with difficulty and shuts it carefully behind him. He has a familiar face. Kathy can't recall his name.

"I'll have a coffee to go," the man says, pulling off his cap as he sits down at the only other table. "Hiya, you been out in this too, I see."

Kathy nods carefully and tugs at her jacket, covering her breast and the head of her feeding baby. The man takes his time checking her over before he looks away. Maybe he recognizes her. He smells of motor oil and sweat.

"You're from around here, right?" he asks.

"No," Kathy lies. Would anyone else be back here in a blizzard? "Not anymore."

"Right. It's been a few years, but I think I know you – you're a Johnson, aren't you? Farm's just south of the correction line, right? You have a sister, takes piano lessons from my wife. You must be Kathy, eh?" He shakes some sugar into his coffee.

Kathy nods.

"Well, you're through the worst of it if you're heading south," he says. "I've got my son and daughter coming out from the city after they finish work, and I sure hope they got the sense to just stay put today."

"It wasn't storming when I left town, not like this," Kathy says, taking a good swig of her coffee. It burns her tongue. "Shit." The abrupt movement pulls Joy off her nipple. Crying.

"Just you and the little one there?" he asks.

Kathy looks around for the waitress, who has brought his coffee and disappeared into the kitchen.

"Just asking," he says. "Look, I've got a little more clearance than you. If you're heading home, why don't you call your folks from here, let them know you're coming in, and then follow my tail lights to your corner. No use taking any chances on these roads." He looks anxiously out the window, apparently not aware of Kathy's discomfort.

She's forgotten. You lift your finger from the steering wheel every time you meet someone here, they always wave back. If they don't know who you are, they will soon. And he remembers her. She's still part of this place, its history, its memories.

Joy cries until she latches onto the nipple again. "That's kind of you, thanks, but I think we'll be okay," she says.

"At least give your folks a call. They'll be worried," he says as he stands, puts on his cap, picks up the styrofoam cup, and drops a loonie by the cash register. "You think you know this country, but something like this comes up and all of a sudden everything seems strange. Well, take care." And he disappears out into the storm again.

Wait, I'm sorry I didn't recognize you, I'm sorry I didn't agree to follow your lights, I'm sorry I couldn't trust you, thought you were a stranger. I'm sorry I can't call home. It's going to be so hard, when I do get there, so hard for us to even be this decent with each other.

The waitress leaves the kitchen to ring in the bill for her coffee. She grins at Joy, asleep in Kathy's arms. "Weather like this makes me wish I could do the same," she says.

Kathy bends her head over Joy, wraps her tightly, covers her milky smile with a blanket. "I think it's settling down now," the waitress says. "It should be easier going from here on."

"Ah, these roads never bothered me too much," Kathy says. She tightens her hold on Joy, half waves as she leaves the café, and pushes into the wind, struggling back to the car.

She'd once heard somewhere, probably on some radio talk show, about the unforgiving highway. A mathematical formula determines how sharp the corners, the slant of the ditches. But this stretch is no more difficult than what she's already been through. The waitress said so. So did the guy with the truck. *You're through the worst of it.*

When she arrives at the farm, will they run to the porch, their eyes glossing over her, going straight to Joy, to the round impossibly soft baby cheeks, the jet black hair spiking comically from her bonnet's edges, the wise brown eyes? Will they instantly fall in love with her, their first, their only grandchild? Or will Mother open the door cautiously, the smell of bleach and fresh bread wafting out in that familiar mix of severity and nurture? Will Mother hug her? Will she see her daughter's still round body and say, *My God, you've changed!*

The swirling drifts settle now, leaving new patterns of dark and white on the blacktop. Like a stop motion of a million ocean waves, the tongue and crest of wind-whipped snow on the surrounding prairie makes it an unfamiliar landscape just for this moment, alien and vast.

Out of the corner of her eye in the rear view mirror, she spots Mother in the ditch again, her arms draped to overflowing with the blossoms of exotic and native plants. A ribbon trails from the massive bouquet, embossed with the words she cannot speak. "With love." Down the highway Kathy can make out a set of tail lights blinking like beacons. Because she can see them, she no longer needs them.

She pulls out onto the road.

Kaleidoscopes

DAMN, HE PICKED A FINE TIME TO VISIT. That quick call from the bar down the street. Boosting his courage with booze. He's going to have to get his act together if he expects to see Joy more than just this once, that's for sure. He'll be right over, he said. Right.

My head's throbbing with a hangover, I've got a sink full of dirty dishes, and the house is a disaster. Joy's got clothing, pots, empty plastic bags – everything she could pull from the lower cupboards and shelves all over the floor. And she's filthy-faced from peanut butter, Ritz crackers, and God-I-hope-not dog shit. Even the dog, Pooch, is working against me. He's dragging last night's soup bone under the kitchen table. Get your butt out of that rut, Kathy, and at least get the place presentable.

The last time I had a visit with Ron was at that fireside party, the night I thought I saw Jesus in the fireplace, standing in the embers. Jesus or some other biblical person who could walk through fire; he was tiny, but he could wink at me, and wave from his hot den. I wasn't loaded enough to reach out and touch him, and when the next log got thrown on, it crushed poor Jesus in the barbecue pit. Ron never did see what I was pointing at; he thought I was crazy. I don't know, doesn't everybody see shapes in things?

Anyway, wouldn't you know it, I'm trying to clean the place up for Ron when I knock the damn brandy decanter down from the book shelves, the decanter he gave me, the crystal one that fractures light into threads of colour. That's why it was up there, to catch and split the morning light. It came crashing down as I scrubbed the greasy dust from lower shelves, bounced against the bottom shelf, and smashed onto the floor, just missing Pooch and his bone. Oh God, thumbnail chunks of glass all over the kitchen counter, the floor, under the table. Back home, there was no worse sin than to break glass. Mother insisted that glass could creep into children's stomachs, knife deadly gouges into the soft red interior; before you know it, you find them dead, blood flowing out of the eyes, ears, anus.

I check the butter, the bread and the fruit on the cupboard for shards of glass. How can glass bounce four feet up from point of impact? A mystery, but Mother threw away even the freshest June-yellow butter and made me wash all the dishes in all the open cupboards if there was broken glass in her kitchen. Not one of us ever bled to death. None of us were ever hurt. If we cried, Mother sang the sunshine song, rocking, rocking, gazing in fixed contemplation out the window that faced the pasture, the round smooth hills, the dugout. There the ducks and sometimes a heron, long-legged and somehow a freak, too graceful for these flatlands, would startle, take flight no matter how we held the old dog, Trixie, back, no matter how we snuck up on them slowly, careful not to wave our arms.

Now the decanter is ruined and it's Ron's fault. I'll blame him, too, for making me scream at the dog and Joy to get the hell out of the kitchen while I scrub the shelves and cupboards again, mop up the floor, clean up this glass.

I kept the decanter even after Ron took off on me, because it reminded me of a magpie feather, each barb of the vane like a perfect shiny rainbow. Of course Mother flipped out the day I came home with one of those feathers in my hair. Besides the mites, the lice and God knows what else, she knew there were sure to be germs torn from the stomach of a dead rabid skunk on that iridescent feather. She burnt it in the cook stove.

Joy's back underfoot, playing with Old Doll under the kitchen table before I even get the mop out. Old Doll's in pretty rough shape – worse than I am – her guts are all hanging out. I lean the broom in this corner over the pile of broken glass, suddenly too tired to scoop up the broken bits, and sit for a minute. Listen to her coo to her baby. Already she doesn't need me so much. Maybe I can use those shards for something, make something neat for my girl, maybe a kaleidoscope like the one I once made at bible school.

I've never been much for church, but one summer, when I was too young to help, instead of spending the summer at my grandparents' in Deer Run, Mother kept me out of her skirts for harvest by sending me to Rock Valley Vacation Bible School. The leaders made us kids sit in jagged semi-circles on the clumpy prairie grass, but I'm telling you, our eyes were full-circle wonder as the ladies in small print dresses told us about wine, *it's better than water,* and lepers, *people whose noses fall off when you touch them,* oceans hundreds of times bigger than the dugout, cut in half by a stick that used to be a snake, stories about blood, and floods, and rainbows. I learned the names of the old time magicians there, and a little magic of my own: a dark hollow tube with three mirrors and smashed glass at the end. On the outside they made me print, *Let your light so shine before men.* I tilted it at the sun, lying down in the slender shade of the old school. How could something broken, a few shards of brown and blue and green, become something so beautiful? It made snowflakes, flowers, nothing that lasts, maybe, but I could see the pattern, how the slivers of glass created something whole and lovely every time. I could have spent the whole week watching the changing shapes, but one of the ladies always found me and brought me in to join the group around the shrill old piano, to sing with the others, *Dare to be a Daniel, dare to stand alone.*

This is what I've come to. There used to be a time, if I knew a man was coming over, I'd have the old makeup mirror out, brushing on the colours. I haven't seen Ron for, what? two years, and all I'm doing is pulling handfuls of my hair from the twist tie that's supposed to hold it back, counting the split ends, trimming them with my teeth. He'd say *Don't do that,* disapproving. Critical. As if I care. As if he cares. Besides, I'm looking pretty good, aside from the post-baby paunch. He'll know when he walks in nothing's changed. It's not as if he's coming to see me, anyway.

God, Kathy, pull back the curtains, let in some light. It's raining. The colours outside are shadowy, intense. Even the new leaves are a glossy grey. Then I see Ron's old half-ton pull up out front of the house.

Why come back now? I don't see the sense in it. Our child is here, fed, happy. But watch me rush to the door, open it before he knocks.

"Hi."

"Hi yourself."

"Well, come in, I guess," and he does. His eyes slip right by my greasy hair and the grease on the stove top, not to the broken glass I missed, not to the pile of glass and dirt under the broom, but to Joy, his daughter, his daughter whom he hasn't seen in almost two years, since the day she was born. She pushes Pooch and Old Doll aside for moment to take a good look at him.

Clomp, clomp, right up to the table. At least he has the sense to crouch to her level. "Hello, Joy. Remember me?" he says gently, hoarsely. "I'm your dad."

Remember you from what movie, Ron? Like she'd remember him in utero? Yes, I told her Daddy was coming over, but what the hell is that supposed to mean to her? Poor kid, a guy tall as a lamp-pole invading her space. And isn't he a specimen: black bushy beard, heavy plaid jacket, stench of sweat and beer, with a booming voice straight from the powerful dark heavens. He does not arrive bearing gifts, I note. Like he'd know what to get her. Joy squints; it's her just-before-bawling look, but she's in control, pausing a moment to glance at me first. I'm hoping she'll scream good and loud. She does, and Ron sensibly backs off while I go in for the rescue.

I carry our child to the front room to smother the strains of her magnificent lungs, but I yell back, "There's coffee on. Get a cup, Ron." And I give him the look that once meant there'll be some explaining to do. We're past explaining. "And there's cream in the fridge somewhere."

But I tell you, I feel a little less satisfied with the situation once I get her settled and find him slumped like a hurt dog at the kitchen table, watching the cream clouds in his coffee. Look at him. His jeans haven't been washed in weeks. His hands, how could they have been so gentle? Grease-lined callouses are rough.

"I'm sorry for the way she acted."

"It's okay, Kathy. She's probably not used to a man around."

What should I say? I've been celibate since he left? No, there have been men enough here, but always in the fumbling drunken dark, when Joy's been tucked safe in bed. And none of them were good fathers, and none of them were good lovers. They grunt and thrash and moan in anxiety-ridden climaxes, then leave me dry and cold and closed in a huddle so they can leave without looking at my face. They don't know what to do with me, what to do for me. They don't want to know. None of them make love like Ron. Can't think about that.

Be damned if I even give him the pleasure of an argument. I won't even touch him, save him the trouble of delivering his personal-space lecture. As if he's the only person on earth who's ever wanted to be alone. In fact, what kind of a clue would he have about what I need? I'm the one doing the twenty-four hour childcare. Not that he'd care.

Holding an unlit cigarette, Ron stares at the spot on the wall where the clock used to be.

"There's matches there on the shelf. Go smoke outside, not in front of the kid. Your coffee need a warm-up?" When I pour more black into the muddy brown liquid, it explodes into patterns. His eyes look straight into mine for just a second over the match flame before he shakes it out. Then they slide past me again, and I know Joy's toddled back into the room, is doing the doe-eye thing to him from the entranceway. Pooch is right there beside her, just checking him out. He remembers Ron, but he's Joy's dog now.

"She'd get used to you soon enough, Ron, if you want to come around again." Why am I saying this?

He shakes his head slowly. "I'd better get going, Kathy."

Just before he stands, Joy diaper-waddles towards him, holding Old Doll in one fist. Ron crouches carefully beside her as she lifts the battered toy up between us. "Broke?" he asks gravely, as he takes it from her. The stitching has come undone again and Doll's insides, coarse seeds of synthetic sand, are spilling on the floor. She'll be empty soon. He touches Joy's head with his dark fingers.

"Yes, it's broken, baby, and your daddy can't fix it." It's the shake in his voice that gets me, and her small hand on his knee, the sweep of his arm as he lifts her face to his, the glittering of his eyes like the crystal I had to keep on moving. Ron got mad at all the marks in the ceiling, but I never did place the hook to catch the light just right. The faceted glass was supposed to burst into a dance of reds and blues and yellows that we could wake up to every morning. But then Ron left, and Joy was born, and she never did get the rainbow show.

So I stay put, while Ron tries to explain to his daughter what a needle and thread are, and how he's her daddy, yes, and she kind of rocks against him, she hasn't got the words yet, but she's going to hum for him, our favourite tune.

I've been singing the sunshine song to her since she was newborn, stroking her fine baby hair away from her forehead, and touching her smooth new cheeks and breathing in deeply that baby smell, so sweet the air from her lungs was better than the air any place else. I'd watch her face while she slept, just as I used to watch Ron's face when he slept. He'd wake up angry, tell me to stop it, what's wrong, what am I looking at? But I'd do it again next chance I got because his face was so beautiful in sleep, and sometimes, softly, so I wouldn't wake him, I sang, *The other night dear, as I lay sleeping, I dreamt I held you...*

But it's a song better sung to babies, and was even better the time I heard my grandpa sing it. He was in the home already, and starting to fail and Mom had tears in her eyes every time we went to see him. Grandpa was part of the choir the time I'm remembering, and we parked his wheelchair in the front row. He sang as if it would save his life, his voice cracking and quavering. Mom was digging for a Kleenex when he looked right at me, making a wish, or pleading, or casting a spell: *Please don't take my sunshine away.*

That was the last time I saw Grandpa, except for the hospital, where tubes and machines controlled his body. His eyes were rolled back in his head. His nose was bleeding a little. Each breath they pumped in lifted his whole chest off the table and then his chest would fall again, as the machine let it go. But the body lying there wasn't really him, only a part of him that had become clouded, no longer reflected light. I think that's what happens when death comes; one facet of the whole is darkened, and it's like that for all kinds of loss, even the end of love. But with a bit of sunlight even broken glass can become, or become again, something beautiful.

"Well, I'll be in touch," Ron says abruptly, passing our child back to me like a big football. He waves at her awkwardly. Doesn't try to kiss her. "I'd like to see her again, Kathy." Then he's out the door, and Pooch and Joy are both clamouring at the screen, bulging it with claw and fist. Joy's still got a strangle hold on Old Doll, fast losing all that's left of her stuffing.

Finally his truck pulls away, and I can let my menagerie out onto the step. Someday I'm going to replace this battered old door with a wooden one. The top half will be beveled panels that splinter into orange, violet and green on the walls and floors when light passes through them, even on a cloudy day.

Women Waiting

Kathy shivers on the back step, watches the pink sky push through the trees shading the garden, onto the grass. Her old dog Pooch, lying at her feet, offers small comfort.

She cradles a cigarette paper between her fingers, pulls the strings of moist tobacco from the bright blue pouch, rubs the poison round and round. Just like Reva used to do, waiting. Kathy used to tell Ron she took up rolling tobacco because of Reva.

Damn it, he should have been back ages ago. He was supposed to take Joy just for the afternoon, but now it's way past the baby's bedtime. He better not have left her somewhere, like in the truck while he's in the bar with his buddies. She doesn't know what he might do. Never has. And he's pretty clueless about children in general. "The jerk. I should go check around." She nudges the dog with her toe. Neither of them gets up.

When Ron came for Joy he seemed really happy to see her, and Joy had taken to him, too, after the initial visits at home. He wasn't a total jerk. Maybe he treated Joy to supper. Somewhere good for her. Somewhere with food for two year olds. Not to one of those cheap steak joints where the meat is so full of tenderizer they dump the leftover bones in special boxes so dogs don't get at them. "Right, Pooch?" Pooch lifts his head to her hand, and she strokes it.

Thoroughly chilled, Kathy grinds her smoke out on the old wood of the steps, climbs them to the fluorescent kitchen for a sweater and a cup of coffee. Before she can stop herself she's at the front window, scanning the street for Ron's truck. This is ridiculous, she tells herself. She'd feel the house vibrate before that old heap turned the corner.

She carries her coffee outside, sits back down again in the dark and waits. Like Reva, she thinks, as she rolls another cigarette. Reva was the greatest lady, could roll with one hand, milk a cow with the other, never miss a beat. Kathy's folks dropped her off there in the summer for a few days, on the way to help her grandma at Deer Run. With Reva, Kathy learned the peace of the habit, concentrating on the tin, the paper, the matches and, after the first drag, on the smoke rising like a curtain between her and everyone else.

Reva always hoped to go to town on Saturday night after the long day in the field, but her husband, Charles, never obliged. He would just smile at her, thin-lipped, and then say, "Why would I want to be seen with an old dirty woman like you?" He himself would be already wearing his good shirt with the pearly snaps. Then the screen door would slam and his car would roar out of the yard before she could say a thing, before she even took a second drag from her cigarette.

On Sundays, Reva and Charles' neighbours always went to the lake for a swim and sometimes ice cream, and Kathy and her three cousins, Diane, a year older, and the two boys just a little bit younger, wanted oh wanted to go, and said so. Reva was silent. Charles said, "No one's going anywhere today, there's too damn much work to be done." And so they never went. Not once. He poured himself more coffee, she rolled a smoke and sometimes he did too, and they sat there not looking at each other, blowing smoke into the space between them, while the kids finished the milking and the other chores. Kathy couldn't stay in the room. She was supposed to be there to help, after all, not go to the lake. She wanted to be as tough as Reva.

Weeks went by when Reva wouldn't see anybody except Charles and the kids. She always seemed glad to see Kathy when she arrived, and happy to see her sister, Kathy's mother, though it was hard to tell sometimes. She wasn't ever mean, anyway. Kathy sat at the table like an adult, drank coffee with her and with the cousins, and listened, listened.

She had never heard another woman talk like Aunt Reva: *goddamn* this, *son of a bitch* that, talking like he did, like the cousins did too. Kathy would practice, mouth the words silently on her way to the outhouse, feeling deliciously bad.

During the summer Kathy turned ten, she noticed that her cousins had all stopped calling Reva "Mom." Now she was "the old lady." People seldom dropped over; Charles was too miserable to be around. He drove all over the countryside with their only town vehicle, an old green Acadian, so that if Reva did go anywhere, hike to the neighbour's to have a chat about how their dog was chasing the cattle, say, people would marvel at how they hadn't seen her for years, and here they were only a few miles apart. Reva would curse them for being so goddamn nosy; she didn't need their sympathy.

Reva, she lost it one night. She and her daughter Diane, and Kathy, were carrying pails of warm milk from the barn to the cream separator in the porch. Reva said she didn't mind milking the cows, though it wouldn't have mattered if she did, she'd be doing it anyway. Charles' bad back, you know. Kathy watched Reva as she poured the cream into the narrow-necked metal cream cans, making them ready for Charles to take to town, to the train station's wooden platform, where the milk was shipped and they got cash to buy groceries – the food and other things they couldn't get from the garden or the cattle. That was all Reva's doing. It was her work that got that money.

They had a pail in each hand, Kathy, Aunt Reva, and Diane, and had just crossed the yard when Charles backed the car away from the house and spun out like a teenager, his cigarette drooping from his bottom lip. His hair was wet from a recent combing. Reva dropped her pails, the frothy milk spilling, soaking into the sandy path. "Where the hell does he think he's going?"

"Probably to see his girlfriend," Diane said.

"Which girlfriend is that?" Reva knew, had to know what was going on. She didn't sound surprised.

"The one the old man bought that new silky blouse for. Where the hell did you think that last creamery cheque went?"

"Is that so?" This time Reva didn't sit on the old three-legged milking stool by the back door, have a smoke, and watch his dust. She rubbed her powerful hands against the outsides of her thighs, and marched directly to the old Fordson tractor, which happened to be free of the hay mower. Her face was like a rock. The fumes from that old beater stung Kathy's eyes as Reva pushed the starter button, revved the motor to a deafening crescendo.

"Where the hell does she think she's going?" Diane asked, trying to be cool, and she didn't expect an answer. Even Kathy knew. They just stood there, listening to the rumble of the tractor. Reva swung it slowly out of the yard, down the road toward Deer Run. Diane kicked at the earth where Reva had spilled the milk. "It's going to take her all bloody night to get anywhere. He'll be back before she even makes it to the highway." Diane picked up her pails and carried them down the path to the house. "Besides," she said, as she passed Kathy, "It's time someone said something here. God."

Kathy nodded, as if she agreed, but she believed in Reva, believed she would succeed in finding Charles and setting him straight. "Well, let's get the rest of this goddamn milking done," Kathy said, hoping she sounded just like her aunt. At least Reva wasn't sitting and fretting, feeling foolish and helpless.

Tonight, Kathy's first instinct is to go in the house, wash some dishes, keep busy, but as soon as she's inside, she's checking the phonebook, calling information, making a list of Ron's old friends, their old friends. She can call them in the morning. Not now. It's too late.

"And he doesn't have a frigging phone." She opens the door for Pooch and finds herself back outside, watching.

No one heard Reva come home, even though Kathy and the cousins slept in the living room and Reva had to walk right past them to get to the bedroom, the only proper bedroom in the house, with a chest of drawers and a bureau with a mirror.

Reva wasn't standing at the stove making coffee and porridge when they woke up the next morning. "Where's the old lady?" one of the cousins asked Charles. He sprawled on a kitchen chair, smoking.

"She's not feeling well, so you just stay the hell out of there." He pointed at the bedroom door with his cigarette. "And that includes you" he said to Kathy, who was crouched on the chesterfield. He kicked at her bum with the toes of his cowboy boots as she walked by him to get a cup from the cupboard. "Isn't it about time you got the hell home, anyway?"

Reva never came out, not at all, not that day or the next. "Shouldn't we check in on her or take her some food or something?" Kathy asked the cousins as she helped them at the barn with the milking and the chores. They just looked at each other and shrugged.

Every time Charles saw Kathy he said, "What the hell you still doing here?"

Diane managed to call Kathy's parents from town, and they drove down to pick her up.

Reva didn't even poke her head out to see them. Kathy's mother walked straight into the bedroom, while her father sat at the table with Charles, not saying a word to him. "Kathy, make us some tea and then take your things to the car," her father said. Kathy put the kettle on. She and the cousins fled outside as soon as they could, but hung around the back door, as if they couldn't bear to be inside and couldn't bear to leave.

They heard Reva's voice and then Kathy's mother's voice through the screened bedroom window. "Get the hell out of here and mind your own goddamn business," Reva said.

"Not until I get you something for that eye," Kathy's mother said. The cousins looked at each other and then at Kathy. It was time to leave.

KATHY'S MOTHER LOOKED LIKE SHE WAS EATING something sour all the way home. After they were on the road a while and she thought Kathy was sleeping, she said to Father, "My sister never was strong enough. A man like that needs a firm hand. Why she didn't leave him long ago I'll never know."

Kathy always thought of her mother on spring nights like this one, and the times they would sit out on the steps at the farm. Supper was ready, overdone really. She and her mother talked softly, listening to the dog barking at the coyotes, listening harder for the throaty rumble of the Massey on the road home. Sometimes they waited many hours.

Mother said once or twice, "I wonder where those men are," and pretended to be worried about the food, but Kathy believed she was thinking about the brush fires and gas tanks and belts and pulleys and teeth and heavy wheels and the sharp hillsides where no one but a farmer or his wife would ever find an outfit tipped over, and underneath, a crushed body.

Neither ever said it, but Kathy played with the idea that it was their waiting there that got those men home safely, the act of willing them to come home in one piece. If you went out looking for them something bad could happen.

Well, it would have. Father would have been mad. He never understood women, their worrying. "We'll get back when we get back," he'd say when Kathy's mother begged him to come in at meal times, for her peace of mind if nothing else. A man who liked to finish what he started, Father obeyed no one's schedule but his own. He never had to sit and fret.

So many other things could happen to a child. Kathy imagines phoning hospitals. Maybe the brakes failed on Ron's junk pile on wheels. Was it impounded for lack of muffler? Was she stirring herself up for nothing?

They could take a bus home. Joy loves buses. She's figured out how the bell works, and sometimes when Kathy's not watching she'll get in a tug or two by standing on the seat and stretching, before Kathy figures out who's making all the noise. There are pay phones too. Would he think to use one? Irresponsible bastard. He always has been. Thinking only of himself. Is that true? Yes.

Even the most self-absorbed person would know that a mother would worry, that Kathy would worry. So what is he doing? How's Joy going to get through the night without big fat Ted Bear? How is Kathy going to get through the night without her baby? What would Reva do? "Guess it's just you and me, Pooch."

As she stands from scrubbing Pooch behind the ears and under the chin, Kathy sees the northern lights wave their colours like tail feathers of magnificent peacocks. They make Kathy think of her friend Leda, with her brilliant gypsy cloth and bangles, stones and metal dangling, jangling, caressing her hands, her feet. Pounds of polished stones draped over her graceful long neck, celebrated her breasts. Leda was the only person Kathy had ever met who believed so absolutely in beauty; Leda was the first to make Kathy believe she could be beautiful too.

Kathy had always known there was nothing special about the way she looked. "Just Ugly," her brother called her, all the cousins too, and her parents never corrected them or yelled at them for saying it. Work was what you were. What you looked like didn't matter. Why all the fuss anyway? No doubt the younger cousins were also a little bit afraid of the power of beauty, especially in a girl, soon to be woman. On the farm, it was important to keep the women under control – even other women understood that. How could they know she'd need all the strength she could get, that she'd be on her own and have to understand this city world where what you looked like was all that counted most of the time, where your skill was not something anyone could tell by driving by your garden or fields or barnyard on a Sunday afternoon?

Joy. Joy has lovely skin. Her eyes are like a grazing doe's, unstartled, in peace. She is so beautiful it makes Kathy's heart hurt, and Kathy tells her, she tells her. How she misses her. Fears for her, if she lets herself go anywhere near fear.

Leda had taken Kathy under her wing at a time she really needed it. She was a woman of generous nature, a woman of flamboyant, European tastes, and she said, "Yes, of course you should wear dresses. Look at those ankles. And you have a waist my dear, why hide yourself under those rags?"

Leda's husband was often – too often – overseas on business, and Leda hated being alone. She would call Kathy to come over and keep her company. Even though being with Leda got in the way of being with Ron, who she was dating hot and heavy by then, Kathy was drawn to her. Leda gave her something she needed.

Kathy didn't understand about appearances, about

how beauty could be not only a source of joy, but also a disguise, a cloud, to hide pain, to feed forgetfulness.

When Leda's husband didn't come back from his latest business trip, didn't come back at all, in fact, Kathy found her friend drinking gin and tonic in the bay windows overlooking her magnificent flower garden, distracting herself by finding fault with the man who worked in her yard. "He never brings in the best roses for me, just leaves them there for the dust of the passing cars."

So Kathy told Leda about how Kathy's mother would wait for the men to come home, and about how Aunt Reva took the tractor to find Charles.

"We worried about Reva not coming out of the bedroom," Kathy said, "So Mother walked right by Charles, where he was sitting at the table, his cowboy boots sticking way out. Mother marched straight into the bedroom. When she came back out for an ice-bag and a cup of tea for Reva, Charles just stared at the toes of his boots, didn't even look up."

Leda didn't understand, or didn't want to understand. "My husband is not violent," she said. "He has never laid a hand on me. I am not in any physical danger. There is no comparison."

"But there is," Kathy insisted. "You're so strong, you don't need a man who hurts you, who makes you wait."

"Who abandons me? You are so very young, my lovely dear." Leda walked Kathy to the door and hugged her hard. The next time Kathy tried to phone her the line was disconnected. Leda had moved away.

"Joy will be fine with Ron tonight," Kathy tells Pooch. Pooch is unconvinced. Joy will miss her blanket. If Kathy had thought he was going to pull one like this, she'd have sent it along. Kathy considers taking a bus or taxi over, grabbing her daughter, and hauling her home. Would that be a sign of weakness? Of lack of trust? Joy's his child too. "A phone call would be nice. Asshole. I'll wait to kill you until you get here with my daughter." Pooch wags his tail listlessly. "She will be back tomorrow morning. He *will* bring her back." Their baby will be fine. She knows that. But what about me, Kathy thinks.

The first time Kathy told Ron she was leaving, he placed his hands on her shoulders. She looked into his face. It wasn't the leaving that mattered, but that he cared she was leaving. Like a whirlwind forced to stop, all that energy was suddenly thrown back, churning. She had wept. And then she had stayed. But at the end, when she told him about the baby, and he said, "Mine?" Kathy knew she had to go away, finally, and leaving didn't hurt. She could get along alone. Now, her head on her knees on her front steps, Kathy cried for Aunt Reva, for Leda, and for her mother too; how alone they really were, still are. At least Kathy has Joy.

When the house is dark the streetlights filter through the front windows, turning the stripes in the rainbow quilt to muted greys. Pooch, on the bed at Kathy's feet, is a warm golden pillow. Joy is usually right here beside her. Always. Alone in this darkness,

Kathy tries to be quiet, to breathe evenly, but clenches her teeth, wishing away the tears.

SOMETHING IS WRONG. "JOY. WHERE *are* YOU!" She's out of the bed she barely slept in, looking through the window at the street. Daylight already and no Ron. No Joy. She watches the kettle heat, the boiling water sink through the fine-grind as if she could see the future in the deep brown swirls, and then she carries her cup of coffee to the step, grabbing her tobacco on the way. She'd just as soon not spend time indoors, tripping over Joy's playthings, over Pooch, who is too lazy to move. The fridge is empty anyway so there's no use thinking about breakfast. Even term papers and books seem too heavy to look at first thing in the morning. This morning.

The neighbour, carrying a hoe to her back yard, waves.

"How's Joy?" she calls.

"Fine," Kathy yells back. She hopes.

"Well, time to weed that garden, I guess."

Kathy's going to do that, too. Just as soon as she finishes this coffee, has a smoke and thinks a bit more about what to do when Ron finally returns with Joy.

But even before she gets the tobacco onto the paper she hears the rumbling of his truck motor, like a massive John Deere. She leaves the tobacco and, carrying her coffee cup, saunters around the corner into the front yard.

Ron has Joy up on his shoulders. Where did he get ice cream this time of the morning? In Joy's arms there's a new plush bear, checkered in every imaginable colour. She's sharing ice cream with her new teddy, and she garbles, "Hi, Mommy." Ron is smiling; my God, when has Kathy seen him look that happy?

Kathy smiles back. Lop-sided. This isn't going to be pretty, but she's tired of acting tough and feeling weak and she's done with the fear of being alone, when she *is* alone. She may not have his love, but she does have his baby.

She's about to have a moment, her moment.

Ron, she'll say, there will be no more waiting around.

Creek Bottom

THE WORLD'S NOT SUPPOSED TO CHANGE this much for my baby and me. But here's her dad, out of the black and murky past and right in our laps. No, Joy's in his lap and I'm alone for the weekend while she has her first *official* overnight with her dad. Ron, no longer my lover, not even my friend. Anymore.

Nothing horrible will happen. Nothing has so far with their visits, the few hours here and there, except for that one time Ron took off with her. That won't happen again. And I've got to let him see her, and he seems to care for her. As they were leaving this afternoon, I told him not to let Joy out of his sight. I mean, what does he know about taking care of a toddler? Now I've got these thoughts going around and around in my head so I just can't stay in this empty house or I'll go nuts.

I grab my driving hat and the keys to my trusty, rusty half-ton, and head out for a drive in the country. I want to walk down to the creek, wade, feel the slippery green on my feet, then climb onto lichen covered boulders, kick at a fly or two, and watch the water wash past. Like I once did back home in the valley. Like Ron and I did when we used to sleep together under the stars.

When I get there I see that this year the creek isn't boggy. In fact there's no creek, only its dry, cracked bed, and I want to get the heck out of there, too, but this rage starts bubbling up, or maybe it's fear, or maybe it's grief. I'm gasping like I'm holding something in my throat, unable to let it out. I was looking for comfort and all I find is a reminder of how very alone I am. I know I'm too shaky to drive.

The last time I drove away from Ron, I was this angry. When I hit the steep grid, the gravel ridges, and lost control. That had felt right somehow. He saw the truck sail down the embankment, saw the crazy way it skidded to a stop, veering wildly but not rolling, and he ran to where I was, shaken and laughing in the ditch. Laughing until I was weak.

But Ron left anyway, and then Joy was born, and now I'm afraid to go too fast when I drive, afraid of losing control again. I've got someone who needs me; it's only today she doesn't because she's with him.

I sit in that same ditch today, in the part they haven't cut yet; tall grasses almost hide me from the cars and semis. The drivers turn their heads like curious dogs to see if I'm peeing or something, out here in the middle of nowhere.

Heads of thistle and squat spidery flowers hug the gravel. It's been so dry this summer and late for moss, that healing green. If I find dry weeds, it's because of the season, not because of me, or anything that may not be going right with me, or with my child.

So I drive home thinking I should go out somewhere like I used to, find someone to drown my sorrows with, someone who doesn't know my child, or Ron, or me. And I can curse, throw glasses of beer, knock over tables. Generally kill the pain.

Instead, like a well-trained dog, I go home. The phone's ringing.

"Hello, Kathy; this is Cherise."

Cherise. He'd have to pick someone with a bimbo name like that, wouldn't he?

"Can we meet somewhere for coffee? We have to talk," she said.

I can hear my heart pounding in my ears. "What's happened? Where's Joy?"

"No, nothing's wrong. She's at the park with her dad. It's nothing like that."

Reluctantly I agree to meet with her. Someplace neutral; someplace where I can have a drink, too, on my weekend off.

I SPOT HER AS SOON AS I WALK INTO THE BAR. She's just what he wanted me to be all those years. Petite, that's the word. Stylish, in a classy sort of way. My cast-offs from the Sally Ann look more faded than usual, and suddenly don't feel as comfortable as they did. I dress in line with my budget, but a lot he knows about thrift. A lot he knows about feeding a child and making ends meet. But he knows about keeping this tiny woman looking good. I'll bet he knows about standing outside dressing room doors as she tries on another outfit, about putting his arms around her little waist as they stroll through yet another boutique, finding just the right shiny doodad to string around her throat. That perfect jewel, the one he always wanted since he didn't want me. Or Joy. He saw her a grand total of once, the day she was born, until he called me from the bar, two months ago now, and I agreed to let him see her. I wanted to see him.

"Cherise?"

She smiles, trying to reassure me as I scratch the chair to the table. Shit, this was a big mistake. I'm perched at the edge of a ridiculous round-seated stool, the kind they always have in bistros. I swing my pack into the corner, narrowly missing the vase at table centre, the obligatory wilted carnation. Cherise has chosen a seat by the wall, so short of sitting right beside her, I've got to expose part of my back to the entire room. Not a power position. The only danger here, though, would be from the odd crumb of cheesecake or cappuccino foam sneezed by a patron across the way.

I know I've got to make the first move, like in a chess game, so I pull out all the stops and order an import. Cherise orders something that must be wine, in French. The waiter smiles his approval.

"So what was it you wanted to see me about?" I ask, nonchalantly digging through my pack for my smokes. She watches me pull out the tobacco and finger it into the paper.

"It's about Joy."

I've been rolling cigarettes for ten years and this is the first time I've torn the papers. "What about Joy?" I'm trying not to sound defensive.

"Well, now that we've gotten to know her –" She digs for words, "We'd like to –"

To what? Steal my kid, for good this time? And 'gotten to know her'? After three hours?

"We'd like to work something out with you."

Why doesn't Ron, the father of my child, talk to me about this "something"? Why send out the death squad? Because I'm dying here. I'm thinking about lawyers and custody suits and strangers with clipboards coming into my home and judges who call macaroni pasta making decisions about my baby and me.

"What did you have in mind, exactly?" I put away the tobacco. There's no ashtray on the table anyway and there's no one else in the whole place lit up. I crumple the napkin.

"We want to see more of her. And," she says, as the waiter sets down the drinks, "It'll give you a chance to do some things for yourself."

Do I look deprived? Does my child? After two years of just me and Joy, and before that, just me, alone in that hospital and the nurses all treating me like a dolt, like a slab of stupid meat because I was alone, because there was no man there, no man to rub my back or breathe with me like the books said, until, out of desperation, they called him. He was quick enough to leave us then too.

I find myself saying not the polite thanks-but-no

thanks, but saying to this woman I don't know and don't really care to, "Pain is always suffered alone."

She looks like maybe she understands that, in a patronizing kind of way, like someone had warned her I might be saying crazy things, that she should just take them in her stride, nod, and keep on talking. "I know it's been tough for you, Kathy. I really do. When I found out Ron had a daughter, I really encouraged him to get to know her, at least make an effort. I'm so glad you let him see her. It's good for him. Really good for him. For them both, I hope."

Right. Thanks. Why does my stupid head always get pain mixed up with anger?

"It's only right a child know both her parents." Cherise takes a sip from the glass with the delicate lemon garnish. "And we'd like to see her on a regular basis."

"You're talking about a visiting schedule?" Not custody, not taking her away. Not yet.

"Well, as you know, Ron and I are both working."

No, I didn't. Now I do.

"But we'd like to see her on weekends, evenings, we'd like to work something out. And I wanted to get to know you, too, Katherine." She stumbles on my name. "I want to know you, I want you to get to know me, so you'll feel more comfortable with all this. I was hoping we could be, well, friendly enough to make it easy."

Easy to take my child away. Easy as it was for Ron to push me away, to walk from Joy and me. It's all been so easy for this woman. You can see it on her smooth face, in the calm way she looks at me now, at the cracks around my eyes filling with water, at my runny nose. I have to search in the bottom of my pack for a Kleenex. "Ron always said I cry at the drop of a – Damn."

In one smooth move she pulls a tissue from her handbag. Then her voice becomes deeper, almost husky, like she might cry too. No. Too intense. "Forget about Ron and what he says," she says. "He doesn't ever think of you."

Forget him? I still remember his shoulders, their squareness, the way his waist narrows to his hips, his lips shy, pursed. I can't remember his kiss, but I can still feel him inside me, and I love to torment myself with the memory. Forget him? "So you can have him?"

"No," she says. "So you can have yourself."

We sit for a while with our drinks and she's watching me, I'm watching her. My thoughts are an eddy and in that mud is hate for this neat woman, contempt for myself, fear for my child, sadness so deep it's almost a sob, but I take another drink and take in a deep breath. A sentence comes to my head. I fight it but I know it's true. She's right, you know. She's right, let go. Let go.

Then it dawns on me that she's pretty perceptive to pick up on that, considering our brief acquaintance. I wonder if Ron's complained to her about me. And then I wonder if I've really missed the point. Perhaps he hasn't let go either.

When spring burst on the white cocoon of snow, I'd rush down to where the icy banks overhanging the valley collapsed into the torrent. These were my only waterfalls, these rivulets cutting into the sand and clay of the ravines. I tested my strength against them, using thick sticks for support, my boots filled, the chill water pressing hard against my naked calves. Nothing had the edge, the thrill of that first snow-ridden run-off. It's like first love: always the most exciting even if it isn't the best, even if it isn't something that will last, even if there's no time to learn how to stand or go with the current before it sinks away into prairie dust and boggy creek again. If I were to go home to the valley when the creek starts to run next spring, I might wonder what the big deal was, but I'll never put my memory to that test. I'll never put my love to that test either.

I can't let go of Joy any more than I have already. I wave my hands, starting to tell Cherise this, as if it mattered that she know, and my fluttering fingers flip over the beer. It flows, foamy and yellow, over the smooth plastic table. I watch it a second too long before reaching with the well-creased napkin to wipe it up. By the time I have the table dry, she's pulling out her day planner and a list of dates and times. Then I'm dictating rules and guidelines for the care of my daughter. Cherise writes everything in the back of her book, drops a twenty on the table and glides out of the bistro, leaving me staring at my hands.

I order another beer, this time a Blue, and pull out the Drum, start to roll another smoke. Cherise was kind enough to leave her glass, which I could use as an ashtray, but I spot a pile of tin flats in a dark corner by the condiments and nab one of them. I breathe easier once I have a rollie in my hand. After my first cigarette, I pull the carnation from its vase and spend a long time pinching the dry ends, then rolling each crinkled petal smooth between my fingers. By the time I'm ready for my third beer, the flower is completely transformed, and looks, I think, better. I splash a few ounces of lager in the vase to help ease its pain a bit in this time of change. But it's still just a rumpled old carnation. Not a rose.

Rat Root

I WAS IN COURT, ABOUT TO CROSS-EXAMINE A respondent father, when the miscarriage began. It was the last day of a nasty week-long custody trial. Living on fast food, little sleep, and lots of adrenaline, I wasn't surprised by the cramps, had been feeling them all morning, but hadn't had time to pay them much attention. In the court room, they grew in intensity, became unbearable, and I had to ask for a ten-minute adjournment, a risk I took on behalf of my client, so late in the day and with a testy judge. But I had no choice.

I lost the baby in the Barrister's Cloakroom in the pristine porcelain of the women's washroom. No one witnessed my distress, fortunately. She slithered from me and I can't recall whether the sudden tears clouding my vision were from pain, loss, or relief. I only assumed it was a girl: unformed, a scarlet, darkening mass in the bowl. I folded sheet after sheet of tissue into a thick soft pad, stuffed it into the crotch of my panties, flushed the toilet and returned to the courtroom.

Perhaps I won't tell Ron, I thought. Perhaps it's

better not spoken of. Although Ron has said he'd like a family, he's always on the verge of running away.

A week after I lost the baby, I still hadn't dealt with the matter. Ron and I were sawing cross braces for shelving in the basement, a place to hold Ron's tools, the fruits I preserve, and the Indian medicine Ron picks and dries in the fall. I held the boards; he held the skill saw. I wondered if anyone had done a statistical analysis of how many domestic disputes begin when one of the combatants is already holding a weapon.

"Why don't you go see a doctor about your eyes?" I asked, thinking about doctors, about his recent complaints of headaches, and how maybe he hadn't noticed my despair.

Ron said, "Why do you keep on doing that to me, Cherise?"

"What am I doing to you? Showing concern is what I'm doing. Can't you take a little concern?" Besides, he's sawing close to my hands and his. Vision counts. Zip, and the first set of cut one-by-fours dropped to the floor.

"Not when you're trying to manipulate. I'll go to the doctor when I damn well want to and your opinion does not matter."

"My opinion does enter into it. I have to live with you complaining." Zip. After the second set, he didn't need me to hold the lengths of two-by-fours.

"I'm always doing things for you, and you're always asking for one more thing." Zip.

Ron hates doctors, hospitals, the whole medical system, and wouldn't go voluntarily. I know that, and was trying to be supportive.

We managed to make up, in bed, in the middle of the night, reaching for each other. I could have told him then that earlier in the week I had lost the baby. My baby. Our baby. I didn't. If he were relieved I'd be devastated, and if he wanted to try again, I still didn't know if I wanted a child. You can't leave a law practice for three months, or however long it takes to nurture a new life, and expect to maintain a thriving business. And he left his last relationship because of a baby.

THAT NIGHT I DREAMT I'D RECEIVED A GIFT from Josh Pine, a former client, a former friend. We faced each other, seated on two molded orange plastic chairs. Josh's round cherub face loomed, larger-than-life. He wore a white uniform. His hand glowed, dark and disembodied as it stretched out, palm up, towards me. He held a twist of rat root, the bitter swamp plant that cleanses a congested head, soothes an upset stomach, sweats out infection. I was crying, and in the dream Josh reminded me of Ron. I accepted the medicine.

Rat root is a deep taproot, difficult to harvest. A wild, harsh licorice that, when chewed or made into tea, alleviates all manner of suffering. Muskrats gnaw it, therefore the name, although what use would those quietly organized rodents have for such healing?

I woke up, my stomach hurting, and then I

remembered my dream. And the dead baby. So I slipped out of bed and slogged off to the office early.

I hadn't thought of Josh for years, hadn't seen him for almost five, despite my promise. But now I wondered if he might have some wisdom for me. Something about loss and death and healing, and yes, about silence.

Once my heart had slowed down and my breathing returned to normal, I phoned, arranged the visit. I knew where to find him – in the same place he was last time I saw him. A place that had become too familiar during my first year in the practice.

The penitentiary squatted, an unfortunate fortress at the far west side of town, a protective custody joint, first stop for rapists, child molesters and informers. An oppressive silence comes over me every time I drive through the fences and gates, walk through the grey metal doors. A silence broken by the jangle of keys, the slide and slam of doors.

Lawyers learn to be especially nice to gatekeepers. This works wonders with maitre d's, security guards, court clerks, all the truly powerful people. No amount of charm, however, worked at the penitentiary. Quite the reverse. The more pleasantries I attempted, the more suspicion I attracted. I learned to state my business briskly, no small talk. "I'm here to see inmate Josh Pine. I'm his lawyer." They knew that. Nevertheless, I signed in, with all the particulars, then shed all metal, jewelry, money, containers, packages, and the contents of my pockets into the locker. Even though I'd phoned ahead with a precise time of arrival, I waited twenty minutes while they brought the prisoner up. After passing the first of the double doors, the odour of sweat caused by anxiety permeated the air. Accompanied by a series of key-laden guards, I followed a maze of hallways and electronic double doors before being ushered by telephone into the visiting area. A guard leaning a meaty shoulder over a half door waved me towards him, even though there was nowhere else to go, and no other possible way to obtain entrance.

My name was the only one on Josh's visitation record. Social calls were reserved for family or pre-approved friends. Josh's family wasn't likely to ever visit. Not after what he did to the child. It was hard to understand, even for me. And I defended him.

I had continued my visits with Josh after the trial, even after the appeal period. He was a convicted murderer, and I had no further role, no business disturbing the ordinary and expected treatment of such criminals. But I feared if I weren't there, Josh would change, would give up.

The joint. That's what they call it. I learned some of the penitentiary lingo from the men who called my office once they heard I was visiting Josh, all to do with shivvies, and sticking pigs and diddlers: a vocabulary of violation.

After the trial, my visits with Josh made me heartsick, the very air thick with mind-numbing, unarticulated sorrow. Finally I just stopped going, stopped taking the calls, as if I'd fallen off the face of the earth. The flood of correspondence from the joint trickled, dried up, except for Josh's annual Christmas card, once with a photo of him, looking fine, by the fence of the exercise yard.

Years passed without so much as a card. When I mentioned my regret, my colleagues agreed that I'd done the only healthy and merciful thing, that Josh would adjust to institutional life, that I was, in essence, torturing him by being there, reminding him of the outside. I let them convince me.

But Josh, the child murderer, was my friend.

The interview room where lawyers see their clients was separate from the chaos of the family visiting areas. The social room was always crowded. Someone had to stand. Another room, for no-contact visits, placed a plexiglas wall between prisoners and their loved ones, a tiny circle of metal slats approximately mouth height for conversation. Not to touch, not to have a moment's privacy, while the next guy shouted to his visitor too; a long line of half-heard conversations. I still claim the privilege of the interview room, where lawyers and clients can speak with some semblance of privacy, closely watched through the glass of the door.

After five years, Josh's empty eyes didn't seem to recognize me. I hardly recognized him. And Josh didn't look like Ron, I realized immediately. Why would he? They are not related, not even from the same reserve. Ron has those classic cheekbones, an angular face and full sweet lips. Josh's face is pudgy, his nose a bit too short and his lips are thin. He looked like an unhappy little boy, even at thirty-five. I had imagined there might be something similar around the eyes, but no.

"Josh, it's me, Cherise."

"Oh yeah, the lawyer," he drawled vacantly. No "thanks for coming." It was like talking to someone in a sensory deprivation tank. His mind floated elsewhere. His shoulders slumped as if weighed down by the wrist irons he wore for this visit.

My voice echoed, overly loud, an intrusion. "Well, I just thought I'd drop by, say hello. It's been a while –"

Silence.

"Josh, I dreamt about you last night, so I thought I'd come see you."

"Yeah." Not "Yeah?" or "Yeah!" He yawned, gulping air.

"Yes, and you and I were sitting across from each other."

His eyes glanced lazily around the plain, box-like room.

"You had some rat root. Remember when I was so sick, and you made me some medicine tea?"

His face remained blank.

"You used to know something about healing, remember? You really helped me then."

"That was a long time ago."

"But I remember it. I'm still thankful for that. You have done some good things, you know."

"Like I said. A long time ago."

"I guess I haven't got much to say." I blushed, a reaction I thought I'd had under control. "You're looking good." A lie. His face was pasty, his eyes tired and a bit drugged.

No response. Nothing here for me at all.

"Well, I'd better get going."

"Do you have a cigarette?"

"They took everything at the door. I don't even have a file with me. Legal file that is." I tried to laugh. Not a glimmer. "You know that, they only ever let me bring in the paperwork."

"Oh."

"Well."

"Hey, lawyer, I didn't do it, you know. I never got a decent trial."

"Josh, I was there, I was your lawyer, remember?"

"And they won't let me transfer out of this p.c. joint and they took my stereo for three weeks and kept some of the tapes and they're holding back my mail and I know one of the guards is stealing my pay."

"Are you taking any classes? Reading? Anything?"

"They've got me cleaning the cans. Mopping the goddamn toilets. There's nothing you can do for me, is there."

"No. I guess I just needed to see you." In case there was something he could do for me.

"I really didn't do it, you know. I was blacked out. I can't remember anything from that day."

"Yeah. Well, I really just dropped by to see how you were doing."

"Why?" Josh asked as I signaled the guard.

"Oh, I don't know. Old time's sake." I walked away before they came to get him.

Why did I bother? What did I expect?

Back at the office I paged through the file, looking for something that could have made this case exceptional, something redeeming. But the details of Josh's case were no better or worse than a dozen others I'd acted on. He went down for life, twenty-five years without parole. His crime generated good press for me at the time, so early in my career, even though we lost. Arguably, the evidence was circumstantial. Josh couldn't remember the actual death, or the events leading up to it. Although they did not materialize, Josh maintained there were other possible perpetrators of this motiveless violation. I'd done the best I could with what we had. There really was nothing I could do for him.

A WEEK AFTER I LOST MY BABY I THOUGHT OF Iris, one of the residents I met the summer I worked in a facility for people with mental disabilities. That job was hard as law, but in a totally different way. There really was nothing I could do for her, either.

It was a dirty job. Many of the girls were incapable of being toilet trained. A few took pleasure in popping the creamy turds in their mouths, or smearing them on the walls, a form of primitive graffiti. I hosed them down, rinsed the clothes, mopped the walls and floors, pried open the reluctant mouths, wiped and brushed them clean. I spent most of the workday trying not to retch.

Iris was, according to her chart, severely brain damaged from birth. She looked like a raven, with cocky, alert eyes. She screeched, striding incessantly around about the ward, testing the edges of her cage. Sometimes, she would perch on the back of one of the lounges, rhythmically rocking, banging her head against the wall, often with something hidden in her hand, something she had found in the yard.

"All right, let's see what you have this time." I spoke to her as if she could understand, or recognize me as anything other than an obstacle restricting her need to move. She was about five inches taller than me, and very strong. Trying to control her was like pinning down a raven, her arms and elbows thrashing unpredictably, dangerously. I pried open her fist, her long fingers scaled and calloused despite the nightly slathering of lanolin. I always let her keep lint, small stones, even buttons, but not nails, toothpicks. This time she held the small light bulb from the nursing station reading lamp. "How did you ever get that, Iris?" She would eat her new treasure, so tackling Iris was routine. I often bore bruises and her teeth marks home from work.

Her compulsion to consume led to Iris's most serious management problem: an object lodged in her lower intestines. Iris occasionally had a powerful urge to push it out. One of the first orders on the ward then was to make sure Iris was not allowed to stay too long in the bathroom, on one of the long line of white toilets, each equipped with a leather strap designed to hold the less focused to her task.

On what would be my last day on the job, the RN tried to cover too many wards, and the other summer student left early, sick. I had just finished mopping a puddle in the day room when the senior aide called me into the bathroom. There she had pinned Iris, naked, face down on the floor, and was struggling to remain astraddle her. Many of the girls crowded around, grunting excitedly.

"Go on, get." I pushed the girls aside. "What's going on?"

"Be very gentle, I don't want her to move too suddenly. Just pull her cheeks apart, really slowly."

"Oh my God." A bright red fold of flesh, the size of a man's hand, hung flaccidly between Iris's buttocks. She had pushed her insides out, like a cow, after giving birth, sometimes cannot stop heaving until she loses her uterus and intestines.

"Get to it, Cherry, before she really hurts herself." The aide was trying to be patient, professional, but I heard the stress in her voice. Clearly no time to track down the RN. "You've got to put her back together while I hold her down. Come on."

I did it. I pushed the intestines back inside Iris.

I can't recall with any clarity the rest of the shift. I can't remember if Iris was given any pain killers. She simply got up and continued her incessant strutting around the cottage.

I left with the aide at shift change. We went directly to the downtown bar where most of the staff seemed to gravitate after hours. For some pain killer. I remember tears rolling down from my eyes, having to wipe my nose on my sleeve because no one had a tissue. The aide, her eyes moist, told me it was all in a day's work. I caught myself rocking, my back stiff, tapping my head against the wall behind me, Iris's rhythm.

I didn't know about rat root then – wouldn't for ten more years. I wouldn't know what it was like to try to push something no longer viable from my body, until I was sitting on that toilet, the red bits of embryo like Iris's red folds of intestines, the bright red blood. Like Iris, I simply got up and completed the trial. Unlike Iris, I can choose to talk about the experience. But would that change anything?

Eight days after I lost my baby, I reviewed my personal notes on the case of Josh Pine. I'd first met him at the Department of Social Services. I'd dropped by to discuss a client. Josh worked as an entry-level caseworker there. He'd drive over for tea, to talk. I'd see him in the bar after work. He knew my address, my phone number. He shared with me the story of the abuse he'd suffered as a child, and how he hoped now to help others. When I was under the weather he brewed rat root tea for me.

He found me by the post office, the day before the murder. He was untidy, sweaty, breathing unevenly. His eyes had a wild look I hadn't seen before.

"What's wrong?"

He kind of half sobbed and blurted out "Not good, not good."

I'd never seen him like that. I wondered how often he was that out of control. "On a binge, Josh?"

"Huh?"

"Having a party?"

"No party, it's not good." We leaned against my car and talked, but he couldn't or wouldn't say anything more specific, except that he was frightened. And that I had to promise to help him. I did. When I got home

I found he'd written *Help Josh* on the dust film of my car door. I turned around and went looking, couldn't find him anywhere.

A couple of days later, he made the call from the RCMP lock-up.

A good lawyer doesn't weep with her client in the cell block. A good lawyer doesn't throw up over the body-ID and autopsy photos. A good lawyer defends to the best of her ability and then walks away. Although I held it together during the prelim and trial, the very act of being a professional required the disciplined dulling of all my feelings. When the jury came back and announced the only finding the evidence would allow, I caught myself rocking, the rhythm of comfort I'd picked up from Iris all those years ago. Rocking, the rhythm of a mother cradling her dead child. Of a woman having had a miscarriage.

Someone had taken the five-year-old out of her home, where Josh had been drinking. Someone had taken her clothes off and opened her from belly to back-bone with something large and hard. And someone then crushed her gut, split her insides with a blunt instrument, left her in the frozen first frost, the west wind blowing new snow in that night.

Josh was still drunk when the parents came looking for the child. Josh helped them look. Josh found the smouldering clothes stuffed in the wood-burning stove. Josh led them to the broken body, split and crushed in the soft snow of the poplar grove. Josh did it.

Every lawyer will counsel their clients to be silent, but sometimes silence is harder to live with. Josh Pine opened up a child, a violation he could not or would not remember. That dull ache, the horror and the guilt, will not go away. There is nothing I can do to help him heal. There is nothing I can do for his victim, the five-year-old child. There is nothing I could do for Iris either. There is nothing I can do to bring my baby back.

Twelve days after I lost my baby, I woke up with a gnawing in my stomach, an ache, as if I was turning myself inside out. As if I was unearthing some sort of understanding, some sort of acceptance, if not some sort of peace. I have tried most of my life to help others. To bring resolution to their suffering. To offer them the panacea of rat root. Some people cannot be helped, or don't want to be, or never could be. Or are blind to their own need. Like Ron and his eyes. Like me. The last time Ron found out he was a father he ran. I don't want to lose him, but if I tell him about her, this child we've lost, maybe it'll help him see clearly what he really wants. If we talk, our anger, our sadness will have names, no longer buried in darkness. Maybe these words will create a gash in our relationship. Maybe these words can heal.

Ron and I are filling the new basement shelves. One half is loaded with the tools of his trade: bits, screws, nails, all the little things that can get lost in the darkness of a tool box now displayed in the light and at eye level. The other half is lined with a winter's worth of canned fruit – dark plums and pale pear halves floating serenely, almost regally, in their juices.

I've just learned the old art of preserving, the rush to prepare the fruit before it's over-ripe, the steam from the sterilizing jars, and then the canner, rising, sweat on my skin. The sweet taste taking me back to a wholesome place. On a top shelf, in the dark recesses between board and floor joists, I store the dried rat root, the medicine of first resort when sickness hits.

Ron knew where to find it all along. When I asked him about it, his eyes lit up. "This is just the right time to dig for it," he said. We drove to the valley where the marsh water is sweet, sloshed along paths better suited to muskrats, knelt in the moist earth and dug the stubborn roots, bringing them, gnarled and tender, into the light. "This will keep us well all winter," Ron said.

TWO WEEKS AFTER I LOST OUR BABY, I LAY THE rat root on the shelves Ron and I have built, and I break my silence. Before the store of food and medicine that promises a winter together, I tell him about her.

For the Love of Strangers

AT THE SWINGING DOOR TO THE BAR RON released Kathy's hand. A little thing, but done purposefully, as if he was making a statement by creating this ravine between them. They were not necessarily connected, not necessarily a couple, just arriving at the same time. She was not to touch him. He was alone. No, she was.

Rosie, eagle-eyed, her face even more of a moon now that she'd lost her hair, nodded her turbaned head slightly at Kathy from where she held court in the corner, her powerful belly laugh and staccato observations audible over the hum of the Indian intelligentsia settled around her. Behind mugs of brew and clouds of Player's, they were well into worrying over the latest litany of injustices.

Ron took the last chair at the end of the table, and Kathy went in search of her own, which she carried over from the other side of the busy bar room and placed gingerly in the only open space at the table, to Rosie's immediate left.

Kathy was on her second beer and third cigarette

before anyone but the barmaid spoke to her. She listened, appearing attentive, as conversations went on around her.

One by one the supplicants came to Rosie, bringing greetings, asking advice. At this moment a black woman in flowing rainbows, her hair a jewel of intricate braids, leaned close to Rosie's bead-work draped ear, discussing the best strategy in a current human rights complaint. A politician, who'd once dreamed of doing something concrete and constructive in office, hovered nearby, twisting his tight braids, waiting his turn.

Rosie glanced up from her intense and clearly private discussion and half-smiled at Kathy. "Hiyah, Blondie."

Kathy automatically held out her hand. "Rosie, how are you feeling? You're looking good."

"I'm dying, how am I supposed to feel?" But she shook Kathy's hand firmly.

"Like you can beat the beast, Rosie, like you can win this one, too."

"To tell the truth, Blondie, I'm tired of fighting. But what would you know about that?"

Kathy was not up to a fight. "Nothing, Rosie. I guess I don't know anything." But there was a slight challenge in her voice she couldn't help.

"Here's what you know: you know how easy it is to let things go, you white women, you know you can fix things, that you can turn things around, or start something somewhere else. If you had no place else to run to, you would have to stay and fight."

"Maybe I just choose my fights."

"That's a luxury of the elite."

"Rosie, Dahling, I'm about as elite as they get." Kathy flourished her cigarette in an airy loop.

"I'm not joking about this. It's your lackadaisical attitude that got us into this mess you call civilization in the first place. Yours. You. Especially you. You who know better and still let injustices happen. You haven't really thought about anyone else but yourself today, have you? I can see you sitting there worrying about yourself. So what if your life goes to shit, so what if your old man is giving you the cold shoulder."

Kathy's right arm jerked involuntarily. She leaned closer, spoke more softly. "You saw that?"

"Everybody did. You look like a little lost sheep, and you're not. Stop feeling sorry for yourself. None of these Indian guys want to be seen with a white woman. Just get over it and get on to the real issues."

"Rosie, the real issue for me is that I love Ron." Kathy was whispering now.

"You don't know what love is." Rosie's voice rose so that anyone nearby could hear. "You're tied up with romance and obsession and what the goddamn media says a relationship is supposed to look like. Love is bigger than that, Blondie." Rosie took a sip from her soda water, and waved her long brown fingers towards Ron, her voice lower. "And that one, he's always going to treat you like shit. You're never going to be brown enough for him." Rosie smiled broadly. "And if you ever have a kid with him, it won't be dark enough." Tough words, but Rosie reached out, touched the top of Kathy's hand.

Kathy swallowed a flare of anger. "I don't want to be brown, Rosie. I just want to be me." Tears weren't that far away. Time to change the subject. "Hey, congrats on the victory in court." The news was full of it. After seven years, the federal government was found to have discriminated against Rosie on the basis of race in her dismissal from the workplace. They were ordered to pay a settlement.

"That was no victory. They refused to release the money until I signed a document promising to take no further court action, and to never talk about the issue publicly again. They'd have to kill me first."

"This conflict is killing you, Rosie." Kathy nodded at Rosie's tidy twisted scarf, where unruly black hair once danced. "And you're killing yourself."

"That's harsh, white girl. I'm going with peace of mind."

"My God, Rosie, you deserve a rest."

"Order yourself another beer, Blondie. You can afford it. I have things to do." A young man with a scarred face was settling into the chair on her right. Rosie turned to him. Kathy was dismissed.

"Ron, I'm heading home." Kathy had her hand on his shoulder, lightly, but lifted immediately when he turned to face her.

"Yeah, sure, see you in a bit." He turned back to the table.

The politician was already seated in Kathy's chair beside Rosie.

IT WASN'T THAT LONG AGO THAT KATHY HAD felt like royalty with Ron. Earlier that summer, in fact, they'd slept under the stars together. They had driven out to the campground, then walked past the campsite, swatting mosquitoes until they found the perfect clearing, mossy and smooth, where no one else would think of going. Ron chopped up a few fresh spruce boughs, soft and smelling like anticipation, like Christmas, like some place really safe. Kathy picked the first saskatoon berries, just ripening, and they shared that simple, wild sweetness before Kathy rolled their sleeping bags out over the branches and they snuggled in. No need for a fire that night; the warmth of their bodies was enough. A gentle wind eased away the bugs, murmured with the poplar leaves.

"That's more like it," Ron's mouth on her ear, his hands around her back, pulling her close to him. His face lost its worried look in the moonlight. He was the man she'd first met, gentle, somehow shy.

"Better than the bar?" Kathy stroked the length of his back. So smooth.

"I think I've got to move back north."

"I think I've got to quit drinking."

"And smoking?" Ron had never really liked the smell of tobacco on her, even though he did sometimes smoke himself.

"Well, no, I'm not going to quit everything!"

"That's good," Ron said as he shifted himself over her. "I'd really miss it if you gave up everything."

When he came into her, she hugged her legs around him, held him to her as the fresh air caressed her face and the stars dipped to meet her mouth. Something deep in her body opened. Kathy knew then, really.

"What if we have a baby?" she asked him as they slowly untangled, so they both could watch the night sky.

"A boy, we'd call him Nightfall."

"Cool. But then he'd be called Nightie for short. Poor kid." Kathy shook her head. "A girl would be Joy."

Ron kissed her fingertips. "That's a silly name."

Kathy pushed herself up, swung herself over him and dug her fingers into his ribs. "What's wrong with Joy, eh?"

They wrestled and hugged and talked most of the night. Dream talk.

Kathy dared not move, tried to breathe as a sleeper would when Ron finally made it home and into bed after the bar. He did not touch her, curled up on his side, immediately asleep, or passed out. Kathy felt that old aloneness, like the earth had opened, revealing again the deep ravine between them. It occurred to Kathy then that that darkness had always been there. When she reached across, finally, Ron groaned, turned sleepily, took her hand and pulled it to his crotch.

Not that Kathy had anything against sex. She just couldn't seem to handle the emotional fallout these days. She was waking up with someone she had lived with for years, thought she loved, feeling like she'd been sleeping with a stranger. Instead of holding him, thinking *wow that was great,* she stood up, thinking *what a waste of time.* How can the celebration of the body be a waste of time?

KATHY LOST RON AT THAT SAME CAMPGROUND, just outside of town. She was in classes that day, and the sun was dipping the entire sky into a paint box when she pulled up behind his truck, parked in the site farthest from the entrance, isolated from the campers and nylon tents, the usual weekend crowd. It was almost fall and she and Ron had plans to sleep under the stars again.

He was chopping wood by his truck "There you are, finally." He was impatient. She was late, and he'd been increasingly edgy lately. She didn't know why. She never was good at guessing at the endings of things. But she had to tell him. Couldn't wait until morning, until the calm of the time away from town had smoothed all the edges away. Couldn't wait in case she lost her nerve, changed her mind again. If she said it once, it would be true that she was going to go through with this, no matter what.

Ron reached over, pushed an empty beer bottle into the open case in the truck box. Kathy leaned over to check. A twelve pack, half empty.

"Let's go," he said.

"Ron, just a moment." She'd grabbed his arm, the one wrapped around the sleeping bag, not the one with the axe. "Ron, I got a call from the doctor today."

Then she didn't want to go on. She wished she could rewind, erase, pull those words back into her mouth. His face, in the brilliant yellow light of the remaining day, was perfect and perfectly still. "The test was positive, Ron." Try to lighten this, try to. "You're going to be a daddy."

In the dusk quiet, his "No" seemed disembodied, a groan made by some wild animal in the bush, an alarm before melting into the shadows.

"Yes, it's okay, I'm trying to, look, aren't you a little, like, happy or something?"

"How could you be, we've been using those goddamn rubbers, for Christ's sake. This is bullshit." Ron shook her hand from his arm.

"No bullshit, and sometimes precautions, well, they're not a hundred per cent, you know. But it's okay. I'm going to go through with it. I want to."

"Are you sure it's my kid? You been sleeping around?" It wasn't so much what he said, although that hurt, but the way his body moved as he said it. Like he'd been cornered in some sort of bar fight, like he'd do anything he had to do to get out.

Kathy stepped away from him, unable to speak. Her head pounding, she stumbled to her car, backed out and sprayed dust and pebbles into the night air as she hit the gas and careened away like a wounded thing, furious and defiant and totally out of control. Her eyes were so full of tears she missed the corner to the highway, bounced over the road and into the ravine, the buck brush scraping the car, holding it up at a crazy angle as she slammed on the brakes.

Ron followed, his headlights sweeping the steep hillside where she'd stalled out, not rolled. Ron at the window, "Are you crazy?"

"Yes," and laughing, not like the laughter with Rosie, but a bitter, choking sound, in the throat, not from the belly. One hand on the ignition key, the other rolling up the glass between them.

KATHY HAD INVITED ROSIE TO GO BERRY PICKING in the valley, having noticed from the corner of her eye as she sat in the ditch, watching the dust settle, wiping tears of anger and loss from her cheeks, the silhouettes of plump chokecherries dangling from the bushes in the ravine. Now their hands were already purple.

Out there, alone except for the real mosquitoes, the possible big cats and bears, talk was easy.

"So, I've got some news," Kathy started.

"Well, if it's that you and Ron are done, that's yesterday's news," Rosie said as she pulled a top-heavy branch towards her. Rosie talked tough, when it was called for; she was practical where Kathy was vague. "And everyone knows you're knocked up. Moccasin telegraph," Rosie shrugged. Her eyes gleamed quick and cold though a gap in foliage, just off the narrow path at the edge of the ravine. Rosie was physically frail already, but still feisty. She glanced at Kathy before she swooped the next branch down over her pail. The tree was dark with berries. "You're still in love with him, aren't you?"

Kathy pulled her ball cap down and steadied her pail. "What?"

"Ron. You still think you love him, don't you?"

Kathy couldn't help it, couldn't stop the tears that were right there. Rosie didn't look at her. "You think you love him, but you didn't even know him, sure as hell don't know him now. You're in love with an idea, and it's a damn small one. Open your mind a bit, Blondie, stop wasting your time."

Kathy could barely talk. "I know. I should just forget about him."

Rosie was silently beside her, patting her shoulder.

"No, you're not listening. Just love yourself and the rest of us more." Rosie had turned to face her through the leaves.

"Yeah," Kathy shot back, chokecherry bitter, "like you love those federal government guys, the guys from your old office, the bastards–"

"Yes," Rosie nodded emphatically. "Exactly like that. Fight the fight, not the people. Get on with your life, Blondie. You've got bigger fish to fry."

"Mmm, that's what I could use, a fish fry," Kathy said and then they were laughing, big and booming over the valley.

Later, at Rosie's apartment, Kathy sorted the berries while Rosie fried up some pickerel fillets for their supper.

"Rosie, would you be the kid's godmother?"

Rosie glanced up. "Blondie, I'm honoured that you that ask me, but you know I'm not into that religious thing at all."

"No," Kathy poured a handful of berries into the

almost overflowing bowl. "I don't mean like in church. I mean like in, you know, in case."

"In case something happens to you? You know I may not live to see this kid."

"So this will give you something to live for. Please."

"So. I will now be known as the Godmother." Rosie laughed.

"It's hard to have a serious conversation with you, Rosie, but God I love you."

ROSIE DID LIVE TO SEE BABY JOY BORN. SHE was a pretty hands-off godmother, but every fall from Joy's infancy on, mother and daughter would join her for an afternoon of berry picking, an evening of laughter. And she lived long enough for Joy to see Rosie the Warrior, too.

It was the summer of 1990, and Joy was four. Emails from far away Québec reported daily on the Mohawk mothers' stand against a golf course development on an historical graveyard. The highways and bridges were blocked, and in the confusion a police officer had been shot dead. The armed forces were called in. Many local people set out to Oka, to help take a stand. Rosie wasn't up to the trip, but helped organize a march across the local bridge to the legislative building in support of the people now under siege in Kanesatake.

There were only about one hundred people out, some carrying signs, but most just walking, talking in small groups. When the police arrived, looking scared, they pulled a couple vans and half a dozen cars across the end of the bridge and began hauling people in. Ten people had already been arrested, three of them under fourteen years of age, when Rosie ran forward, Kathy and Joy a few feet behind her.

Rosie carried an eagle feather. "Let those people go," she demanded, knocking the palm of her hand on the hood of one of the police vans. She dove into the doors, trying to pull people out. Two officers yanked her from the vehicle, threw her to the pavement. One of them gave her right side a kick. "This is for our boys in Oka," he said.

Rosie did not get up. Kathy and Joy were kneeling at her side as the police van doors slammed and sped away.

"Rosie fights," Joy said.

Every police car in the city was out. Kathy counted over a dozen passes in front of her own home, as she debated whether to take Joy with her to the protest that night. Nothing felt safe. What if a situation arose that a sitter couldn't handle? The police weren't acting reliably at the moment. What if she wasn't able to come home to her daughter? What if Joy got hurt? In the end, she and Joy joined the much larger group gathering in front of the police station that night.

Rosie was already there. "Hello, Blondie." Her smile reminded Kathy of one of those showy harvest sunsets, when the warmth suddenly pales in the face of the first bite of fall. "Look what those bastards did to me." She was in a collar bone brace, and her right hand and arm were scraped and bluish purple above and below the bandages. "We're going to demand the release, at least of the kids."

There were many speakers, each more impassioned than the last. A cold stone lodged in Kathy's stomach – this could turn out bad, very bad. The stone turned to fire as Rosie climbed the steps of the police station to speak. Kathy kept a tight hold on Joy's hand. Rosie's face, coloured by the deep rays of the setting sun. Rosie's arm, thin but muscled, raised above her head. Rosie's voice, carried away by the wind that comes up on summer evenings, cool and clear. "...exercising our right to protest!...not fair...an uneven playing field. In-jus-tice."

"Injustice," chanted the crowd.

"In-jus-tice" Joy said from her perch on Kathy's arm.

The police station doors remained locked. There wasn't an officer in sight, even by the solid reception desk you could just make out through the glass doors. The police failed to respond in any way to the demands of the crowd, refused even to show their faces. As the mosquitoes came out in hordes, the crowd dispersed.

The protesters were released the next morning without charges.

Five days later and three provinces over the troopers loaded the buses at Kanesatake.

ROSES TOPPED ROSIE'S CASKET AND WERE GIVEN to the mourners after the service. But they were tea roses, sedate and heavy-headed, not the wild, scratchy roses of the sand ravines where the berries are thick. Joy, eight, managed to find a thorn, blood drops on her new dress.

There was a head-dress of eagle feathers propped above the coffin, and Rosie's mom carried a feather the whole time. She wasn't so old herself. Hell, Rosie had been only forty five.

The disease had eaten her, so she was hard to look at in death, but it was important to see that, and to greet her family as they stood by her earthly remains. Kathy and Joy remembered to shake the elders' hands in greeting as they filed by the open coffin. Joy was just tall enough to peek in without lifting. "Bye bye, Rosie," she whispered, and dropped a crumbled piece of coloured paper into the coffin by Rosie's right hand.

"You wrote Rosie a letter?" Kathy asked her.

"A poem, and a promise," Joy said. "I promised I'd help take care of you, Mom." Then Joy turned her head. She had seen her father, and now she was watching him as he slipped outside with the smokers. He hadn't seen her.

Kathy watched him too. "You know, he was always after me to quit, and now look. You really think I need taking care of?"

"Sometimes." As they followed the crowd out the door, Kathy approached Ron and held out her hand.

Ron's eyes were everywhere but on Kathy as they shook hands cordially and then he focused only on Joy. She held out her hand to him, gravely. "Hi, Daddy."

They shook hands, formally, then Ron swept his daughter up so she was looking over his shoulder. "Mommy. Daddy. Mommy. Daddy. Mommy. Daddy. Rosie!" Joy mouthed the words silently, but Kathy could see her daughter's face from where she stood, just a half step behind Ron.

When the drummers started, the pallbearers carried Rosie out of the hall. The people stood on either side of the walkway, respectfully. No one touching or holding hands, but pulsing through them for that moment was the love Rosie had fought for all those years. Here it was, the love for everyone, lovers and strangers alike.

In the sweetgrass-clear air, instead of sadness Kathy felt gratitude. To have known such a person. Gratitude and a great surging freedom, clean and healing as the wind over the ravine where the saskatoons and the chokecherries grow like grapes even in – no, especially in – a dry year.

Bird Bones

I SPENT A LOT OF TIME AT GRANDMA'S AFTER Grandpa died, even before I could help her out much. And I thought I knew a lot about her, but I didn't. Now I'm going through her things, wanting to uncover that part of her that was hidden, forgotten all these years. It's difficult. There are a lot of other things to dig through as well.

Going to Grandma's was the only holiday I knew until I was ten, when we went to the mountains. Mom, Dad, and I drove to Deer Run to pick up Grandma, to give her a break from Uncle Merv, Mom said. Merv was Mom's brother, Grandma's only son. He still lived at home even though he was already old, too.

Dad drove the whole way in that boat of a Mercury, south and west across the prairies for what seemed like an eternity. That was the longest trip of my then short life, the most boring, the hottest and stickiest. So when we suddenly dropped into the hoodoos near Drumheller, the red walls like the edges of a giant jigsaw puzzle, I knew we'd see something spectacular, something that would make it all seem worthwhile. Even though I knew Dad would not stop, said it wasn't safe, I begged to be let out of the car *right now* so I could climb those amazing cliffs, the layers of orange and sulphur yellow, grey and charcoal black, the eyes of coal mine shafts, even the lazy winding river hinting at dark and ancient secrets.

And there was one revealed, in a tiny island of green, right across the street from the gas station, where Dad said we could stop and stretch our legs: a dinosaur! Massive hind legs and a white stomach. Vicious flipper-claws at its chest. And the head: gaping jaw and the knife teeth of a true monster, a night-time terror in crude effigy.

"Just like a big green naked chicken," Grandma said, "patched together with cement and wire." I was not allowed to cross the street and climb on it. Instead of stretching my legs, I stood in the fumy lee side of the car near the pimple-faced gas attendant, and committed to memory every crack and contour of Tyrannosaurus Rex. Why didn't I think to take a photograph? To be close to something so large, even the symbol for something so large, filled me with an awe I have never been able to explain. Now they teach my daughter in school that birds and dinosaurs are first cousins, because of the way the pelvis and hips connect. How can something as ordinary as chickens be related to something so grand?

The Rockies didn't move me like the scudding, heart-shaking colours and ever-changing shapes of the massive sky of home. At ten I was taller than my mother and my grandmother, and feeling a surge of new power in the fact. I was capable of dealing with the bigness around me, celebrated it, felt connected to it. Unlike Grandma. She found the mountains oppressive. Too much vertical and not enough sun. We both took a big breath as we headed east, glad to be back on the prairies.

On the long trip home, Grandma sat beside me in the back seat. When we got tired of looking out the windows, she opened up her purse. "When I was eighteen, I weighed ninety-eight pounds," Grandma said, pulling out the photograph, this photograph, of her and her boyfriend, the one I never met. She's eighteen and looks twelve, wearing a flapper dress and smiling, really smiling, not the straight-lined imitation they gave her in the coffin, nor the twist of fatigue and pain she wore daily for as long as I knew her. In the photograph, she looks elfin, playful. The fringes of the dress blur, delicate feathers, as she turns to the camera. It must be Christmas, maybe New Year's, because there's snow, and a man seated in a sleigh; her boyfriend, the man with no name. He wears a tailored suit, his long legs thin and razor-sharp at the knees and his face square and full of health. He's looking uncomfortable, maybe unhappy.

"What's his name? What happened? Where is he now?" I asked then. Grandma nodded as if I already knew, and leaned back in the car seat, glowing like a woman in love, but she never explained. Now I see the possibility of an unfulfilled love: the great sadness in even her most careful moments, her change from the sprite in the picture to the ample-breasted, matronly woman I knew as a child.

The picture is taken on Grandpa's farm, where Grandma worked as a housemaid before she married Grandpa, had his kids and became his house*keeper.* I don't remember seeing Grandpa out of his coveralls, and I can't remember ever hearing him talk directly to Grandma. I don't remember ever seeing Grandma out of her house dress and plain apron until I was ten and we went on that trip, except for funerals, when she'd ask me to go the closet for her good dress, her best apron with orange rick-rack trim. Her hair was braided firmly, sensibly coiled against her head as long as she was able to lift her arms. Many nights, when I was supposed to be asleep, I felt I was seeing something I shouldn't when Grandma pulled the hairpins, one by one, let the braid down, unraveled it slowly in front of the flame-warped mirror. The light of the coal oil caught the ripples, an ocean of reflections, like the marcelled waves worn by the child-like woman in the photo in her purse.

Grandma was the eldest child of twelve, born in the old country. When the next girl was old enough to take over, Grandma was expected to leave. There was a gap between her and child number two, while Great Grandpa was away in America, working the lumber camps and ore deposits of Minnesota. When he'd saved enough money and found a good place to live, he sent for his family. Meanwhile, times were tough. When they came to Deer Run, times were even tougher. After the lean years, Grandma never grew, remained a full half-foot shorter than her mother when she was fully grown, eight inches shorter than her sisters. Her bones were bowed. She had aches that she sang to whenever she moved too quickly, whenever she sat too long. "Voi, voi, voi, I'm no good," she sang. Which meant I had to go and help her.

Summers at Grandma's included the interminable rows of potatoes, peas and beans; she never did learn to cut back at seeding time, loved to give pails of vegetables away in the fall. She'd grow as much the next year, just in case. Helping her, I would stop frequently to wipe the sweat from my eyes, black earth scrubbing my skin. Horseflies left bloody patches where they bit hunks from my arms and legs. I couldn't see the end of the row yet, and there were six more to hoe. Some years, I was there for seeding, weeding and harvest. From beginning to end.

On the days when the July breezes were light and it wasn't too wet, Grandma and I would go to the ditches and meadows, Grandma already too stiff to move much, but still bending over, pushing aside the tall grasses to uncover the ground-hugging strawberries, little pinheads of sweet sugar. Those were the times she got closest to playful, when she laughed or pretended not to see the pails never filling, our lips and hands bright with juice.

Mornings at Grandpa and Grandma's, I'd wake to the quiver, stomp, munch of horses with hooves the size of pie plates, grazing just outside the screen window. Grandma and Grandpa had two wonderful

Clydesdales, Billy and Pete. Their velvet noses and toughened lips whispered over my palm when I offered them the sugar Grandma cut from the block in the chimney cupboard. The fine sugar was for company, so I had to sneak it. Sometimes it was easier to grab a peppermint from the enamel candy dish that squatted at the centre of the crocheted doily on the treadle sewing machine. When Grandma caught me feeding them sweets, she'd say, "They aren't children's horses, they're work horses, just leave them alone. If they step on you there won't be much left." But I knew they wouldn't harm me; even fly-startled, they had a sense of where I was, were always the most courteous of gentlemen.

Grandpa would put those horses to work, but occasionally we'd all get to go for a wagon ride. I remember the first time I was lifted onto Billy's barrel back. It was all Grandpa could do to reach so high. My legs jutted perpendicular to the ground.

Grandpa died suddenly, as they say, when I was nine. No one touched the harnesses after his death, and Uncle Merv shipped the horses to the glue factory.

Uncle Merv killed the pigeons, too. Every last one of them. Took the twenty-two, locked the doors to the loft, and shot them all. Maybe it was the right thing to do; they were messy and noisy. But Grandpa had let them live in the barn, and Grandma called them her pets. Talked to them, cooed to them, as if they could understand. And when Uncle Merv shot those birds, it wasn't because he was asked to, his stubby fingers hot on the trigger. Dust and feathers and blood spattering on his crew cut head, his short thick neck.

Uncle Merv liked to drink, and when I was kid, Grandma would keep food on the table for him hours after meal times. From my bed on the pull-out couch, I could see Grandma walk the floors from time to time all night, waiting for him to come home. Even when he was fifty, and she nearly eighty, she kept her vigil, worried for him. Like a teenager, he refused to tell her where he'd been, when he'd return. Sometimes he would bring his friends home, and Grandma would stay in the kitchen to make sure they didn't do anything stupid, like fight or break bottles. Once, after she went back to bed, one of them came into the room where I was sleeping. I didn't move, pretended I was sound asleep, his stench making it hard for me to breathe. I never knew who it was; I never opened my eyes. I never told Grandma.

Uncle Merv would pout when he lost at cribbage, accusing me of cheating. He remembered debts and was not inclined to give favours freely, and he hated "Indians." When I was a teenager and felt in control of my life I thought I could change things in the world, and I believed Uncle Merv could not be serious in his racism. When I started dating a guy who was part Cree, I thought my uncle was joking, that he'd never do anything mean just because of a guy's background. But when Ron came to pick me up, Uncle sicced the dog at him, threatened him with the gun. Ron had to run for his life. Grandma must have seen this happen from the kitchen window, where she was finishing up the supper dishes, but she never said a word.

RON DID, A FEW DAYS LATER. AND I REMEMBERED then the night we got back from the mountains, how a bunch of men came into Grandma's yard. They were really drunk, which wasn't new; Uncle Merv and his friends were often like that, but this time there was something really wrong. I peeked through the curtains that separated the bedrooms from the kitchen. Grandma and my parents formed a barricade between the kitchen and the porch: "Get on out of here, go get cleaned up," Dad was saying. I could hear the men outside, yipping like a bunch of teenagers who'd just done something really bad, that kind of wicked delight. But they were grown men. I looked out the kitchen window and saw that they were dressed in strange clothing, like bathrobes. One of them wore a long, dark wig. They were yelling something, I could hear through the screen, something about killing them all. Dad strode into the yard, the only voice of reason: "Just get on your way, on your way, boys, on your way, now." Over and over until they left, Uncle Merv with them.

Mom and Dad and Grandma spoke in whispers for a long time after that. I never got a straight answer about what had happened, not even the usual shrug, the "Oh, nothing." It was as if those men had never been there.

And I still don't know if they had anything to do with the unsolved murders. Just down the road that night, someone had taken an axe to the powwow grounds tents while everyone was asleep. An eighteen-year-old boy died on the spot. A child bled to death before help came.

But Uncle did build Grandma's short cupboards, shortened the chair I sit in now, with the press-back phoenix swelling out of the carved back. Grandma's cupboard was so small I had to stoop to reach the sink. She would sigh with relief when I told her, "Sit down, I'll do the dishes." She'd set herself in her chair, not far away, lean her cane on the table edge, and tell me how much water to use, how much soap, where to place each dried cup or plate or pot. Although I'd done it thousands of times, she would not just rest, she would remain in control even of that little detail of our daily lives. Or making coffee, twice a day, she would tell me to use fresh well water, not rain from the barrel, and which dipper to use, the orders coming at me an irritating half second after I'd already done exactly that. As if her timing was off.

She started having terrible falls. She'd get dizzy, she said, and just keel over. No one actually saw it happen, and the doctors didn't have an explanation. One night she spent on the floor, couldn't get up, no one to help her, no one around, except Uncle Merv. He said he never heard her call, didn't notice a thing until morning. She got really sick that time. Pneumonia. Bruises.

Uncle Merv wasn't so good with kids either. It was just two years ago when my daughter and I visited

Grandma at the farm. It wasn't my daughter's fault. Joy was just being a kid, only three, and of course she wanted to climb, and look at things. When I turned from making coffee she was cowered on the floor, Uncle's arm already swung back, his face red with fury.

I scooped Joy into my arms, passed her to Grandma and tried to face him down. "Don't!" I screamed. "Don't you ever touch her." Nothing is more dangerous than an angry mother. "Get out right now, leave, get out." I may have even pushed him before he pushed me. He was little, but tough, like a rooster, ready to fight. I glanced to where Grandma sat passively, a silly-looking blank smile on her wide lips, to where Joy peered at Merv and me with more interest than fear. I stepped in front of them, about to push him back again, but there was a nasty, gleeful shine to his eyes. He could definitely take me down. He would enjoy it.

My uncle wouldn't leave; it was his home.

I wouldn't go there again as long as he was there.

Uncle Merv is nothing but a stick man now. Dried like a brittle bone.

Feeling haunted by old mysteries, I called him today. What harm can there be in a phone call, with Grandma dead over a year ago now?

As if nothing had ever happened, we chat; I ask him about the photograph, and he says, "Oh, her old boyfriend is still alive, lives in the next town down the line. His wife died here, just a month or so before Mother passed away." Grandma never saw the man,

Uncle Merv said, never talked to him in all those years.

Uncle is happy I called. I hope right to the last word that he might apologize for what he did to Joy and me, to Grandma. He doesn't. That's how these hurts get buried, but like the ache in old bones, they never quite go away.

UNCLE MERV HIT GRANDMA. THIS TIME SHE ended up in the hospital. Yet, she went back home. "He can't get on without me," she said.

There was no way to make her safe. The family could have had him committed. We could have had him arrested; but Grandma would just say she fell and he'd be out in a couple of days, madder than blazes. But two weeks after she got out of the hospital, things got worse for Grandma, and the police came. Uncle Merv found a place in town.

There was no peace even then. Grandma's phone would ring and no one would be on the other end. But she would always answer. The night unwanted visitors arrived, walking in as if the door wasn't even locked, taking what they wanted, she lay in bed, afraid to move or call out. She never even got a glimpse of them.

After a month at the farm alone, Grandma admitted she couldn't get around on her own anymore; her hip had finally given out, she said. She left her home of sixty-two years to get her bones fixed, but didn't make it back. Uncle Merv took the fridge, the beautiful round table, even the oil-cloth cover with the print faded to white at the edge. Mom took the best dishes, leaving cracked cups, worn mats and Grandma's cut down press-back chair.

Eighty years of living: cracked cups, dusty sealer jars full of fruit and pickles, and this photograph. No one dared use the food in the larder and the cellar; there was no way of knowing how old it was. Even the grandchildren who carried the jars down, placed them on the shelves when she could no longer climb the steps herself, even they were not sure when she put up those preserves. So everything, all her hard work, ended up in the dump.

Just before she died, Grandma shrank to ninety-eight pounds, became frail, something she had never been. She said she'd never want to live without walking, so they opened up her hip, but her heart wasn't strong enough.

And this is the photograph I found in her purse afterward, still there after all these years. She stands at the shoulder of a stranger, herself unrecognizable except for her mouth, the curious straight-lipped smile, as if she is afraid to laugh, is holding it all back, as if the world isn't quite safe.

I saw the dinosaur at Drumheller again this summer, on a trip west with my five year old daughter. All these years later it no longer inspires awe: Joy is accustomed to animated, scientifically accurate half-scale models that roar and have names like parasaurolophus, pachycephalosaurus, archaeopteryx, words she loves to spiel out.

Joy will appreciate, one day, how things have a life of their own in memory, that even in the face of reality, in the face of death, some things live on. Like family secrets. Like lost opportunities. Like dinosaurs, once real and alive, then buried deep for millions of years, and then found in bits and pieces, put back together, even if all that's left are their bones.

THE SCREEN DOOR SLAPS GENTLY, AS IT ALWAYS did, the last time I see Grandma at the farm. She wants me to stay longer, but I don't. I want to take her picture, and she has me comb her hair, just so, to hide the fading bruises on her forehead. Her hair had been cut in a short bob by then; "Easier to care for," she said, although she loved it when one of us took the time to pin-curl it for her, her hair now thin and fine as a baby's.

Grandma leans over her walker in the doorway of her home, those big eyes still unreadable, unfathomable, her lips stretched across her teeth, not a smile so much as a grimace.

"I may not be here next time," she says, just like always.

"Oh, you'll be here," I say.

She was just a bird by then, bones and beating heart.

Perfect Strangers

On the deck he'd just built, Ron watched Cherise paint her toenails flame red. The colour clashed with the hot pink of the webbed patio chair but not with the jet black of her bikini. Third swimsuit this season, he figured. Why would anyone need more than one swimsuit? When he'd asked her, she'd done that thing with her eyes, that blank *I can see right through you as if you were never there* look, and didn't bother with a reply. He flipped the skewered, marinated, tarted-up lamb. Ron preferred steak, but Cherise had pointed out how special this shish la something was. She'd even forbidden ketchup with the meal.

Not that he didn't approve of the results. She looked great, all the time. The house looked great. They ate great food. It was all so fucking perfect. And that's why he was here, and working his butt off. His one chance at a beautiful life, even a beautiful family. And today, with one punch, he'd blown it.

Cherise had even got him seeing his daughter. At least Joy looked like his daughter. With Kathy, his ex, you could never tell. Like today, Joy was supposed to be having supper with them. Kathy storms in like a house on fire, grabs the kid, and says, "We gotta go," just like that. And he'd only just put the meat on the grill. Not a moment to take her aside, to warn her about Adam.

"She's a bloody strange one." Ron stepped back from the flaring barbecue, grabbed the spray bottle from the patio table.

"Why do you say that?" Not bothering to ask who, Cherise stretched her legs out to admire the results of her toenails, then reached to pull the cotton puffs from between each toe.

"Well, like the things she says sometimes. Like the way she named the kid. Joy, for Christ's sake."

"What would you have named her? If you'd been around, that is." Cherise squinted up at him.

OK, we'll let that one go. Ron clenched his jaw. "Amanda."

"Amanda. That's nice. Maybe we can use that sometime."

"Oh, I don't know about that." He started, then changed tracks when her eyes narrowed, her teeth glinting a grin. "Sure."

He never could figure a good way to shorten her name. He hated the name Cherise so he rarely said it. In fact, whenever he was angry, and damn, she could make him angry, or excited, making love, Kathy's name was on the tip of his tongue. After five years with Cherise. So he usually made a practice of saying nothing at all.

"Cherise," he whispered carefully, and the jolt of hostility he'd felt just a moment ago melted. "How hungry are you?"

Cherise stood, her hands flickering, nails scratching down the length of his back, each finger a small flame. He turned off the propane.

"Damn, it's hot," he said, as he opened the French doors to their condo. Cherise rubbed her open palm down his chest and slid one thumb beneath the waist of his shorts. She pulled him through the door. His hand rested on the back of her neck, on her pulse as she led them into the cool shade of their home.

During the drowsy early after-sex evening, only their hands and feet touching, Ron lay wide awake beside Cherise. No talking tonight.

STRAIGHTENING THE BLOUSE SHE INTENDED for work tomorrow, Cherise caught herself moving the iron to the rhythm of the television sports announcer. She'd brought her work into the family room to be near Ron. Maybe they could have a conversation? Cherise suspected something was troubling him, had for weeks. She felt like she was walking on a bed of spikes.

The game blared and Ron smoked and sucked back another beer. He hadn't even glanced at her since the national anthem. He spoke only to the players on the screen.

Ironing was a depressing chore. Some day she would hire someone for such menial tasks. Law degree, partnership, good condo, right neighbourhood.

Just getting here is success, Cherise assured herself. Even Ron seemed like just the right choice for the times. So why did she feel so out of control?

The ashes from Ron's cigarette were spilling from the over-flowing ashtray, falling directly on the highly polished glass and brass of the end table and onto her prized Asian rug.

"Ron, the ashtray!"

"Shhh. Right after this inning."

Damn. There was no need for such slothfulness, no need. She couldn't understand why Ron didn't empty his own ashtrays. She loathed the way the smoke yellowed the walls and curtains, smelled up her clothing, and carpets. Ron would never empty the butts, even though there was nothing but beer commercials for a third of whatever game was on. It didn't seem to matter. He'd watch it all.

"You're going to start a fire if you keep on dropping your ashes on the carpet."

"Umhum."

"I do the cooking and the cleaning and the laundry and the goddamn ironing while you sit around all night watching other people exercise. You can keep your damn cigarette ashes off my carpet."

Now she had his attention. "I've done my share of cooking and cleaning this week. Now leave me alone, I said I'd get to it after this inning."

"This isn't a mud hut."

"All right, then. Get out of my fucking way." He rose from the couch, whirling the contents of the flame-red ceramic ashtray. The ironing board clattered to one side, iron clunking to the floor, and he stood over her, his breath heavy, his face unfamiliar. "You just don't know when to stop, do you?" He dropped the ashtray, with a dull thud, on the carpeted floor in front of her. "There, it's empty." He turned back to the chair, facing the television.

Cherise did know when to shut up. She also knew Ron could hurt her. He had come close before, and she had done what she always advised her clients to do: walk out. But it didn't seem fair that she'd have to leave the furniture and art she'd selected and lovingly arranged, the condo she had paid for. She had more right to be here than he did. He'd moved in with the clothes on his back, a box of old record albums, and his television. Even the ashtray was hers, damn it. A souvenir from Ron's home town.

So last time, she hadn't even waited for him to find her and apologize. She had walked back into her house, shouting, "If you can't take the heat, get out of the damn kitchen," something Kathy might have said. But then she added, in as cold and commanding a tone as she could muster, "Get out of my house, now. Get out." Every blood vessel pumped fear and anger at the same time. If he moved the wrong way she could duck or run to the phone. But this was her stand.

Like a child caught doing something he shouldn't, he had shuffled towards her, head held down, and said, "I'm sorry, I'm a real shit. I won't let that happen again." He had appeared to be waiting for her to hug him or say, that's okay, but she hadn't been able to. If she had spoken she'd have cried. She had just held the door open and he walked out. She could tell by the way he slammed his truck door he was still angry.

Ron had come back that same night, smelling only of coffee and cigarettes. "Are you ready to forgive me yet?" he said with that charming little boy grin of his.

Tonight she knew nothing had been resolved. As she stooped to pick up the iron where it spat and steamed on the rug, a flare of anger erupted in her brain. "Clean this up, Ron."

"Fuck you."

"Clean this up, right now."

"Listen, woman." He was right over her again, snatching the hot iron from her hand and holding it threateningly, its sharp wedge towards her face. "Listen, I do what I want when I want. I'm under the boss all day. I sure as hell will not take it at night."

Cherise willed herself to stillness. To staring him down. If she showed weakness, the balance of power would never be the same.

Who was she kidding? He could hit her anytime. Everything depended entirely on his decision.

It would be easier if he did just brand her with the iron, whip her with the electrical cord, give her a black eye, something she could wear as a badge. Instead of the clarity she was experiencing this moment, she wanted the smoky veil of pain; she wanted to be able to huddle in a corner and dream of a perfect life somewhere. Somewhere, there were two lovers speaking to each other about music, art, and literature. They would be pushing their intellects, their imaginations; they would delight in the dance of their entwined thoughts. These perfect people would not watch the game on television, iron, or stand defiant and terrified before each other.

SON OF A BITCH, WHY DOES CHERISE DO THAT, *pick at me until I blow up? And then stand there, as if she wants it.* Ron grabbed the ironing board, set it upright, and placed the iron gently on the covered surface. His jaw clenched so tightly his molars hurt. His fists throbbed. He realized he'd been holding his breath. Brushing past Cherise, who stood like a statue, her face white and expressionless, Ron marched out of the room, returning with the vacuum cleaner. Before he turned it on, he said, not looking directly at her, "We've got to talk."

The roar of the vacuum was just the right sound. The aggressive thrusting of the brush over the carpet felt good. *Just because I work with my hands, just because I don't have my own fucking prim little office, I have to do the goddamn vacuum cleaning.* Ron pushed the coffee table aside and felt his pulse slow down.

He could no longer avoid telling Cherise about the job. He just had to work out in his head where to start.

RUDOLF DIDN'T SAY MUCH, BUT AS THE OLDEST guy on the crew, what he did say got heard: "Never work for a short man."

"So what are you doing here?" Ron asked.

Rudolf shrugged. "Union posting, same as you. But I almost turned it down when I saw the boss."

Ron hadn't had that kind of premonition. He'd thought Adam was okay. Adam had met him on the site, introduced him to the rest of the crew.

Odd, Ron had thought. The general contractor isn't usually so hands-on.

"All right, boys, I want this job to go within budget." Adam was walking among them like a sports coach, slapping one or two on the upper arm. The response from the team wasn't exactly warm, though. At least a couple of the carpenters displayed a mix of embarrassment and disdain.

"Adam Blitz is the name, speed is the game. I've got jobs lined up until next Christmas for the right crew."

Music to Ron's ears.

"Just play by my rules and let me worry about the big stuff."

Big stuff turned out to be quality and scheduling, but eventually it was clear Blitz was going to show up at every break too.

"Doesn't the guy have a life?" Ron asked Rudolf.

"His father calls the shots, but you'll never see the old man. Sends little Adam to the site to keep him out of the way."

"Well he's in the way here."

After the first few weeks the tension was tight enough to draw a catgut bow across it. Adam knew how to get the men's attention fast.

"Rudolf, you old Kraut, pick up the tempo." Rudolf didn't speed up or glance at the man. Ron saw his knuckles whiten against the stud he was sizing.

Ron just couldn't put up with it.

"Cut it out, Adam. No one's laughing here."

"What'd you say, Wellson?"

"Leave him alone, Blitz."

"Let's get something straight here, Wellson. I'm the employer; you're the scum. You do what I say and you call me *Sir.* Got it?"

Rudolf's hand on Ron's forearm distracted him. "Okay, man."

"Sir."

Ron hammered the rest of the two-inch spike in with two blows.

The next day Adam was waiting at 7 a.m. for Ron.

"I checked up on you, Wellson. Lots of northern crews, right? Well you're out of the bush, now, Tonto. Things are different here in the city. I'll be watching you. Don't think I won't. I've had my share of troubles with you breeds."

Ron walked by him and onto the job.

A few days later Blitz singled Ron out during lunch break. "Got some chicken in your bucket there, Wellson? Got some white meat? I hear you're getting some white meat at home, too. Your little lady lawyer friend."

Cherise. She was a lawyer. Not the kind of thing that makes a guy popular on the work site. The day he had walked into Cherise's office, asking for visiting rights so he could see Joy, like a moth to light, he was distracted. Cherise was so completely unlike Kathy, so fiery, so delicate and precise.

Cherise claimed he was perfect, too. Totally different from any man she'd ever known. Being perfect for Cherise was scary and frustrating. It sometimes entailed reading her mind. There were things she wanted him to be, ways she wanted him to behave. He often sensed he was disappointing her profoundly. If she'd just tell him what she wanted, he'd try. Really try.

Things improved at the work site for a week or so. Adam was gone, starting a new site, and everyone relaxed a bit. Then the worm re-emerged.

"Hey, Kraut-meister, how's the old war wound?" Something Rudolf had never mentioned. His ruddy cheeks were blotching scarlet. Adam patted his back patronizingly. Rudolf looked down, kept on working.

Ron couldn't keep his big trap shut. "This is your idea of a good time, Blitz? We're trying to do a job for you."

"Come on, Wellson, you know a man has to get to know his crew. If my team has weaknesses, I need to know right away. I depend on you guys to do the job right. I don't want anyone who can't keep pace. No room for laziness, right? By the way, Ron," he said, "I understand we have a mutual acquaintance."

"I doubt it," Ron mumbled.

"What was that?"

"I really doubt it."

"Oh, but we do. And she's such a delightful little piece. Your ex-girlfriend, there. She's doing some work for me across town." Blitz made a couple thrusting motions with his hips.

Kathy? Pretty damn unlikely, but it had to be Kathy.

"Fascinating." Ron tried to remain cool. With her mouth, Kathy wouldn't last more than a couple of days working for Adam.

Kathy was a nice comfortable lay. He'd said that to one of his buddies once, felt bad about it afterwards. It was true, but not the kind of thing you should say about someone you care about. They were just teenagers when they met on the beach near Deer Run. She wasn't his first girlfriend, for sure, but in some ways she was his best. It was like Kathy was the earth, something you could walk on, live on, love because what's not to love? A guy could leave her, because he knew she'd be fine on her own. She was that basic, that strong.

When Kathy had told him about the baby, he'd panicked. He knew then he could not stay with her. He had thought he could just leave her, just do it. But he really hadn't yet. Now Adam Blitz had designs on Kathy. She was contrary enough, too, that if Ron tried to warn her, she'd be all the more tempted.

Adam was just using her to pick on him again. What the hell was that suit doing, always hanging around while they were trying to work. Little turkey gobbler, what with *hurry up* and cutting corners and *why did this take so long,* and the fewest nails the Code would allow. When Ron came in a few minutes late Adam said, *Thought you'd split to drink up your pay-cheque, Tonto.* If he came early Adam would ask him if he was trying to make up for all those other lazy

Indians. If he took a break he was *typical.* If he made a mistake he was *stupid.* Cherise could have probably built up a human rights case against the prick. But Adam was the man with the action these days, all the big jobs. From his cousin in some government office, according to Rudolf.

Adam swaggered up to Ron the next morning, grinning. "Been lucky lately, Tonto? How's the lady lawyer?"

"What's with you, anyway?"

"Just some friendly banter. Not up to it, Wellson?" Adam obviously had something more to say. Blitz lowered his voice, almost growled. "I wanted to tell you what a good job your ex does when she sucks my dick, Tonto."

Ron wanted to hurt Blitz. Stopped himself, walked away. Why bother? Over what? Two consenting adults? It was none of his business.

Ron had a chance to talk with Rudolf at lunch break. "I never had anything against short people until now."

"It's not short people, I think. It's short men who want power too much. I've seen it before. He's out to get you."

"And you."

"Yah, but I have years of patience." Rudolf bit into a boiled egg. "You stood up to him in front of the crew. He'll try to crush you."

"I don't understand him." Ron rubbed an apple against his pant leg.

"It's control. You or I may be the boss at home,

yah. Maybe not, with a lawyer." Rudolf's elbow nudged Ron's ribs. "But we know it's give and take, win and lose. Blitz, he wants only to win, and puts himself in a place where that can happen. It's a game to him. People's lives don't matter."

"Like Kathy, my ex. I don't see how she could possibly go for him. God, it makes me sick."

"You know he probably doesn't care a bit for her, but he can be charming like a snake when it suits his purposes. Besides, you know women, they have their needs. Maybe she misses you, yah? But why does he think that would get to you?"

"Kathy's got custody of my daughter."

On Ron's last day, Blitz was at the jobsite at 7 a.m., greeting everyone.

"Good news, boys. I'm getting married!"

When no one responded, Adam went out of his way to single out Ron.

"You know, Tonto, Kathy, your old ex, the whore has agreed to be my bride."

"I don't believe it." Ron walked away, but Blitz followed him to where he was nailing a cross brace to a frame.

"Believe it, my Indian friend."

"It's none of my business, Blitz."

"Oh, but it is. You see, when I marry Kathy, your sweet-bunned little daughter will be mine."

Ron must have dropped his hammer. He couldn't remember dropping it; just suddenly he was pummeling Adam.

Adam's weightlifter chest and arms had not compensated for Ron's speed. With a crack, the shorter man's square jaw had turned abruptly. One blue eye bulged in outrage. Thick blood spurted from Adam's nose, dripping on his crisp white shirt.

"Crazy bastard, you're off this job." Adam's chest was heaving, as if he was trying not to lose control.

The rest of the crew had scrambled into a loose circle around them, and Ron felt Rudolf's scarred hand on his arm. "Easy, fella. Let's go for a walk, yah?"

Ron shook loose and snuck in one more quick blow to Adam's unprotected gut, a satisfying delivery. Adam bent over, gasping for breath, speechless for a change. Like some smart-ass, Ron had picked up his hammer, blew on it and slung it on his tool belt. "I quit." Before the trembling began he had been able to stride smoothly to his truck, start it and drive away with some dignity.

Ron left town, pulled off at the first stretch of uncultivated land, swinging the door open before the half-ton stopped rolling. He kicked at stones and dirt bike ruts, climbing a steep, sandy ridge, holding on to wolf willow and buck brush to make the last few feet. He dangled his legs from the top, and glared down at the rock and scrub wasteland, the dump site of a retreating glacier. The tops of the stunted aspen and poplar swayed in a fitful wind over his truck, door open, red and rust in the alkali dust plain. Why couldn't he be a better worker? Just one more week and he'd have been finished. Adam would have been out of his hair. Except now Ron had hit him. Christ, maybe he'd get charged.

Ron's heart rate sped up a few notches. He really hated the thought of going to jail. But Adam wasn't the type to run to the police with a bloody nose. He'd get Ron some other way. Like no more work, not in this province, not ever. He'd try that, for sure. Pull Ron's journeyman papers maybe. Adam was just way out of line. Way out of line. Ron picked up a fist-sized stone and threw it hard against a black poplar trunk. Damn. He was a lousy fighter. Cherise sure as hell wouldn't see this as a win. No, he'd lost big time. A fighter doesn't moan and cry afterwards, either. A fighter doesn't shake like a child. What was he going to tell Cherise? Nothing. He'd tell her fuck all. This was his problem.

Cherise's catnap ended with the sour after-taste of a re-occurring dream. She was a child living in a mud hut. No sun penetrated the sooty windows of their dreary home. An astonishing gleaming plate of glass, stretching from earth to sky, appeared suddenly by the hovel. Behind it the two most beautiful people Cherise could imagine laughed, danced, picked morsels of fruit from silver trays, and drank from tall goblets. Cherise pounded on the glass, knowing if she could only get beyond it, she'd be like them: beautiful. Many of the people around her struck at the barrier too, but one by one, they all gave up and went back to their hovels. Only Cherise remained, her fists raw from the effort. Behind her, her mother watched until Cherise collapsed in the darkness. "I knew you couldn't do it,"

Mother said before leaving her there. Cherise woke burning with a child's helpless rage.

She was still feeling out of sorts an hour later. For months now she'd awaken in the morning with a twist of pain in the gut. Even eating dry toast, swearing off coffee didn't relieve the burning. "Pre-ulcer" the doctor had said, "very common in stress-filled lives."

When your success depends on letting people think you can help them, there is certainly an element of stress. Nina, her partner at law for the last six years, said Cherise was exhibiting the first signs of burnout. "You do not and cannot control your clients. You do what you can and get out. They've devoted a lifetime to messing up their lives. You're not responsible for fixing everything. Just the legal problems, Cherise. No one will thank you for being a social worker." Nina paused. Ron fit into part of the lecture: "And if you think that they are your friends, you're crazy." A frequent theme in the office these days.

Nina was as cool and professional as the doctor who'd walked into Cherise's mother's hospital room that day so long ago, and said, "I'm sorry, there's nothing further we can do for you. You have two months," and walked out.

Her mother had turned to her and said, "Well. At least he was sorry." And they'd cried and laughed at the same time. Cherise took her home, tried to make her comfortable, and her mother had done what she'd always done: rejected help.

"I don't want to get in your way. If I only have two months, I'd like to do some traveling." The wisdom of travel was questionable, but it was easier to try to distract a charging bull than dissuade her mother. "I have some friends in Arizona," her mother had insisted from her deathbed. That was five years ago, and Cherise still received weekly calls from her mother, and a plane ticket south each Christmas.

"It might not have worked for everyone," her mother would often comment, "but that callous fool of a doctor saved my life." As repulsive as the notion seemed, Cherise thought now any healing the doctor had brought about in her mother was a byproduct of his own instinct for professional and personal survival, his willingness to admit it was out of his hands. Like Nina said, even with the best intentions, controlling others is a dangerous business, and now Cherise's survival was at stake. She needed a break, or maybe just to learn to let go a bit.

Custody fights exacted the most angst in Cherise. Affidavits full of sometimes spurious, often mundane, occasionally bizarre allegations. The health and happiness of those too young to speak for themselves in court lay in the balance, caught in the crossfire between two powers out to destroy each other, and suddenly given a weapon to do so. Children were at the mercy of judges who did not always have the courage to look into the heart.

It was in this arena that Cherise began, from time to time, to doubt the justice in the results of her work. She would focus on the code of ethics. As a lawyer she was *duty bound to fearlessly raise every issue, advance every argument, ask every question, however distasteful.* Fearlessly.

When she thought she'd listened to every accusation, there was this last file: the cross-burning father, drugging his own children, making weird kiddie-porn flicks he sold to Satanists, raising funds for the high-powered munitions he stashed in a rural barn awaiting the day the righteous would arise and take over the world. She had it all in the affidavit, signed by the frightened and frightening Mrs. Murray, who even explained why the children would have no memory of this: ground glass, silica surgically implanted in the stomach lining, and hypnotic suggestion, causing the implants to grind away at the poor kid's gut at any attempt to remember or articulate such memories.

It was the wildest, most terrifying story Cherise had ever heard. Her client looked like she'd walked through Hades.

"We don't get many cases like this," Cherise had commented after taking the information needed to prepare the documents.

Mrs. Murray had stared at her hands, at the desktop. Then her eyes met Cherise's directly. "I just need one person to believe me. Just one so I know I'm not crazy. I know what it sounds like. Please."

I've represented strange cases before, Cherise thought. Like whose-it, who'd insisted his name was a number, the woman who liked to get married so much she had done so seven times, and the kid who knew no remorse after bludgeoning his buddy's head to a pulp.

Mrs. Murray was no different than most of the desperate ones who entered Cherise's office. Desperation makes even the competent, the attractive and the likeable, appear despicable. Cherise studied Mrs. Murray's lined face, eyes made dramatic by the dark bruises of exhaustion. "Mrs. Murray, it is my job to act on your behalf, my duty to respect and represent your point of view to the best of my ability. What I believe does not matter."

There were tears flowing down Mrs. Murray's thin cheeks.

"What have you done to ensure your safety?" Cherise asked.

WHAT HAVE I DONE TO ENSURE MINE? CHERISE wondered as she slung the perfectly ironed blouse over the back of a chair.

"Cherise," Ron switched off the vacuum, "Cherise." She hadn't moved, as if she was waiting for him. "Listen, I'm sorry, I'm sorry. I never want to hurt you."

She let herself be guided to the couch, and sat beside him, his arms around her. "Help me through this," Ron said.

THE MORNING AFTER RON TOLD HER ABOUT Adam Blitz and the jobsite, Cherise was at work early. Her chin was tucked close to the telephone, one hand flipping through files, the other furiously scribbling notes, plowing through the things she dreaded, the things she feared.

"Nina, remember that child custody case with the burning crosses?"

Of course she did. As her partner, Nina was the only one she could talk to about any of her files. They regularly compared notes on the most difficult, the amusing and the bizarre.

Nina slung herself across Cherise's client chair. "Let me guess. Your client's moved in with you? You've filed for adoption of Mrs. Murray's children? You're organizing a one-person vigilante movement against the KKK? Umm, you could call it MASC: Mothers Against Sadistic Control-freaks."

"I went over the salient points of the case with the lawyer for the other side this morning. He won't be filing a response."

Nina smiled at her. "Now you can close the file."

Cherise nodded. "Mrs. Murray's on her own."

Nina leaned over the desk, reaching for her partner's hand. "I knew you could do it. And I, dear friend, have nothing new to report." Nina turned to leave. From the door to her adjacent office, Nina called, "Have a tiff with the charity case?"

"With Ron?" Nina had never approved of Cherise living with a former client. "What makes you say that?"

"You're here early."

"We had a good talk last night. He thinks I'm trying to control him."

"Umhumm," Nina said significantly, closing the opaque windowed door dividing their workspaces.

Cherise could see her own reflection dimly in the glass, muddied and twisted slightly. "And he lost his job," she murmured to herself. She took a breath and reached for the next file.

Women In Trade

As it turned out, being with Adam was like slapping a thick coat of paint on an unprepared surface; a person had to do some scraping first or it was just a rotten job, and it wouldn't last. But at the time, Kathy thought maybe her heart needed sanding, maybe her lack of trust was gumming up her ability to accept anybody, even Adam.

Now a person doesn't just put out an ad and start painting. Kathy was a grad from *Women in Trades.* See, when she finished her Arts degree, she wouldn't stay in university; she wanted to live in the real world. Having crossed professor off her list of careers, she was left with service industries, and lord, she'd done enough of that; a person gets real tired of smiling when she doesn't feel like it. Or the helping professions, when she needed help herself half the time. Working with your hands is an honest day's work, her dad always said. So she became a house painter. Skimpy pickings, but when a person does a good job she can look at the finished product, so perfectly fresh and clean-smelling, glistening, and say, "Now that's beautiful."

True, there weren't many women doing house painting. Kathy and Anna got mostly interiors. It was surprising how many homeowners thought a woman could do a better job inside, a neater job. In the case of Kathy's crew, they were right. Kathy had met her partners in the classroom. Anna and Janine had been on the street, had worked the street, and were jittery on the rough road to the straight and narrow. It was tough to give up the good money. The entire crew still called their clients *johns,* just among themselves, of course. To their faces it was always "Sir."

Adam was one of the johns in town who owned a lot of houses and kept calling Kathy, Janine, and Anna back. In fact that's what he seemed to do for a living: buy and fix up and rent and sell those old clunker houses. In fact Ron, Kathy's ex, worked for him on a project across town, so at first they thought he must be fine. They saw a lot of him. Typically, Anna would do the deal; she had a good business head. Kathy did the public relations. Janine would play the heavy. If it looked like they were going to get ripped off, if a john wasn't going to pay them for a job, Janine would have a word or two with the party in question. If necessary, she would call on some friends for enforcement. Kathy never asked too many questions. They always got first rate treatment as long as Janine was around. But then Janine went back to the street, at first just once in a while to supplement her income. That was about the time she broke up with the guy from Narcotics Anonymous. Anyway, she finally left the business, no hard feelings, and Kathy and Anna missed her like hell some days. Oh, they'd still see her around, but it wasn't the same.

Adam wasn't the kind of guy you'd ever lock eyes with across a smoky barroom. Certainly not photogenic. Kathy's tastes ran towards the raw-boned outdoors type, a good set of cheekbones, strong chin, broad shoulders; Adam had none of these. He had a pudding face, a puffed-up chest and bulky forearms from working out, not working hard.

One day, Anna and Kathy were cleaning up and he came through and offered them a smoke. Kathy was a sucker for a man who shares tobacco. Suddenly Adam was a human being and from then on he'd drop by often and say, "Hey, you women, take a break."

He'd only called them 'girls' once; Janine had given him that stern look of hers and he corrected himself immediately. He'd also always say, "You work too goddamn hard," which was true, but these words only spurred them on to working harder, faster.

And he had money, being a major contractor and all, so the first time he asked Kathy to go for supper – no, he called it dinner, although any working person ought to know dinner's what you have at noon – he took her to the kind of place she'd have to save up months to go to, where they have a guy to take you in, one to pour your water and shake your napkin and another to take your order. All guys, likely paid more for doing one tenth of the job the average female waiter does. God, they had to smile a lot and somehow flirt with both Adam and Kathy, so she was wishing Anna and Janine could be there to see this, because it was a good example of how the service industries make prostitutes of us all. Kathy tried to be kind to the waiters, and hoped Adam was a good tipper. She always left a healthy tip for waitresses when the meal was on her; they deserved it.

But this was on Adam, which was strange for her too. It was one of the hazards of dating in these liberated times; her 'dates' always felt free to expect she'd pay her own way. She was her own woman so she did; she thought there was something sordid about letting a man buy you a meal. A woman knows he's making a deal, that she's putting more than her scintillating conversation into the pot. Not that paying for it is wrong, it's just this falsehood, pretending he's not, the deception that she hated.

This time, though, her daughter was overnight at a friend's, and she hadn't had a night out or a man across the table or between her legs for a long time, so she let Adam be generous, even let him order for her. His boxy BMW floated them directly from the restaurant to his house, without so much as a "Care for an after-dinner drink?"

It took all Kathy could muster to go into his house. All that space for just one person, she thought, God, what a waste. She admired it anyway, although clearly someone else had done the decorating. It was a tad too frilly for a man. When he showed her the bedroom, bigger than the apartment Kathy shared with her daughter, all in a bold peachy pink, except the Jacuzzi, which was a masculine brown, she had to ask: "Who did the paint job?" But Adam was already pulling down his pants, without so much as a warm-up kiss.

Adam was a strange one. Sexually, he was reliable but not spectacular, certainly not passionate, and not very considerate, although most men can be trained. Interpersonally, well, Kathy couldn't put her finger on it at first, but there was something wrong. He never asked how she felt. He'd tell her what he thought she thought, like he'd already decided. Somewhere he'd heard, they'd kept it no secret, that certain members of his painting crew were formerly of a more lucrative profession. He was in love with this idea, so Kathy let him think what he wanted to, never told him she was just a dull Arts grad. Somehow, at first all this dishonesty seemed harmless. Why not, if it helped him with his little fantasy, and it was getting them work?

Adam didn't go away, and Kathy just sort of let it happen. Eventually he came over to her apartment. She watched his eyes for some sign of criticism, of disapproval. Just one wrong word and he'd be out on his tail. But he looked around, gravitated to Kathy's reading chair, her books, looked at her inquiringly and said, "So what are your plans for dinner?"

When he met her daughter, Joy, aged five, he treated the little girl with the same lack of curiosity he expressed for the rest of Kathy's life before him.

"Hello Joy." No 'My, what a big girl, you must be starting school soon,' no 'Did you draw that picture on the fridge?' or 'What a clever girl and what a pretty dress you have on.'

Just as well. Joy hated him from their first meeting. She wouldn't look at Adam, clung to Kathy's legs like a two-year-old all night, so Kathy couldn't even kiss the man goodbye when he finally left.

That should have been the end of that, but he came back. The very next day. "Slumming it," Anna said, and laughed at Kathy's predicament, a little sadly. But then Anna seldom really laughed.

Kathy got used to Adam and the little cracks she felt sometimes were smoothed over by familiarity. It was good to have someone to wake up with. But Anna was right; after awhile they never did go back to Adam's. He'd show up at her place, whenever.

When he offered to take her away from all this (all what? Kathy wondered) to come live with him, she couldn't laugh in his face. She paused long enough for him to add, "Of course, we'll get married first."

Kathy's stomach and bowels went into high panic mode. "I have to think about this. Excuse me," and she ran to the can.

So there she was, stuck in the middle of a bad job, and unless she could go back and start all over again, someone was going to get hurt. She didn't know how she felt about Adam. One of these days he'd have to meet her folks.

"Nice simple people" he'd say. Somehow he'd let it slip, his misinformation about Kathy's past. Then the folks, would they believe him? For now, Kathy's main worry was how to say no without losing her painting team's best john. So here was the quintessential dilemma; she was caught mixing business with pleasure.

"Mom." Joy was tapping at the bathroom door. It was a small bathroom. Kathy could reach the doorknob without even lifting one cheek from the throne. She let Joy in.

"Mom, Adam came into my room." She paused.

"Just now?" What the hell was he doing in Joy's room?

"Uh huh. I told him to get out, but he says you're going to get married."

Kathy's stomach cramped into yet another knot. "Honey, that's not for sure yet. I'll want to talk to you about it, anyway."

"Well, I say no, Mom. He's yucky. He's a yucky snake." Then Kathy's daughter, her rock, the apple of her eye, the joy of her life, wept.

Every mother's done this a hundred times, comforted a child while sitting on the toilet. Moms don't get many solitary moments. But every time, Kathy would get this strong mental image – what they must look like, and she'd giggle. Which always exacerbated the anguish of the poor tiny comfortee. This time, Joy was angry.

"Mom, it's not funny. If you marry that guy, I won't live with you anymore." She marched out, swinging the door open, leaving Kathy reaching for the bathroom doorknob.

Most women, unlike their children, weep in the tub or shower. No one can hear you there, and it's easier to explain away the face. Kathy had found the two or three seconds between flush and washing hands just as useful for those sobs a mother sometimes has to save up – or the ones that strike unavoidably – just because she refused to think about it for a long, long time. So long she's forgotten what "it" was; all she knew was that it's overwhelming and unavoidable and unutterably sad.

Kathy knew she was not going to marry Adam. She couldn't. It wasn't just Joy's reaction, which was the deal sealer, really. There was so much that just didn't feel right about him. So she did what every self-respecting woman would do: she coaxed Adam out the door with, "I'll think about it." Then she tucked Joy into bed, with an assuring "Don't worry." And she called Anna. Who laughed.

"You remember that story about a frog and a princess? Well, Adam ain't under no spell."

The frog part kind of worked; but as soon as Kathy started visualizing Adam as a frog, she developed a fondness, a warmth for him and a defensiveness she hadn't expected. "He's not that bad, eh? Sort of sweet."

"Emotionally underdeveloped," Anna said.

"Show me a man who isn't."

"And not half your intelligence." Anna was starting to sound worried.

"Oh Anna, I don't know. He knows stuff I don't have a clue about."

By the time they'd finished talking, Anna had, much to her dismay, turned Kathy around completely. Kathy thought maybe she could learn to love the bug-eyed little guy. "I'm going to give him a chance, Anna," she said.

Anna sighed. "He doesn't deserve a chance. Not with you and not with Joy."

You're both jealous, Kathy decided.

She had never been married. Oh, she'd been in love, at least once, with Joy's father. She still felt a physical heat in her gut remembering how he'd come up behind her and hug, his mouth on her neck. Ron wasn't a talker, but once he told her she had beautiful feet, no, the most beautiful feet he'd ever seen. She'd have settled for that and his arms around her waist. But somewhere along the road he had taken a different turn. She still cried too much about that even though it was a long time ago. So she figured maybe now she really did love Adam, but didn't know it.

Kathy loved her daughter. Joy was one of those kids who really are too good to be true; quiet, even as a baby, contented, but watch out when the girl's been thinking. When Joy came out with whatever she'd been mulling over, it was etched in concrete. Kathy always asked her where she got that stubborn streak. So when Joy decided she didn't like Adam, that she wouldn't live with him, Kathy had to take her seriously. If Kathy had to choose between her and anything else, even life itself, well, she'd choose her daughter.

There was another thing. Joy's dad. Like all kids with parents in two households, Joy knew the or-I'll-go-live-with-daddy routine. Oh, Joy was subtle. The threat, Kathy's fear of it, was there.

One Thursday late in August, Kathy took Joy shopping for school supplies. Joy was starting "the big

K" and had some decisions to make about glue and crayons, new clothes and stuff. So they booked a shopping night; no Adam, no Anna, just the two of them.

At the rack of sweatshirts screen printed with moon-eyed female cartoons, Kathy held a purple-trimmed number to Joy's chin and said, "So what do you think of Adam?"

"I told you. He's a yucky snake."

"How about a frog?"

"Still yucky."

"Why yucky?"

"He's not nice."

"Why not?"

"He just isn't. I don't like that shirt."

On to the next rack and lace trimmed blue jeans.

"You have to have a reason, Joy. Why don't you like him?"

"He's going to do something mean."

"What?"

"He's going to be mean. Can I get these ones, Mom?"

The price tag distracted Kathy.

When they got home Kathy knew her ongoing relationship with Adam depended now on *him* convincing Joy.

A week later, Adam and Kathy were watching a video, *Lolita,* Adam's choice. Kathy was seated on the floor in front of Adam, her lower back on the edge of his chair, as he massaged her shoulders and neck, something she never asked him to do, but had come to enjoy. Kathy had just tucked Joy into bed but was finding it hard to focus on the film. The story was giving her the creeps.

"Adam, Joy and I have been discussing your proposal." Kathy choked on the word 'wedding.' "It's going to take a while for her to get used to the idea."

"That's fine," he said, smoothly.

"I can't give you an answer until she's comfortable with us. I know she hasn't given you much of a chance." Adam was Kathy's first serious man after Joy's father but he didn't need to know that.

"That's fine. Watch the movie."

He was only around the house a couple of nights a week. When he was there, Joy always kept to herself, played outside or in her room. Joy had taken to drawing reptiles and amphibians and posting them on the doors and walls of their apartment. Adam certainly could have commented on the huge fanged cobras or the bulgy-eyed toads he faced, eye-level, each time he came over. From Kathy's perspective, Adam did nothing to strengthen his relationship with Joy: no friendly questions about starting school, no pats on the head for colouring in the lines, nothing. "Maybe you could make an effort to get to know her a bit."

"Sure. Now shush. You'll like this part." Kathy leaned her head against one of Adam's knees and closed her eyes. She'd seen enough of the movie to know it was all about male fantasy, male ego, and not at all about the little girl. Kathy felt really tired.

She stood up in front of the TV screen. "Look, it's Joy's first day of kindergarten tomorrow, so I'd like to get a good night's sleep." To her surprise, instead of pulling the movie and leaving, Adam pulled the movie and stayed. She rolled away from him and stared at the ceiling for an hour or two before sleep took her down.

The next morning, Anna called Kathy about 6 a.m.. They were to do a big job on a downtown project, but it had to be done quickly, as in yesterday. It was a two person job – Anna couldn't start without her. She had to be there by 8 a.m. Kathy's plan to walk Joy to school for her first day of kindergarten, and to pick her up at noon, was in ruins. Their sitter had a houseful of little ones, and couldn't do the here's-how-you-get-to-school routine. So Kathy turned to Adam, and asked him to walk with Joy. No problem, he said.

Kathy gave him addresses, names, room numbers, times.

Kathy apologized to a very sleepy Joy as she braided a ribbon into her daughter's hair. "I've got to go to work, my girl, but Adam will walk with you today. It's only three blocks. I'm sorry Mommy won't be there. Will you be all right?" Joy nodded, then looked at Adam distrustfully. She seemed to understand there should be an adult with her. It should have been Kathy. Maybe, Kathy hoped, this would be the icebreaker, the time when those two would do something important together and get that father-daughter thing going.

Joy's first day of kindergarten. At noon, Kathy phoned from work to see how things went. There was no answer at home, or at Adam's, and the sitter said Joy wasn't there yet. Kathy got panicky, and Anna said, "Try back in a while, they're likely just late." But a little later, Kathy phoned the kindergarten. Joy had never made it to school. Kathy ran to the truck, yelled to Anna what happened; and Anna cursed, dropped her brush, and ran too, saying, "I knew it, I knew it."

"Knew what?" Kathy said, angry, really angry, and Anna yelled back at her "He's a creep, Kathy. Your girl needs your protection."

"Get in the truck, Anna. And shut up. Don't you think I know?"

Anna shut up. Kathy drove home, shaking. Where else do you start?

The door was locked. She unlocked it, calling and thinking of all the lost children, all the poster kids, all the kidnappers, and she screamed for her baby girl – and she heard her.

She heard her. Joy was hiding as far back as she could go under her bed, her new clothes all dusty and her hair ribbon yanked loose.

Kathy said, "What are you doing way down there, come on out." Joy's face was streaked with tears like rain down a dusty window. "Joy, what are you doing?"

Anna reached under the bed, pulled Joy out, then held her and let her cry. "Can't you see?"

Kathy marched to the phone; Adam had some explaining to do. No answer. Good thing. Kathy was trembling; she couldn't have spoken anyway. Besides, she wanted to kill him. For not getting Joy to school, for not letting Kathy know, for leaving her little girl terrified.

"Get rid of that creep. Forget the work, forget the money, forget your goddamn sex drive for a minute." Anna had Joy on one hip and her thin fist in the air like a gospel preacher's. "He doesn't deserve your spit." Her fist became a wing that pulled Kathy's head to her shoulder, and the three of them stood there a long time, Anna just holding them both and saying "It's okay." Joy finally crawled into Kathy's arms.

"You'll never see that guy again," Kathy told her. "Now Mom's going to pour you a bath, get some of that dirt off you."

While Kathy bathed her carefully, Anna checked her clothes. They both knew how the legal beagles could tear apart a woman on the witness stand; Kathy wasn't going to expose her little girl to those dogs unless it was an open and shut case. Adam could and would launch a rigorous defense. But there were no marks, no blood.

Kathy couldn't bring herself to ask Joy what Adam did to make her hide under the bed. Not yet. She thought she'd leave it up to her child to talk about it if she had to. And Joy had bounced back as if nothing had happened, and was busy at the business of being a kindergarten student. Kathy took a pay cut so she could be there morning and noon for her daughter, and Anna called Janine back in for the big job.

"Whatever happened is my fault," Kathy told Anna. She did try to call Adam once or twice, left messages on his machine. She took to stalking his office on her breaks and after work until five, but either he had totally different hours now, or he'd spotted her and wished to avoid the confrontation. Kathy wasn't sure how she would confront him, but she could imagine making a loud accusation, followed by a threat He was still around town, but whenever she saw him, he always seemed to be going in the other direction, fast.

Mid-September, Janine dropped by the new residential job Kathy and Anna were doing, bearing cups of steaming coffee. Kathy practically slid down the last two levels of scaffolding. She had been cutting in the trim on the third story fascia. They took a smoke break, crouching under the patchy shade of an overgrown caragana.

"I think someone ought to show him the error of his ways," Janine said. "Is the prick paid up or does he owe us money before I go for it?"

"He's paid up. This would be strictly for pleasure," Anna said.

"I have a few friends who'd be happy to do that for pleasure, pay him a house call, discuss the matter." Janine was serious.

"For what? For scaring my little girl?"

"Scaring? Is that what you call it? You're going to have to live with yourself for the rest of your life, Kathy. I'm trying to help, or can't you see that, either?" Janine took a long drag from her cigarette.

"Come on, Kathy, you know he's scum," Anna said. "The next kid may not be so lucky." She grinned at Janine. "Anyways, I figured you'd already looked into the matter, given chicken-livered Kathy here hasn't been able to even get the turd to talk to her."

Janine flashed a feral smile at Anna, and then turned accusingly to Kathy. "You have talked to Joy by now, right?"

Kathy ground the butt of her smoke with the toe of her boot.

"You haven't," Anna said.

"I thought I'd just let it go. Maybe he's learned something from all this."

"From all what? I'm here to teach you something, woman. Adam tried to take you for everything you had. Everything. Including your daughter. He didn't love you or Joy, didn't even like you, hell, didn't even know you. The man had the emotional capacity of a paint brush." Anna lifted her three-inch slant cut, heavy with paint.

Kathy agreed. It was one thing to trade for money, for security, for sex. This wasn't straight business; it wasn't even pretty.

"Where I come from, a man only gets to do that once. No one worries about rehabilitation or his troubled childhood." Janine stubbed out her cigarette emphatically. "Kathy, this is every woman's revenge fantasy, and you're quivering like some bleeding heart."

That night, Kathy took Joy out for pizza. Ham and pineapple, Joy's favourite. They were well into their second pieces when Kathy asked, "So, do you want to tell me what happened that time I left you with Adam?"

"What time?"

"The only time I left you with him. The time I found you under the bed."

"Oh, nothing." Joy twirled a crust on her plate.

"Nothing makes you crawl under the bed!"

"Mom, I told you, he's yucky. I ran away."

"Did he do anything to scare you?" Kathy's voice quavered a bit, intense.

"Not really."

"Did he lay a hand on you?"

"I told you, Mommy, I ran away." Tears were brimming in the girl's eyes.

"I'm so sorry, honey, I shouldn't have left you. I'm so sorry."

Joy never spoke to Kathy about Adam again. Kathy wouldn't push her. A woman must trust her gut instincts and stick to her principles if she wants to do a good job.

Cut Flowers

CHERISE LEANS OVER THE BATHROOM SINK, doing her hand wash again, all these delicates. Trying not to focus on her sorrow. What's it about anyway? She's not PMS'ing. She has a great career, a fantastic business partner, a wonderful man in her life, and she feels so alone. It's Nina's birthday and they aren't celebrating together. Is that all? Cherise is an expert in self control and here she is, pitiful. Crying melodramatic tears. Biting her bottom lip so Ron can't hear her.

She's not sure how he'll react to her crying. Of course she can't stay here forever, sudsing her silks, so she hums the first thing that comes to her mind – some old Rod Stewart, and finds herself laughing, switching all the pronouns: *knowing that I lied, straight-faced while you cried.* The rest of the song is just as inappropriate. Cherise believes in nothing, has no reason to believe. Except in herself. She excels at that. Isn't the mind a marvel? But you can't trust it.

Cherise doesn't trust Ron, a man and never to be trusted. Not Nina, her friend and partner in law.

Cherise holds her hand to her mouth and bites down on it. Her parents have problems of their own. Her mother sees fit to call only occasionally from her warm hide-out in the desert, and her father, well, he has been out of touch.

Cherise has become distanced, too, from what she has felt over the years.

Physical sensations disappeared first.

Not a lovely child: tall, ungainly, tending to pudge, Cherise skulked around the borders of the crusher-dust schoolyard during the long recesses and even longer noon hours. Anyone smaller than her received a pinch for getting too close. Hardly anyone did. "That's my swing," she'd say, and no one argued. "I'm skipping next." But the other girls gave up the rope, slinking off to play hopscotch. She couldn't quite get the knack of how to play with other children.

Then she discovered wild horses. Cantering the length of the chain-link fence marking the school property, she became a stallion, strong and free and somehow superior to but responsible for the poor, less vicious mares and geldings in her imaginary herd. She neighed abruptly, slashed her hooves, not about to be tamed by anyone.

Her mother insisted she wear girl-clothes: knee socks, skirts with netted, itchy crinoline, lacy see-through blouses, which revealed her early breasts and generous tummy. She fought, as any wild thing would, for proper attire, a pair of jeans, please! Something that wouldn't make her stand out so much from the denim and work shirt herd. But Mother was firm: her girl, her only child would be a woman, not a tomboy.

All this made Cherise's life dangerous, especially with the big boys. "Hey, let's catch that girl who thinks she's a horse." Bobby easily withstood the flailing hooves, pinned her against the fence. She bit and hissed, but did not scream or cry when they caught her. There were three of them, bored with their endless game of catch. "Nice pony, nice little pony. Here, why don't you take us for a ride?" They rubbed up against her rump, ran their grubby hands down her front, pinched her nipples. Andrew tried to push his hands down her blouse, but she fought too hard. "Ouch, you little bitch. You cunt." He cuffed her, holding his arm, and she ran to the safety of the ravine.

Cherise often came home bruised and scraped. So did they. In fact it was a phone call from one of the parents, complaining about a particularly deep bite on her son's arm, that prompted Cherise's dad to pick her up each lunch hour and right after school, an arrangement that didn't work out much better.

She missed out on organized softball, which seemed to become the thing everyone was busy with just after she left the schoolyard. She would have been good, even in her frilly dresses, would have been a slugger and popular, the first pick on anyone's team. But maybe not. Sometime during grade six, shortly after Father took over, she stopped growing and soon she was smaller than the others and not nearly as able to fend for herself. Her schoolmates remembered her vicious days as a stallion, however, and most gave her a wide berth.

From then on, Cherise learned much of her etiquette in dealing with people her own age from books and movies. She turned to horror thrillers. It was a comfort. Nothing that bad would ever happen to her. She'd never be consumed by a demon or bitten on the neck by a vampire. If Frankenstein's monster approached her, she would not scream and run. She would reach out a hand and say, "Brother," and he would never betray her.

Despite her mother's insistence, she found worn jeans, finally, in her father's abandoned wardrobe. His yard and garage pants, scarred by battery acid, cut to length, frayed and belted, gave her a start in her high school dress code. Her mother's makeup, readily available, perfectly produced that wan, dark rimmed, sloe-eyed look, and her already bloodless lips provided a vampirish mystique, which attracted a certain admiration with the high school fringe. She was embraced by the druggies, who hung out at the nearby Chinese restaurant, drinking too much coffee and slipping out for tokes.

"I hereby declare school attendance optional." She held court around a café table. Anti-establishment rhetoric flowed from her lips. She kept her honours marks a closely guarded secret, although her Mother clung to them as the only remaining sign of hope.

"You could be anything you want," Mother consoled herself, having already crossed dancer and actress off her list. "A doctor, a lawyer–"

Cherise screwed her face into a repulsive scowl. She'd had quite enough of playing doctor, thank you. Although a pain doctor had some appeal. She experimented with pain, poking needles through her arms and the flesh of her hands, a favourite entertainment in the coffee shop. Nothing ever seemed to hurt after the first pin prick, unless someone distracted her and she lost her focus.

"Maybe I could be a shrink, Mother."

Mother's disapproval ended the conversation. Mother had spent a large amount of hard-earned money on mysterious sessions from which she would return weepy, even more deeply depressed. She didn't, she said, believe in the profession of psychiatry any more.

Though many of Cherise's teenaged companions were boys, young men, she was not date material – untouchable and cool. Too cool to ask out. What would a guy do? Go to a horror movie, make out in the graveyard? Although she hadn't, everyone was of the opinion Cherise had been there, done that. Besides, she didn't flirt. Conversation was never casual. She was diving deep into the dialectic of materialism, way out of their league.

Cherise grew up a lot tougher than the fluffy girl her mother wanted. Too bad, Cherise muses, wringing the soap out of a pair of nylons. Cherise has become concerned about her ability to recall her past with accuracy. Details loom larger while important days, like graduation, and whole chunks of time, like law school, slip her mind. Recent events are particularly perplexing. Like Nina kissing her. They'd been out for drinks; that would make things fuzzy. Did she say something, do something different? How could she let that happen?

She knows the scene with her father happened. Her mother confirms it regularly. "Have you heard from that molester?"

Her father reaffirms it, too, by his absence.

But it's like one of those old box frames, trying to see the picture inside, but moisture and dust have lodged between the levels of glass, so you sort of see a pastoral scene, a cottage home cozy with flowers. But you don't see it, and you sometimes see something you know you shouldn't: you see yourself.

Leaning over the end of the high bed, the pink chenille flower petals swirling patterns into her stomach. The old man behind her, kneeling, making noises. She won't remember feeling anything. Her face is pressed against a stuffed Bambi so she doesn't see the door opening, Mother home from work early, not feeling well, she said. She will remember the sharp intake of breath, the quivering groan from her father. She lifts her head, and knows this won't happen again. She is twelve.

Did Cherise say or do anything? She doesn't know now. She imagines the way she must have looked to her mother, is reminded of it whenever she sees a doe, headlight-blinded.

The rest is a kind of death by suffocation. No matter how hard she tried to be the best little girl, the perfect student, and later, the most outrageous, her mother never did recover enough to love her.

And then Ron came into her life.

For Cherise, the first hours she spent with Ron were really alarming, as if she'd been underwater for a long time, and suddenly had surfaced, seeing and hearing clearly. He had come to her office as a client, but she would glance up and catch that momentary uncertainty in the way his brows pinched together, and she knew he'd been alone a lot, maybe all his life. He'd look off, behind her shoulder, for a few heartbeats before answering a simple question; he'd been loved and betrayed. Every once in a while his hands would grip his knees and he'd be explaining his relationship with Kathy, who, it sounded like, had the grace and tact of a Mack truck, and Cherise could see an innocent bewilderment, like a wild thing about to strike out. Complete vulnerability, total decisiveness. Like her, Ron could drop that melancholia, as if it were a haunting of some sort, and bounce back, smiling.

Cherise is practicing now in the mirror, this is what smiling looks like, and gently wringing the soap, 99.9% pure according to the box, from her favourite nightie, the snowy one with dozens of buttons and tucks and a pink ribbon woven through the eyelet at the neck.

Like the pink ribbon from around her waist in Grade 3, before she became a stallion. The kids all pointed and jabbed and tore the ribbon from the lace, running with it, shimmying up the flag pole, *Cherry, Cherry, Cherry.* They tied the ribbon so high she could never reach it. The next day they all pretended nothing happened. The pink ribbon fluttered above their heads, a banner.

"You done in there yet, Cher?" Ron calls from the hall. "Come on, open the door, please."

"It's open, Ron."

Ron humps against her back as he squeezes into the tiny bathroom, sliding his finger up the slit of her linen pinstripe skirt. Then he sees her face in the mirror.

"What's bugging you anyway?"

"Nothing," she says. "I don't know." Technically a lie.

"Look, if you're not going to tell me what's wrong, don't tell me nothing's wrong." He flips up the toilet seat so hard it bounces back down again. "Maybe you should see a shrink."

Cherise refuses to comment. She will not willingly look at this sadness straight on. A little sideways is easier. But if she avoids it, it rears up, viciously; she detests surprises.

Ron doesn't want to hear her out in any event. As she flings laundry over the shower curtain pole, he pushes by her, and in a moment she can hear the slam of the outside door. "Where are you going?" she calls, too late.

Okay. Okay. Talk through it, a counsellor had once told her, and let yourself feel. So she starts talking through it. Simple.

God, how she wishes she was someone simple. Like Kathy, Ron's ex, someone with a simple life; just her and her child, and her single-minded emotional attachment to Ron. Ron swore there was nothing between them anymore except the child. Well, tonight Kathy can have him, if that's where he's gone. But that creates further problems and doesn't fix anything, really.

Cherise is dancing around the pain. Talk into it, talk into it.

SHE HAD SHARED WITH NINA AS SHE IMAGINED one would with a sister. Nina knew all Cherise's secrets, her lonely past, her need. Nina had said she understood. Cherise preferred to not trust others. "You can't live like that, girl. You've got to talk these things out." So Cherise told her everything. That had been a serious error in judgement.

You don't hurt a sister. There was money involved, a job. A career. Political issues Cherise understood but did not consider paramount at the time, being immersed in her very first friendship, her first real love of another person. Nina. She loved Nina.

Nina and Cherise, Barristers and Solicitors. An unbeatable combination that started right after law school ended. They'd had their Chinese astrology done over lunch one day: business compatibility is exceptional between Nina the tigress and Cherise the sure-footed, determined racehorse. But the teacup reader in the café had warned: troubles loomed on the romantic front.

Cherise had shrugged. "Romance is the opiate of the masses," a quip from her late teens, one she hadn't thought about much since. Here she was, almost thirty, and opiate sounded good. Being part of the masses sounded good. Living the unexamined life sounded good.

There were big holes in her understanding of human nature, interpersonal relationships, Cherise realized, wondering if she couldn't blame that, too, on her parents. But she had been completely blind-sided by Nina, the first person in her adult life who'd meshed so perfectly with her. Nina would grab a file, tear through it; Cherise would study each document, correct typos, query fine points. Nina would spout strategy while Cherise proposed technicalities. Nina would fight fiercely, passionately. Cherise darted, sought out safety.

They were spending too much time together, dashing, right after the office closed, to the bar, dinner together, to the clubs. Cherise felt alive when Nina was in the same room. She knew it was mutual.

Cherise had never been comfortable with touching others, while Nina touched hands, rubbed shoulders, hugged. They were walking back to Nina's car, left by the office while they slipped out for dinner on a glorious summer night, the kind that should never end – perfectly calm, pleasantly warm and miraculously mosquito free. Flowerbeds of nicotiana and evening stocks poured an exotic spice into the air. The deck of their favourite restaurant had been full of other office refugees, lingering over the sunset. It was no special occasion, but the atmosphere was celebratory. Cherise had had more wine than usual, and was, much to her own surprise, giggling. Nina was up to the occasion, witty and theatrical.

Nina, once an ambitious actress, regaled Cherise with favourite quotes, to which Cherise responded as best she could, with remembered bits of her own. Nina had the kind of memory for this, could cite chapter and verse in law as well. Cherise found herself a bit at sea, having the memory of one who knows where to look something up, but not precisely what she'll find when the correct page is finally turned.

"The retort courteous. The quip modest. The reply churlish. The reproof valiant. The countercheck quarrelsome. The lie circumstantial." Nina paused for effect, *"The lie direct."*

"Oh, one of the comedies, isn't it?"

"The degrees of a lie, *As You Like It,* darling. Your turn."

"Oh, umm *We shall have an association in which the free development of each is the free development of all."*

"Communist Manifesto, 1918."

"Yes, Engels and Marx. *All great events and personalities in world history reappear in one fashion or another. The first time as tragedy, the second as farce."*

"Same guys?"

Cherise nodded. "I'm a one trick pony. Your turn."

"Friendship is a constant in all things. Save in the office and affairs of love."

"Dunno. How about: *Let a hundred flowers blossom*

and a hundred schools of thought contend. Chairman Mao."

"Mao Tse Tung? What are you, Cherise, some kind of closet leftie?"

"I used to be Snow White, but I drifted."

"Mae West! *Give a man a free hand and he'll try to put it all over you."*

"Too true." Cherise drooped for a moment. *"There's rosemary, that's for remembrance; pray, love, remember; And there is pansies, that's for thoughts."*

"Ophelia. *Her clothes spread wide, And mermaid-like, a while they bore her up; which time she chanted snatches of old tunes, As one incapable of her own distress.* So tragic."

"Not a farce?"

"Marx wasn't always right."

They rose to leave, the last ones, having put departure off as long as possible. The café staff had all the tables cleared but theirs, and was turning out the lights.

When she stood up, Cherise found her feet were quite unsteady. Nina gallantly allowed her to lean as they strolled. "Need a ride? I think I should give you a ride."

Cherise agreed immediately. She could barely focus.

"Tis almost morn; I would have thee gone; And yet no further than a wanton's bird, Who lets it hop a little from her hand." Nina stopped expectantly. "Cherise, this is your line."

"What?"

"Romeo and Juliet, your line. *I would I were that bird."*

Cherise almost snorted. "Sorry, I don't know it."

"You see, her eyes are open. Ay, but their sense is shut."

"I know that one! *"Out, out damned spot. Who would have thought the old man had so much blood in him?"* Cherise's voice rang overly loud on the empty street, and echoed back to her, eerily.

"Macbeth. My favourite. *Eye of newt and toe of frog."*

And here Cherise chimed in, enthusiastically. *"Wool of bat and tongue of dog, Adder's fork and blind-worm's sting, Lizard's leg and howlet's wing, For a charm of powerful trouble, Let a hell-broth boil and bubble."*

Cherise fumbled for the passenger door. Nina placed her hand over Cherise's, opened the door smoothly, and leaning close, she kissed Cherise, not just a peck on the cheek, but a real kiss, on the lips, her tongue flickering, tickling the tip of Cherise's. It was not a surprise. But it was still shocking. At least Cherise went into shock, couldn't move. Couldn't respond. Couldn't react. Nina stepped back, waited for some movement, some reassurance, anything. Finally she walked around Cherise, hugged her from behind, her face in Cherise's neck, blowing into her hair.

"It's okay, Cherise. I just have to get these things out of my system once in a while."

To love another woman. She did, of course, love Nina, but to make love with her? This was beyond her.

Or rather, it was a difficult reach. Not that either. It just wasn't safe. To be intimate with another person, anyone, was a risk. But with a business partner it's a fatal error. She knew that in her head. It was her body, maybe her heart, that was guilty of betrayal.

Then to complicate matters, or maybe it was to simplify, the very next day Ron appeared at their door. He was a walk-in client, Cherise's turn. It was a standard case. Dad makes kid, takes off, has change of heart, wants to see kid. Standard loser case, unless the client's really willing to make substantial changes to his lifestyle and commitments. Ron said he was willing.

And every time she raised her eyes to his, she felt she was willing too. He was physically strong, with the wild, yet tidy appearance she'd always appreciated in men who worked with their hands. There was something exotic about him. Clean high cheekbones. He was beautiful.

By the time he left the office, he had a Notice of Motion, complete with Affidavit, and they had a date for dinner. Cherise's cheeks were warm to the touch and she startled when Nina leaned against their mutual doorjamb, smiling tightly, almost sadly, at her. "Conflict of interest, Cherise. Don't fall for the client."

Of course Cherise denied it. The first lie. "But I do have something on tonight, Nina, so I can't make it for dinner and drinks."

"You can expect a complete cross-examination in the morning," Nina promised, with more spirit in the words than in her slumping body.

"Of course. You bringing a Bible, or are you prepared to accept my Oath?"

"Nah, I'll trust you on this one." Nina turned, her hand on the door handle, and pulled a tragic/comic face. *"Hark, doest thou hear the sound of heart strings breaking?"* She closed the door very softly. That Nina, what a ham.

They were still having fun together, still practicing law in perfect harmony. As it became clear Ron was going to be more than a passing flirtation, there was stiffness from time to time. Nina would ask Cherise, "Are you sure this is accurate?" or, over dinner "You've got time for this? I don't want to keep you from anything, Cherry." Whenever Cherise said anything about Ron, professionally or socially, Nina's eyes would cloud over a bit, as if she wasn't listening, didn't want to hear.

Nina began double-checking limitation periods, spending more time than she needed re-reading Cherise's memos. The day the workmen built the new and separate office entry, blocking off the door between them, Nina only shrugged. "Professionalism, my dear."

Cherise started locking her files.

Their work, Cherise and Nina's, was full of judgement calls, full of small decisions that often had huge repercussions on people's lives. Sometimes, being human, they missed doing something that would have strengthened their clients' cases. Now, with the new Nina, Cherise didn't care whether every document was in perfect order, or filed in proper time. No, that was a lie. Only a small part of her wanted to let things go.

When she was about twelve, maybe younger, just after her father started to pick her up after school, her cousins decided it was time for her to learn to do the dead man's float. They led her to deep water and pushed her under, their hands heavy on her as she tried to fight, tried to scream, dulled water sounds filling her ears. Finally the cousins' arms relented, pulled her up, and they laughed as she gasped, choked, sputtered at the water's surface. "This is our little secret, kid. You tell and we'll do it again."

But there was a moment under the water when she wanted to stay there, wanted to drown.

The day Ron moved in with Cherise, Nina brought in the accountant, although year-end was still two months away. "Just covering my fanny, Cherry, dear. Clearly your financial situation is about to change." Their accountant looked at Cherise only obliquely. Cherise lasted until noon, took the afternoon off.

There was nothing wrong with the books. And nothing wrong with her work; she just didn't feel like doing it. That was a year ago. They held on to the practice, managed to remain civil, persisted in working together. It wasn't much fun anymore.

Nina, smiling as if she cared, saying, "Cherise, take care of yourself first."

Nina does care. Too much. Cherise should just say to Nina, "I love you, but not like that. You're hurting me." She should say to Ron "Please don't run away."

The first night the tears came Ron listened to Cherise about the problems at the office. She didn't tell Ron about the kiss, the feelings she couldn't focus on yet. If only she could find this sort of thing in the Statutes, in a casebook. If only there was some precedent.

Ron reacted strongly in her defense anyway. "The bitch," he said.

"No, she's my friend, don't hurt her, don't say anything."

"Well, what do you want me to do?"

"Nothing."

"Are you sure there's not more to this? What's really bugging you? I've done something, haven't I?"

Cherise couldn't tell Ron about her father, about the boys in the schoolyard, even about her cousins; all those things she would rather not bring back to life, would rather forget.

Now she wished she'd talked to the counsellor, instead of Nina. Instead of Ron. Yes, Ron had done something, by being part of her life. So she lied. "This has nothing to do with you."

There is nothing to feel bad about, really. No one has lost anything. She and Nina are still friends, aren't they? She and Ron are still lovers. Time will cure all. Ron is a man, couldn't hope to understand. Nina is a professional; the friendship was in the way. If Cherise concentrates, puts a rein on her feelings, they will not betray her, and every one can all carry on as usual.

Cherise is in control again when Ron comes home. "How's Friday night for you? I'm thinking of asking Nina over for dinner. A belated birthday celebration." Already she feels the beginning of excitement, of joy at the prospect.

"Sure, great. Here," he says, dropping a green paper tube in her hands. Cherise tears the tissue back. Roses.

"I thought they'd make you feel better." Ron is already seated, right hand on the remote control, eyes on the television.

Two roses, one full and throbbing red and the other a pale ribbon pink. Purely coincidental, like the song she can't get out of her head, the one she is still humming while she makes new cuts across the rose stems, keeping them submerged all the while, precisely according to the "Instructions for care and preservation of freshly cut flowers." Careful of the knife. If she slips and nicks her thumb, she knows now she will feel it.

Bad Habits and Parasites

So I've got my head under the hood of my trusty, rusty half-ton, doing some fine-tuning. Damn timing chain's always a little out. Not that running rough is a sin, but I always feel a little better when the engine purrs. Sort of a sign that all's well with the world. When along comes my ex, says, "Hey, Kathy, want to go for a ride?" Not "How's the kid, our daughter, Joy?" Not the "I'm a little tight for cash this month" jig, either. I know that tone of voice by heart. Besides, it's mid month, and maintenance payments are due on the 30th. So this is different. And he's grinning at me like I'm made of gold, so I guess I haven't got too much grease on my forehead yet.

"What's up, Ron?"

"Nothing much. What're you doing?"

"Adjusting the timing. Nothing much."

Ron leans over, looks at my rust bucket's mighty motor with the most interest he's shown in anything of mine for years. Eight years, the exact age of our daughter Joy, to be precise. Since the birth of our daughter. Well, almost that long. For sure since he moved in with Cherise, the slick as a pin-stripe lawyer type. So it doesn't take a rocket scientist to figure out what's happening.

"Broke up with Cherise, eh?"

Ron winced like I'd hit him in the gut. "Yeah."

Right, and so you're on my doorstep, lover, and the balls, no pun intended, are back in my park.

There was a time when I would have grabbed them too, no question, when I would have pushed my obvious emotional advantage at a prime moment like this. But now that I'm a professional, with a potential for a salary and all that, I can choose my own time, take it easy, in short, decline instead of recline.

"Come on in and cry in a coffee cup, Ron." And he follows me inside.

The way Ron tells it, it was like he had no clue, no hints, except maybe Cherise had been a bit mopey, but he'd been too busy with his residential renovations biz to ask what was up. It was spring and everyone wanted more space, bigger rooms, after a long hard winter spent indoors together.

So Cherise asks her law partner Nina over for dinner one night and sends Ron out for more wine, and when he gets back, well...

In my cross examination I discover that Ron was actually gone a long time, several hours, most of the evening, in fact, and that maybe there had been some harsh words exchanged before he left, and it is possible Cherise was in tears as he stalked out and slammed the door.

When he gets back with a bottle of bubbly and a dozen red roses – Ron thinks you can pull anything out of the fire with presents – the lights are out. When he switches on the living room lamp he sees their condo is not in its usual perfect order; the sculpture of a horse by Joe Fafard wading in the hardening puddle of red wax, all that's left of the last Christmas candle, thick and shining on the hardwood coffee table. Nina's pants in a crumpled heap on the floor, slide, apparently disembodied, into the next room, and Nina, caught, peeks around the door frame. "Just checking out the navel wool, here, Ron." That Nina always did have a mouth. Then Cherise walks out of the kitchen, her silken blouse buttoned uneven, with that sickly sweet grin of hers. "Oh, you're finally back. We were so worried about you."

"That's sure not what it smelled like," Ron tells me.

Why has he run to me anyway? As if I were his mother or something.

"I can always smell another woman, even on myself. They all smell different."

Ron, I need to hear this?

He asks for more coffee and did I happen to have any tobacco anywhere? Of course I did, and for a long time he looks at the red and white tin, at the papers and not at anything else. When he raises his head, finally, I have to find something quick to do with my hands before I pull his face to my breasts, let him cry on me.

I strike a match, light a cigarette. The usual silence. Have a smoke, see the kid, leave. Only this time he doesn't even ask to see Joy, which is just as well, as she's not due home from school for another hour.

He doesn't stay much longer, likely going to soak his head in a tub of booze, sniff some strange and safer crotch, do some lip stands in a ditch somewhere. One thing about Ron, he never makes the same mistake twice.

Like sleeping with his best friend.

Like moving in with a meal ticket.

At least that's what Ron said to me when he teamed up with Cherise. I used to laugh my head off about that every time I drove over there, which used to be often, in the days when Ron and Cherise had visits with Joy. Cherise had to have the finest, the tidiest, the most mondo-looking condo in the city. Had to, not necessarily wanted to. In a good neighbourhood, with a decent yard, well maintained. This was, for her, a professional requirement. In fact, much to Ron's dismay, Cherise didn't make any more money than I did slopping paint on interiors. Some months she made less. After overhead. It was all appearances. The appearance of a successful, young, female lawyer. In that way, Cherise was even more a victim of the system than I was in the house painting business. We both had to do a bit more schmoozing for the dollar, had to smile more often, and for sure we both got slotted in terms of the kinds of work we could do best, but I never had to dress up for anybody, never had to pretend I was rich when I was hungry. Ron told me before he'd come along there were weekends when Cherise would have absolutely no food in the house, no toilet tissue even. Wining and dining realtors and adjusters and doing the service club circuit all week. All on spec they'd send some clients her way. Parasitic.

And Ron, like some blood-sucking tick, hung onto the neat and tidy, hell, barren and superficial witch, long after it was clear she was bored with him. I mean, what does a man who works with his hands really have to say to a lady lawyer, after the first few hellos? After the chemistry fades and the renovations are all done.

So a day after our conversation, Ron heads up north to Deer Run, and Joy sees him as often as she needs to. I was fine with that, and thought that was it for any connection Cherise would have with me and my little family.

Then about three months later I get this phone call from her.

"Hello Kathy? I need your help."

No formality, no preliminary niceties, but it's Cherise, no question about it. "It's a matter of some delicacy, Kathy. Please come over?" The lawyer asking me, the lowly painter (well, almost, if I ever finish the last class), for something. Too good.

A woman in need shall not be turned down. That is a basic. Like never stealing from a sister, never cheating on her. Though Cherise did steal from me and cheat on Ron. The fact that Ron and I had been apart for at least two years before he stumbled through Cherise's office door was irrelevant. And when Cherise did her number on Ron, man, there was never a sadder case of being cheated on.

But I'm not really into the situation anymore. Emotionally anyway. This is just idle curiosity. Maybe. Just a flash from the past. Right. I glance over at my daughter, still in her nightie. "Look, Joy and I are in the middle of something here." Yeah, in the middle of Saturday morning cartoons and sugary cereal in the living room and couch potato heaven.

"Please, Kathy, this is urgent." Cherise sounds really stressed out.

"All right, then, we'll be right over."

"Thanks. Oh, thanks."

CHERISE OPENS THE DOOR BEFORE JOY GETS TO reach for the doorbell. Doorbells and elevator buttons are favourites with my eight-year-old, and her piercingly clear voice demands opportunity nevertheless. "Let me push the bell, Auntie Cherry."

And she does, five times, before I grab her ladybug overall straps and pull her inside. Cherise looks frazzled, and it's obvious the constant ringing is not wearing well on her nerves as she skitters, leading us to the dining room table.

"Hey Cherise, long time no see, what's up, what's happening?" I just can't seem to stop with the chatter. "You're looking great. Hey, I love where you put this oleander."

"Hello, yes, thanks. Coffee, Kathy? Hi Joy, how are you doing, darling?"

Cherise is the only person in the world who calls Joy 'darling.' Joy scrunches up her face, looks at the ceiling, enjoying her moment in the spotlight. "Oh, fine. Could I have a cookie? Do you have any candy?"

Right, excellent manners; I taught her myself, but Cherise doesn't even wince.

"Just a second, darling," Auntie Cherry says.

In her formal dining room Cherise slowly pushes on the golden coffee plunger and waves Joy and me to the table set with porcelain mugs, a crystal glass of apple juice and, oh perfection, chocolate chip cookies on a pedestal plate. One thing about Cherise, she sure knows how to please a guest.

"Thanks for coming. I didn't know where else to turn." Cherise's hands are in constant motion, pouring coffee and pushing the plate to each of us as if we couldn't reach and then her fingers scratch and tug at her sleeves and her flesh above her elbows, arms crossed over her small breasts.

"Christ, stop fidgeting, you'd think you have ants in your pants or something." That's me, renowned for my tact.

And Cherise, famous for her sensitivity, hands flat on her cheeks, head flopping abruptly forward, cries, "Oh my God, it's that obvious!"

"What's obvious? What?"

"I've got, Nina gave me – I mean it must have been Nina, it's not as if you can get them from a toilet seat or something, and she's the only one, I've never been with anyone else since I've been with her!"

"So you've got –"

"Crabs! Oh God I feel so filthy." Her hands going again make me scratch in sympathy. And it's clear she's never parented a curious, attentive kid as well. An explanation will be requested sooner or later. It's sooner.

"What kind of crabs?" asks Joy.

"Little wee crabs, Joy." I squeeze thumb to forefinger to show her how small. "No big deal."

"Like hermit crabs?" She's seen these on The Nature of Things.

"No! These are different. These ones go on people and bite."

"Yuck."

Yuck indeed. I pass my child another cookie to distract her and turn back to Cherise. "And Nina?"

"Gone, I kicked her out. Oh what do I do? What do I do?"

"You're asking what to do about Nina? Sounds like you did something already. Kind of tough, losing your business partner and your new live-in lover over a little bug, though."

"But don't you see, she's been cheating on me!"

"You want my sympathy?" How do you spell irony?

"No," Cherise says.

"Besides, these parasites come and go, all over the place," I say. "You could drive yourself crazy trying to figure out where they come from, and what's the point of that anyway, really? You could have picked them up from a bench at the Y, in the Value Village change room, even from the laundramat."

"*Value Village?* I don't think so," says Cherise.

"I want to see the crabs," Joy says eagerly, peering into the kitchen.

"Don't be ridiculous." The suddenly dignified Cherise remembers her young audience.

Way too late, so it might as well be a science lesson. Which could be fun, I think. "No, honey, these ones aren't like the ones in the seafood store window. They're more like the lice you had in your hair this fall. Remember?"

"When you had to wash everything three times and Tumble got wrecked?"

"Just like that, baby." Tumble had been a favourite stuffy, but not strong enough to withstand the hot water for at least five minutes, the hot dryer for ten. "Except these lice aren't on Cherise's head." Ah, I just can't help myself, hunker down, as if to tell a secret. "They're down there." I point at my own crotch.

"Oh, gross!" Joy looks totally horrified. She claps her hands to her mouth and sniggers. "How did they get down there? Do they bite? Do they have little crabby claws?"

Cherise is not enjoying the attention, to say the least. "God, I feel so dirty, Kathy you've got to help me. You're the only one I know with any expertise at all in this area."

Expertise? In this area? Huh. Suddenly everything is painfully clear. "You want me to tell you what to do about crabs? You want me to prescribe a treatment? How the hell would I know? You know more than I do. I've never had the beasts, and for all I know I'm catching them now, sitting on your furniture." I stood up.

"Come on, Kathy, I know Joy gets lice every fall."

"Yeah, like clockwork, about the third week after school starts. So?"

"And you've handled that. It can't be that much different," Cherise says. " A parasite is a parasite. What works? What's safe?"

I sit down again. She makes a mean cup of coffee. "In this case, I don't know. The first thing you need to do is get to the pharmacy."

"No, I can't."

"What, you can't physically, or you can't mentally?"

"Socially. Everyone knows me. They'd talk," she says.

"Oh for fuck's sake. Sorry, Joy. Mommy didn't say that. Oh for Christ's sake, Cherise."

"Oh please Kathy, it would be so easy for you."

"Yeah, everything is so easy for me. Try living in these boots for a day or two." There is a no smoking rule in Cherise's house and I suppose I may have recently promised Joy I'd quit cigarettes, but if there was ever a time to break rules and promises, this is it.

"Do you mind?" I don't wait for an answer, pull the tobacco out, and start to roll, leisurely, meditatively, then take a moment to admire the perfect cylinder, all the while listening to Joy's little chant, "Don't smoke, Mommy, please don't smoke."

I strike a match on the underside of Cherise's designer table, light up and narrow my eyes. "Okay, Cherise. But you owe me big time. Come on, Joy." I'm packing the lit cigarette and burnt out match. I figure Cherise doesn't have ashtrays anyway, and I hate using saucers. "We'll be right back. You might as well get started with the laundry. Same thing you do for lice. Everything you've touched for the last month, and if it can't be soaked in hot water pop it in a garbage bag and put it in the freezer. None of this delicate wash stuff, Cherise."

Cherise looks like she isn't going to move from the table, where she still has an almost full cup of coffee. I'm almost at her door when I notice her usually clear eyes are red and puffy. "You know, Cherise, it is possible to love someone who has hurt you. It's even kind of normal." The waterworks start flowing big time. Joy hasn't moved an inch from Cherise's side, even though it's not the closest spot to the cookie tray. I do a slow spin and return to the table. "You just have to decide how much to trust them. Because that's all your decision, all under your control, girl."

"Thank you for this, Kathy." Cherise doesn't look like she believes anything is under her control. Yet. "I knew I could trust you to help." She hugs Joy. "I've missed this girl so much. How are you, Joy? Kathy, isn't there any way we can visit sometimes?"

Joy is doing the "Oh, yes, please Mommy" hop while Cherise opens a buffet drawer by the table, and smooth as a dream pulls out an ashtray, a heavy ceramic number, red with black and orange bleeding on the edges, and sets it on the table by my coffee. In gold lettering on the lip of the ashtray it reads *Deer Run Hotel.*

"Oh, I guess visits are possible from time to time. You know, this is where I met Ron." I point to the ashtray. Deer Run was Ron's home town.

Cherise waves me back to my chair. I shrug, obedient this once. "This ashtray is one of the reasons we split up." Then she tells me how he used to fill it to overflowing with filthy, smelly butts, how the ashes would spill on her pristine Asian carpet. Oh boohoo. How Ron might have even thrown it at her once. I can't picture that.

When I'm finished my smoke, I say "Okay, I'll do this for you. Joy, do you want to stay with Cherise for a few minutes?"

Cherise looks tense, then pleased, and Joy is, well, overjoyed.

"Auntie, can we look at your sparkly necklaces?"

I get back with the stuff for the crabs and read Cherise the directions while she scrabbles to the bathroom, and I even time the application from my spot by the ashtray while she applies the salve.

Joy is pulling chains and baubles from a velvet lined box. The bathroom door is open, but even if it were closed, an unmistakable sharp odour permeates everything, even over the cigarette smoke. "Yuck, Mommy, it smells just like that lice medicine."

"Yes, sweetie, and it will take Auntie Cherry more than one shower to get rid of that stink," I say, then turn to the bathroom door. "Time to rinse that stuff off, Cherise."

After she showers, Cherise pours me another coffee, I roll another cigarette, and she tells me a story or two on Ron. I tell her one myself. Joy eats all the cookies and it's all a bit more than civil, now that I've solved her problems – or some of them – for her.

Now she owes us. And Ron owes us. And I'm so contagiously cocky I grind my last cigarette on the sidewalk as Joy and I depart. "That's it, my girl. Your mom is a non-smoker." We walk hand in hand to the car. My daughter offers me a high five before I open the passenger door for her. And man, that truck's motor hums like a precision instrument as we roll down the street and head back home.

Water of Life

CHERISE POKED HER HEAD INTO NINA'S adjoining office. "I've invited Joy."

Nina stuffed a note-tagged volume into her briefcase, already overflowing with neatly labelled accordion files. "You have what? Listen, big mistake, dearie, big mistake."

"So you're not saying no."

"What are we going to do with a twelve-year-old on our trek over the Highlands? And she's not old enough for the pubs. Have you thought of the expense? Kathy can't afford it."

"A definite maybe, then. Great. I've booked her ticket already, and it may be a non-redeemable seat. Let's talk more when you get back."

"Do not even think about it until we talk. Promise me that?"

Cherise handed Nina her daybook, which her partner dropped into the side pocket of her case. "I promise." Cherise opened the office door and walked Nina to the elevator. "Remember, if you get Chomsky, keep it short and sweet or he'll fall asleep."

"In this case, that may be an advantage."

"But His Lordship wakes up in an absolutely foul mood, Nina. And don't be too witty if Conrad's on the bench. He's gone a bit simple."

"Speaking of simple, Cherry, have you asked the mother of the aforesaid burden about this excursion overseas?"

"Kathy will be informed in due course. It's an opportunity she could never offer her child. How can she possibly refuse?"

At Cherise's invitation, Kathy's choice, they met in the Sports Bar, where the larger-than-life television screen roared with race cars. Kathy's attention was focused on the jocks at the next table, playing a casual game of pool. Cherise looked over her gin and tonic with a squeeze of lime, her eyes intense. "I did not know you were homophobic, Kathy," she said.

"Cut the defensive crap," Kathy said. "You've never had the kid around for more than overnight. When you want to do adult shit, you just can't leave my Joy in some hotel room while you and your over-dramatic squeeze go party. Have you considered the logistics at all?"

"Not totally, perhaps."

"Well, a twelve-year-old can't stay in a room by herself. She's still a kid, for Christ's sake. And I can't afford to send her decent pocket money even." Kathy took a swig of her domestic beer.

"Don't worry, Auntie Cherry will take care of that," Cherise said. "It's a wonderful opportunity for her: The British Museum, the National Gallery, the –"

"I thought you were going for a walk in the country?"

"Of course we'll visit London and Edinburgh, perhaps York."

"Not on your life. She'll get lost for sure. And she won't want to spend however long touring cathedrals and galleries."

"It's an opportunity you can't offer her, Kathy. A chance to get some culture."

Kathy clunked her bottle on the table. "And what's wrong with this culture? Or her dad's? She knows more Métis wood lore than you'll learn in a lifetime." She slid the brown glass in a tiny circle. "All right, here's what I want to know. Why do you want to do this anyway? I'll bet last week's pogey cheque it wasn't Nina's idea. You do understand Joy's a kid, eh? A person, not a toy?"

Leaning forward, Cherise rested her hand on Kathy's denim-clad arm. "I know that, Kathy. How old was Joy when she started seeing her dad and me? Two? She's the closest I've ever had to a child of my own."

"No, Cherise. No go." Kathy knocked her knuckles on the arborite table top to emphasize her decision, and pointed at the pool table. "How about a game? Let's challenge these jokers." Kathy was up with a loonie in her hand before Cherise could object.

"I don't play pool," she called weakly to Kathy's back.

Kathy didn't even turn around. "Time you learned."

She returned, stood expectantly by the table, and reached for her beer. "We're up next," she announced.

"I'll play you for the holiday," said Cherise. "If I win, she comes. If I lose, you come too."

"I suppose I could go with her," Kathy said.

LOUNGING IN ONE OF TWO DINING ROOM chairs she had lugged in front of the glass of the French doors, Cherise waved Nina over. Her face glowed in the peaceful azures and sunset mauves streaming through the perfectly placed cloud bank, reflected artfully in the manmade lake, part of which formed the back yard of their condo. "Nina, do you remember travelling when you were twelve?"

"The year our drama troupe did Europe. Changed my life." Nina flounced onto the chair by Cherise, her eyes flashing in the vibrant reds of the dusk light.

"Everything this bright young girl will never see unless worldly aunties open that door," Cherise said.

"But I want to travel with *you.* Explore the hills with *you.*"

Cherise reached for Nina's hand. "You will, Nina. Kathy's got a bum knee, can't do the heavy walking. We'll set them up in a pleasant village nearby, and do day trips."

"I'm not sure we can handle this together. It is *madness.* I'll have nothing to do with it. I will not be responsible for the brat and I certainly will not be exposed to Kathy for two weeks."

"Nina, it's something I have to do. Soon Joy will be a teenager and out of reach. She's the closest thing

I'll ever have to a daughter. She's – family."

"Oh." Nina breathed deeply, emphatically. "Cherise, we've been through this. I thought we were on the same page: no children. None."

"This is only two weeks, Nina. I have to try this. Please?"

In front of the computer Joy squirmed, her face lit an eerie green by the monitor's flashing. "This is a piece of shit, Mom. When can we get a new computer?"

"That one's fine for now, kid." Kathy lifted her feet from the milk-stool ottoman and leaned forward to rub her knee. When she bent it towards her chest, there was an audible crackling and tearing. "There's got to be a few games you like that don't need bells and whistles."

"Not the good ones, Mom. Auntie Cherry has a better computer than this," Joy said.

Kathy smiled at her daughter. "By the way, I booked my flight today."

"Yeah, with my college education money. Why do you have to come along anyway?" Joy said. "You'll slow the rest of us down."

Kathy sighed. "Well, I won't slow you down for the first few days. Everything was booked up until after the long weekend and even then the only connecting flight didn't really connect." Kathy would have to fly into Glasgow and take the train to Edinburgh. "I'll have to catch you up. Jolly good, eh what?"

"Right, then." Joy grinned at the screen, her right hand frenetic on the mouse. "Just try not to embarrass me. And don't pick fights."

"Not unless Nina picks one first. You and I have never been out of jolly old Saskatchewan." Kathy kicked her left leg out, stretching.

"Have so. Remember that time you took me to Alberta to see the mountains and that cool dinosaur museum? Akk! Ah, I'm dead." Joy turned from the screen.

"This time you'll be climbing the mountains," Kathy said.

"I don't think there are any mountains in England. Here, let me rub that for you, Mom." Joy leaned over Kathy's knee, kneading the lateral muscles.

"In the U.K.? We'll see, but my guess is the hills at Grandma's farm will seem pretty puny once we get to Loch Lomond." Kathy grimaced as Joy massaged the skin around the kneecaps. "Are you sure you can handle those two ladies until I get there?"

"Cherise is okay, but she's not used to kids. I don't think Nina likes me much," Joy said.

"Yeah, well I predict between you trying to take care of them and them trying to take care of you that I'll just have to show up to referee. Don't take any guff from Nina. She's never had to deal with much shit, at least the kind that stinks."

"Gross, Mom! Don't worry." Joy grinned at her mother. "We're going to fly over the ocean! I'm so excited."

"WHY DIDN'T KATHY SHARE WITH US THE possibility that the girl would get air sick?" Nina leaned as far from Joy and Cherise as she could in the rigid airline seat, one hand delicately shielding her nose.

"I've never been on an airplane before, Nina," Joy said greenly, leaning over the tiny sick bag. Even the Gravol hadn't stayed down.

"A bit more air, Cherise, if you please," Nina said, ignoring Joy.

Cherise reached over their heads and opened the airflow to its maximum.

The cabin was darkened, and humid with human odour. An infant whimpered in the front row. Joy leaned her forehead on the cool, blank window.

"At this moment we are flying over the North Pole," Nina announced to Cherise.

TEN HOURS LATER, JOY HAD CLAIMED THE remote and was surfing channels on the black and white television. "They've all got English accents, Auntie Cherise!" she called from her cot.

Nina emerged from the bedroom of their London bed and breakfast, stumbled to the tv, and pulled the plug. "Cherise is asleep. I suggest you do the same." She marched back to the bedroom and slammed the door.

"Ouch, jet lag," Joy murmured, and finally settled into silence.

Late afternoon the women re-emerged. Joy had her jacket on, her face to the window, watching everything that moved on the street below. "Let's go, aunties! There's a McDonald's over there on the corner!"

"Oh please!" Nina said, making no effort to hide her disdain.

"Let's let Nina choose where we go tonight, okay, Joy?" said Cherise.

"Okay, as long as they serve hamburgers. I'm starving!" Joy said.

"I believe fish and chips are the British take-out favourite, with a side of mushy peas." Nina pulled Joy away from the window and scanned the street. "And there's a chippy across the way too!"

"Chips are fine," Joy said dubiously.

Nina swept by her and led the way out into the cobbled streets.

THE NEXT DAY, NINA STOPPED TO EXAMINE every postcard stand along the way to the British Museum, critiquing garishness with enthusiasm. "Look at the buxom beach goddess on this card, Cherry. If her breasts were any larger, they'd have to charge extra postage."

Cherise ducked into three shoe shops, searching for quality British shoes.

Joy sank into silence, with the effort of one who wishes to memorize every cobblestone, each new expression.

"What do you think, so far, Joy?" Cherise asked.

"The buildings are sure big. And the trees. There are lots of people, here, aren't there?" The street swarmed in an exotic jumble of skin shades, hair colours, dress styles. Joy's own brown eyes and skin fit right into the mix.

Cherise took Joy's hand. "A bit much, is it?"

"It's so much more than I thought it would be." Joy held on to Cherise as they walked, although it was difficult in the press of people. Nina darted ahead, then let them catch up by the great stone lions guarding the museum gates.

"Sorry I was such a bother on the plane," Joy said to Nina. "And in the hotel room. And in the restaurant last night. I just didn't expect mushy peas to be that..."

"Mushy?" Nina grimaced. "I'm sorry too. Don't let it happen again."

"Right." Joy smiled, catching Nina by surprise.

Nina and Cherise examined the exhibit guide. "What do you want to see at the museum, Joy?" Cherise asked.

"Oh, I don't know. I bet the gift shop has postcards." Joy sat on a bench just inside the doors, as if just being there was far enough.

"The gift shop is a must. Would you like to see the Elgin Marbles?" Cherise asked.

"I could look at marbles, I guess," Joy said doubtfully.

"Let's start there. Come on."

On the way to the marble room they admired a motherlode of exhibits, but they each seemed drawn by different items. "There's sure lots of old stuff," Joy commented, always a bit ahead.

"Turn right here, Joy. There, those are the Elgin Marbles."

They stepped into a room full of statues, broken and cracked. Joy gave the stone people with no clothes a wide berth and scanned the carved deer hunt on the white walls. "Right. No cat's-eyes in here," she announced.

"No, no honey, these *are* the Elgin Marbles," Cherise said. "You were looking for something else?"

Joy blushed, and shook her head. "I think I'll go to the gift shop now."

Cherise ran to catch up to her. "Come with me for a minute, Joy. There's just one thing I want to show you."

"Nah, I don't think so."

"Come." Cherise tugged at Joy's sweater hem, pulling her back into the hall where Nina strolled from piece to piece, ohhing and ahhing. "Come, I know it's here."

Cherise hurried Joy by the naked statuary, the stone pillars and walls. "There he is!" A huge horse head, as tall as Joy, carved from white marble. Cherise stroked the well-defined neck, the alabaster cheeks. "Beautiful, isn't he? Feel him."

"You're not supposed to touch things in a museum, Auntie."

"This horse is older than history. No one knows who made him. Look at those flaring nostrils. What spirit!" Cherise said.

Joy dutifully rubbed the cold sculpture. "Okay, Auntie. I want to go to the gift shop now. I'll be all right by myself, really."

"If I lose you, your mother will have my head on a platter. I'll come." Cherise dashed across the hall to talk to Nina, who glared at Joy, then waved them both off.

"She'll be along in a bit, too," said Cherise. "Let's go."

"You like horses, Auntie?"

"I used to pretend I was a horse when I was your age, maybe a bit younger," Cherise said. "Didn't you?"

"No. We played cats a long time ago." Joy glanced sideways at Cherise. "When I was ten."

"You *have* to see the Egyptian room, Joy. Have I got a cat for you."

NINA FOUND THEM IN THE GIFT SHOP, PURCHASING Bastet postcards, Bastet note-pads, even a miniature carving of the Egyptian black cat on a key chain. "For my Mom," Joy explained. "Isn't she beautiful, Nina?"

"Bastet was the goddess of love, sex and fertility," Nina said.

In an attempt to catch Nina's attention, Cherise dropped her hand firmly to the counter. Nina smiled in mock oblivion, and then lifted both hands as if asking for guidance from elsewhere.

Ignoring the pantomime, Joy responded all the same. "Don't worry, I'm not planning on getting pregnant or something. I'm too young to really appreciate sex, Mom says."

"Perhaps your Mom is too young to appreciate sex," Nina said, dodging Cherise's surreptitious kick.

"She says that stuff is easy," Joy said. "Love's the bitch, she says."

Nina nodded, grinning wickedly. *"She* certainly *is."*

"Nina, I think it's time we grabbed a bite to eat. Your sugar is getting low," Cherise said, as she paid for the icons, and catching Joy's arm, steered her out of the house of old gods.

Joy's hand felt positively clammy in Cherise's as they navigated the warren of tunnels and stairs, the press of bodies cramming into the coaches that took them to the Tate.

"You're not going to get sick on us again, are you?" Nina looked alarmed. "I think you'd better sit here."

Joy moved willingly to the forward-facing seat, snug up against a robust elderly man, his ebony skin shiny against a crisp white shirt. He glanced at Joy with disinterest, as Joy pretended to stare at the route map, all the while stealing glances at his hands.

"Wasn't he beautiful, Auntie?" she whispered when the man got off at his stop. "It was like sitting beside a living statue or something."

"A man with presence is a thing of beauty, all right," Cherise agreed, and grinned at Nina.

"Although staring at strangers is not good form, child," Nina said. "Not good form at all."

Joy dropped her head and watched her own feet for the next two stops.

"Aunties, let me just look by myself. I'll be fine. I'm almost thirteen!" Joy begged as they climbed the steps to the gallery. "I'll see you later!" She darted into the first room and disappeared in the swarm of a guided tour.

The Tate Gallery, although massive, seemed a safer place to let Joy wander where she wished. "Besides," Cherise told Nina, "you know where we'll find her."

"The gift shop?" Nina rolled her eyes.

"Maybe, but I'd wager the Pre-Raphaelites; that's where I'd be at twelve."

"Sentimental. Melodramatic. Yes, I can see where an uneducated child like Joy would appreciate the Rossettis," Nina said.

"Really." Cherise paused before a large painting of nymphs dancing. "You don't have a romantic bone in your body?"

"I live my romances, not view them." Nina pulled Cherise into a narrow alcove and kissed her fingertips in a courtly fashion, from bended knee. "I do love you, Cherry."

"And I you, fair warrior. Arise and kiss my lips." At that moment the ubiquitous security officer stalked around the corner, eyeballed them and walked firmly away.

They resumed their viewing of the exhibits.

"Joy's a joy, isn't she?" Cherise asked.

"I'm doing this for you, Cherry. Excuse me if I don't exude enthusiasm."

"But it's not horrible?"

"No, it's not horrible. She's been sick on me, she gets panic attacks in crowds, she doesn't appreciate art and she stares at strange men. Our conversations cater to her interests, to her education. And we're not spending quality time, you and I. But otherwise, I'd hardly know she was along. I'm not complaining. You did ask."

Joy was not among the Pre-Raphaelites, not fingering postcards in the gift shop, not studying heaven and hell in the Blake room, not even eating ice-cream in the cafeteria. Nina plotted out a systematic search, but when they met back in the hollow echoing foyer, Cherise pulled at her hair, near panic. Security agreed to a search of the galleries as the speaker system announced ten minutes to closing. Nina and Cherise turned expectantly at each resounding set of footfalls in the main hall. Unless she was very well hidden, Joy was not anywhere in the labyrinth of galleries. She was lost.

"Maybe she's been abducted," Cherise whispered.

"Don't be absurd. This is an incredible inconvenience, that's all. She's likely gone back to the bed and breakfast, in some sort of sulk," Nina said.

"She would never go on the underground alone. Does she have our map?"

"Damn her. You don't think she'd go near the river, do you?" Nina asked.

"You're worried, aren't you? You've started to care," Cherise said.

"Scared shitless, as her mother would say. We are responsible, aren't we?"

Cherise nodded. "I should have stayed with her. I should have kept her with us. I should have–"

"Oh, stop it. Let's go, they want us out of here."

Security waited, rather apologetically, by the

doors. They were indeed the last to leave. No one lingered on the steps and greens by the entrance. Cherise and Nina half ran to the street, glancing back to search the shady recesses of the broad steps and stone building.

"I've been waiting for you guys." A voice wafted to them from across the street. Joy waved from an elevated bench facing the Thames, where she could have been watching ships being tugged though the bracken water.

Cherise reached Joy first, grabbed her by both arms, and paused, not knowing whether to shake her or hug her. "You do realize we've been looking for you."

"For the last two hours." Nina's voice was an odd mix of frustration and relief.

Cherise opted for the hug, her voice catching slightly. "We've been very worried."

"You didn't tell us you were leaving the building!" Nina caught herself waving a scolding finger.

Joy pushed herself away from Cherise and gestured toward the grand entranceway across the street. "I'm sorry. I didn't want to bother you. I knew I'd see you leave."

"But we didn't know you knew. What if you were looking at a ship or something and missed us completely?" Cherise waved at the tired, brown river. "What if you got lost, or were bopped on the head and robbed, or worse." Cherise tried to stop herself but her own mother's voice had taken over. "Whatever possessed you?"

"The Lady Ophelia. She possessed me. She looked so peaceful lying in the water. Clear water, not like that stuff." Joy regarded the Thames. "After I saw her I didn't want to see anything else, and I didn't feel like talking, so I came out here. Besides, I knew you and Auntie Nina would want to see more."

"So you were trying to be considerate of us by disappearing?" Nina sat on the bench beside Joy.

"I didn't disappear. You only thought I did. I was right here," Joy said. "Besides, I need my space too, you know."

"And space you shall have, Joy," Cherise said, "but let us know when and where you're taking it."

"Ophelia died, you know." Nina prepared to perform. *"Thought and affliction, passion, hell itself, She turns to favour and to prettiness."*

"And so did the model for that painting. Caught a chill from that cold water and died." Cherise seated herself on Joy's right.

"No, you must be thinking of the Lady of Shallot. Elisabeth Siddal? And it was an overdose, on laudanum," Nina said. "Meanwhile, her husband, the painter, was screwing Fanny, 'the artists' friend,' and Jane, his best friend's wife." Nina delighted in the story, apparently oblivious to Cherise's pointed shush. "Jane was the dark one with the interesting nose. Fanny was the blowsy one."

"So she died for love." Joy almost sighed.

"Yes. Or lack of it." Cherise stood up. "They have posters of the paintings in the gift shop, I should imagine."

"I didn't like them that much," Joy said.

"Just as well; your mother would have hated them," Nina ventured.

Joy looked at Nina curiously. "No, I think she would have liked that one a lot."

"DO YOU KNOW WHAT I WAS DOING WHEN I was twelve, Nina?" Cherise stared at the high ceiling, bordered in mouldings of pink, green, and pale blue. A grey dawn crept through the windows. Cherise had not slept well, anticipating their early departure from Victoria Station.

Nina slung a sleepy arm over Cherise's belly. "Servicing your father?"

"Yes, that. And losing my mother to her own sorrows. And losing my horse fantasies. I was crazy for horses."

"Never had one, did you?"

"No, I never even mounted one until I was in my twenties."

"Mmm." Nina nuzzled into Cherise's shoulder. Cherise's temples were gleaming with tears. Nina licked the streaming salt from Cherise's left eye corner. "You're one tough lady. You know that?"

"But not the teacher that Joy needs," Cherise said. "I thought I was, but I'm not."

"Neither is her mother."

Cherise lifted herself to one elbow. "Neither are you."

"Hey, don't bring me into this. I'm on vacation. I'm not the one mourning lost opportunities." Nina rested a massaging finger on the ridges forming between Cherise's eyebrows.

"I would have been a good mother. It's just so much more taxing than I thought. And I sure would never want to be a child again."

"Aunties!" Joy was at the bedroom door, fully dressed, carrying her packsack. "The train!"

"To the Cotswolds, then," Nina cried, and leapt to her feet atop the bed, one arm waving above her head like a military leader's.

"Don't you think you should get some clothes on first," Joy said, turning away from the door. "You're naked, Auntie."

"Nina, for Christ's sake." Cherise's exasperated laughter didn't totally subside until they reached the station.

"We're getting off here." Nina closed the guidebook decisively, stood, and reached for her pack from the rail above.

Joy and Cherise looked at each other, shrugged, and pulling their luggage from the racks, followed Nina to the door of the rail car. "Do you know where we're going?" Cherise asked. "The Cotswold trail doesn't begin until Chipping Campden."

"Hold onto your hats, ladies, you're about to experience a breathtaking visit into the dramatic past. And Cherry, don't sweat it. We can always catch the next train."

Nina shrugged into her backpack and led the way along a narrow cobblestone lane opposite the train station, along an even narrower way, and, consulting the guidebook briefly, turned, after a few yards, into an arched courtyard. All around the courtyard a covered boardwalk opened into the centre. In that alcove a pub, sleepy in the mid-morning, offered tables facing out, beneath the second and third level balconies, prettily framed in carved filigree. "Behold, the Coach Inn, a prime example of the first theatre in the round."

"Post-campfire," Cherise added.

"Yes, but definitely pre-Globe," Nina replied.

"Globe?" Joy asked.

"Let's at least stop for a drink," Nina said over her shoulder, moving into the shade of the first level pub and dropping her luggage by a table.

Joy followed Cherise uncertainly from the table, and perched on a bar stool to better examine the colourful taps, the lines of glistening glasses hanging from the racks overhead, and the exotic bottled beverages behind the frosted glass doors.

"How old is the child, there," the pub-keep asked.

"Sixteen," Nina lied.

"All right then, ladies, what'll it be?"

Joy surreptitiously studied the shelves of bottles. By the time Cherise and Nina had decided what draught they wanted to sample, she'd settled on a label she didn't recognize. "I'll have a shandy?" she said as casually as possible.

Cherise shook her head emphatically.

"Don't you worry, Ma'am, I'll fix her up a nice light one, just as I do for my own young ones." He winked at Joy and began pouring their drinks.

"Where'd you get that from?" Cherise asked her.

Joy pointed to the shelf, where bottled shandy sat, as tempting as any ice-cold soda pop.

"All right, you can drink it," Cherise said, "but take it easy, it is not candy, and do not, I repeat, do not tell your mother I let you have a drink."

"I promise. What's pre-Globe?"

Nina assumed her tour guide role. "Everything here, child. The courtyard, where the acting troupe would bring their horse-drawn flatbed, complete with a secret door hatch about mid-centre. The paving stones where the poor members of the audience stood. Those who could afford it took shelter from the weather here, and the very well-off purchased the balcony seats, where there are now rooms to rent for the night. Shall we stay?"

The drinks had arrived, and Cherise nodded, cheerfully. "Why not, if there's one open."

"And the Globe?" Joy did not have a look of comprehension on her face.

"Joy, the Globe was a theatre back in the 1600s, in London. Your Auntie Nina used to perform Shakespeare." Cherise touched Nina's arm.

Nina rose from her chair, and bowed. *"Now my charms are all o'erthrown. And what strength I have's mine own, which is most faint. Gentle breath of yours my sails must fill, or else my project fails, which was to please."*

Just outside the village, they hiked along a river, lush from the reflection of massive willows leaning gracefully over the water. The well-worn path burrowed through knee-deep clouds of lacy flowers

Cherise called cow parsley. Joy stared into the clear green water. "This is where Ophelia died," she said with certainty.

Cherise decided they should try the path higher up.

Nina pointed out a shy robin, not at all like its bold and stupid namesake back home. Their eggs are not blue here either, Nina informed them. Joy thought that would be a loss, no robin's-egg blue. Undeterred, Nina ventured forth, in search of other mysteries, while Cherise and Joy lolled on the hillside.

"Auntie Cherry, I could live here forever." Their rest stop was marked by an ancient shepherd's byre, a crude stone and log structure. Blue sky glimmered through the slits and cracks of the crumbling lean-to. A few sheep dotted the valley, like broken pieces of chalk. "I wish Mom could have seen this. She'd love it."

"You miss her?" Cherise asked, loosening the laces of her hiking boots.

"Nah, but she'll be missing me." Joy sprawled under the shade of a young oak. A blackbird, so unlike the raucous slough dwellers back home, trilled melodically. "Of course if she died or something, I'd really miss her." Joy looked at the waterway below. "What made Ophelia drown herself?"

"Well, let's see. Her boyfriend appeared to have gone crazy, rejected her cruelly, and then killed her father. According to the play, that softened her judgement." Cherise watched Joy's face. "Perhaps she had no place else to go."

Joy skipped one of the smooth white stones from the hillside into the stream, creating rings of ripples, distorting the perfect reflection on the water's surface. "Auntie Cherry, have you ever wanted to live someplace else, far away?"

"Of course, always. In fact I did for a while." Cherise nodded at the stream. "Then I started to see myself as a river. It's like, you're always yourself regardless of where you are, or who throws something at you, and you take that with you where ever you live. For better or worse."

Joy put down a stone, and stared at the river. "Do you think I could come and stay with you and Nina when we get back?"

Cherise glanced around, but Nina was out of earshot. "Maybe for a weekend. But your Mom wouldn't want to let you go for long."

"Yeah, I know, she's pretty over-protective."

"Your Mom is a special woman." Cherise paused for moment, as if wondering where that came from. "And she loves you."

"Of course she does. She's my Mom," Joy said. "Auntie, you look like you're about to cry!"

Cherise rubbed her eyes, and leaned forward to tug at Joy's ponytail. "You're a lucky kid, you know that?"

Nina appeared at the edge of a clump of beech. "Cherise, Joy, come over here. There's an entire field of wild lilies."

Nina had arranged their lodgings in Edinburgh, the home of lawyer friends who were on holidays and glad for someone to live-in for a few days. The suite was accessible through a door facing a narrow arched alleyway, a close.

Gathered around the unlit fireplace, Cherise and Joy lounged in each closed-in corner of the high-backed wooden settle that served as a couch in the sitting room, as Nina pointed to the compact map in the Guide. "Old Town, where we're staying, stems from a mile long central street which begins up hill, with the castle, and ends downhill, at the palace."

"Can we go inside them?" Joy bopped up and down before her, grasping Nina's arm. "Nina, what's the difference between a castle and a palace?"

"Don't maul me, child. All your questions will be answered anon. But first, to the station, to meet your mother's train."

"I told her not to bother coming." Joy glanced nervously from Cherise to Nina and back. "I told her I'd be okay alone."

"It'll be fine." Cherise looked at Nina, her brows raised in a question.

"We can hope," Nina added.

AT WAVERLY STATION, KATHY EMERGED FROM the train, totally enmeshed in small bags and totes.

"Couldn't afford a suitcase even?" Nina wondered softly.

"Not her style." Cherise lagged back with Nina as Joy finally ran to her mother.

"Hi, Mom, here let me help you."

Kathy unburdened herself with Joy's help, and

then opened her arms. "Well, I see the wolves haven't got you. Big hugs, my girl."

"No wolves on this island, Mom," Joy said, wrapping her arms around Kathy's waist, then picking up a couple of her mother's bags. "Let's go, Mom. We've got lots of stuff to do. You've got to try to keep up."

"I've already spotted a hill I want to try in this town." Kathy pointed in the direction of the basalt crags and the lion shape of Arthur's Seat, the ancient volcano towering over old Edinburgh. "Cherise. Nina. You've been good to my girl?"

"She's been good to us." Cherise grappled with a couple satchels from the platform floor before Kathy's feet. "It's a five minute walk to the apartment."

There was no such thing as a five minute walk that day. Joy stopped to exclaim at everything: the view from the bridge, the Scott Memorial, the castle, the palace, and the Covenantor's hill. Nina, in her début performance as guide, and having by now memorized the touring book *verbatim,* burst into her role as information central. "The old town is medieval in character. We're off the Canongate section, by the palace, and Holyrood Park. The Salisbury Crags, and rising above those, Arthur's Seat at 823 feet, are the central feature of the park."

"As in King Arthur?" Joy asked, swinging a satchel recklessly over her head.

"No one knows. It is said that King David the First, son of St. Margaret herself, was confronted by a stag on those hills, and was thrown from his horse." Nina paused for effect and began to pantomime the struggle. "As the stag attempted to gore him, the King grasped its antlers in desperation, and found himself holding," and here Nina looked down into her own empty hands, "not an antler at all but a crucifix."

"What happened to the deer, Auntie?"

"It ran off," Nina said, casually. "But Holyrood means holy stick."

"Yeah, well I bet it wasn't always a crucifix that boy ended up with, back in the mists of time." Kathy adjusted the bags on her shoulder again. She turned to Nina. "Good story, though. Now take me to the nearest couch and let me catch a few minutes of sleep. I haven't closed my eyes for two days."

Nina led Joy in a chorus of "Holyrood" to the tune of "Hollywood" as they trooped down Canongate. Kathy lagged behind. "Cherise, you're very quiet. I can see Nina's fine with Joy, at least as long as it's part of a performance. Tell me, how's it really going?"

"Kathy, that's a beautiful daughter you've got there," Cherise said.

"Don't I know it. Takes after her old mother, here."

"And her father." Cherise paused, somewhat defensively.

"Don't *we* know *that.*" Kathy watched Cherise, waiting for her to make the first move, then shook her head slightly, and lowered her eyes.

"You know, Miss lawyer-know-it-all, there are a few things you don't have a clue about," Kathy said.

Cherise nodded. "Motherhood perhaps? I'm here to learn."

"Yeah, well now that I'm here, I'm going to play," Kathy said. "Funny about that deer story. Did Joy's dad ever tell you any of his deer stories?"

Cherise shook her head no.

Kathy adjusted the satchel straps on her shoulders. "I met a country woman on the train." Kathy spoke breathlessly, as they turned into the close. "She told me some local lore, and since we're doing animal stories, here's one for you, Cherise. Mary, Queen of Scots, would not speak after seeing a white horse in the streets. People hereabouts flip a silver coin for good luck when they see one."

They'd caught up with Joy and Nina at the doorway to the apartment. Joy lifted her onyx cat key chain for Kathy to admire, and the ornate key, which Joy then carefully pressed into the door lock. "I found lots of cats in London, Mom."

"Yes, I think I heard a story about cats in London once." Kathy adjusted her grip on her satchels as the door swung open.

"Well, this cat was supposed to be for you, but I need to keep it for now, because I'm carrying the key."

"I see that, Joy. Good work. And maybe, since you found that cat, you need to hang on to her too." Kathy dropped her luggage in the front hall and stepped into the sitting room. "Joy's dad used to say once your animal found you, it could help you, like from childhood to puberty, the rough stuff, eh," she said to Cherise.

"So, Kathy, what animal picked you?" Nina's voice had a barely civil edge to it.

Travel-worn, Kathy did not rise to Nina's challenge, but took a deep breath and dropped to the nearest corner of the settee. "Drink and the devil may find me first, but I'm damn well going to check out old Arthur over there right away."

"After you get some sleep, Mom? Nina and Cherise were really tired when we got here too." Joy took Kathy's hand and led her to the bedroom just off the kitchen.

"Right. My girl, I'm so glad I came here."

"So am I," Joy replied, with warmth that surprised even herself.

WHEN KATHY WOKE, THE APARTMENT WAS IN darkness. She found the light switch and, on the little kitchen table, a note in Joy's hand: *Dear Mom, We've gone out to catch a bite. Will bring some back for you. Later, Joy.* xxxooo

Kathy wrote below it *Gone for a walk,* and grabbing her smallest satchel, set out.

"Be prepared for the cold shoulder, Kathy, once you hit Scotland," her well-travelled friends had told her in the bar the night before she left. They were referring to the Scots nature, but Kathy had fully expected a cool breeze from a closer quarter. "Hell, people are people," she mumbled, and besides she was dressed warmly.

Uphill first, walking briskly, Kathy passed lively, laughing groups in the street-side bars. Couldn't be any rougher than what she was accustomed to back home. Still, walking in a strange city alone at night wasn't such a good idea. About to turn back, Kathy almost stumbled into a memorial, a fountain. The plaque read: *In memory of the 300 or more women burned at the stake at this spot on charges of sorcery.*

Kathy pulled her cigarettes from her pocket. Shredding one, she sprinkled tobacco on the Witches' Fountain, a little bit of ceremony she'd picked up from Joy's dad. A gift to the ones who've passed on before.

"Guide me, old ones," she said, "And may the devil of intolerance be resting tonight." Kathy walked down the hill to search out the pleasures of a nip and a hauf.

"Everything here's got mashed potatoes." Joy did not sound unhappy at all.

"But who would have thought bashed neeps, chappit tatties and stovies were all mashed potatoes?" Cherise complained, not as impressed.

"Neeps are turnips, dearie. And the scotch was just fine." Nina paused below a pub sign. A great lot of singing and stomping was taking place inside. "The Jolly Judge. Cherry, I must see if they have keepsakes."

"T-shirts for the Saskatchewan Bench," Cherise said. "The power of positive suggestion and all that. How old do you feel tonight, Joy?"

"Sixteen, and I'll have a–"

"Ginger-ale, this time, darling. Remember, we're going home to your mother."

"I don't believe that will be necessary, Cherise," Nina said from the doorway of the pub.

Inside, Kathy swayed amidst a clump of singers, linked arm over shoulder. So tightly meshed were they she could not rise or gesture, only call over the song, "Cherry, Nina, my girl, come over and meet my friends here! And what the hell are you doing in a bar, Joy?"

"So this is your wee lass," said Angus, the singer on Kathy's right. "Aye, and she is bonnie. Come, scoot in by your Mother, dearie."

"They're teaching me to speak Scots," Kathy said.

"And Gaelic," the man on her left, Roddy, said with a bit of a lilt.

"You think we have language problems back home, girls," Kathy said. "They're tri-lingual here."

Chairs were brought around, handshakes exchanged, and drinks ordered. "A soft drink for the young one, please."

"Ulsage Beatha all around, then." Roddy waved a circle at the bar keep.

"What are we getting?" Cherise asked.

"You mean, what are we getting into?" Nina looked perfectly comfortable under Angus's meaty arm.

"Water of life, my dears. Water of life." Angus had to free his hand to hold up a glass.

"It's your first words of Gaelic." Then Kathy commanded: "Repeat after me: *oolsaye bea."*

"I can tell you she's butchering the mother tongue." Roddy performed an energetic wince. "It's the old name for whiskey. A lovely one at that."

They practised until they got it right, which took the best part of the evening, as Gaelic was ever and always a difficult language.

They discovered the wool shops the next morning, on the way to the palace and the climb to Arthur's Seat. "We must purchase something warm for the climb," Cherise decided, although they were appropriately dressed for the cool and blustery morning.

"You love to shop, don't you?" Nina said, patting Cherise's shoulder.

"This is the kind of weather I love, contrary as hell. It's like fall in the middle of summer," Kathy said. Her arm was linked with Joy's, so they had to untangle to enter the store.

The knits were incredible. Pictish design from the Shetlands, open weaves from the Orkneys, and wool soft as a sigh.

"Joy, these are for you," Cherise called from a rack of deep green sweater vests. Nina was drawn over to the grey heather tones.

Kathy glanced around quickly, and headed outside again. "Going for a smoke, girls," she called, but no one responded. She stood on the narrow side walk, and when she got tired, she crouched there, looking rigidly away from the glass windows of the shop.

As they approached the cash out, Nina poked Joy. "Go ask your mother if she wants something."

"She can't. She won't." Joy's happiness at her new find diminished almost entirely. "Auntie, she'd never be able to afford these. They're, like, hundreds of pounds!"

Cherise turned to stare at Kathy's back through the plate glass window. "I do this to her every time. I can't believe I'm so insensitive."

"So, what to do? Buy her a sweater?" Nina fingered a rust coloured knit.

"Right, buy her something, that'll make it all right." Cherise grimaced.

"It will," Joy said, "if I buy it. Moms can't question a gift from their kids. It's one of the rules. Can I borrow some money, Auntie?"

THE FOUR OF THEM, DECKED OUT IN THEIR NEW woollens, began the climb. Dry and pebbly, the path narrowed so they walked single file, especially through the gorse, which looked like four-foot high buffalo beans with nasty four-inch thorns. The hillside vibrated with the brilliant yellow of the blooms and the sun stole the bitter edge from the cold, wild North Sea wind. About a third of the way up, Kathy's knee popped loudly.

"Just give me a moment," She rubbed her left leg vigorously. "Okay, let's go." But it popped again as they approached St. Anthony's ruins.

"This is a good place to catch our breath," Cherise announced, and they took turns leaning through the empty window of the only remaining wall of the Chapel. Even from there, the ducks and swans in St. Margaret's Loch below were small as ants. The port of Leith stretched out to the north, as did the waters of the Firth of Forth. Directly below, the palace grounds appeared inconsequential, and all Edinburgh, the castle and New Town, glistened in the clean, bright air.

"I can't believe we're in the middle of a city," Joy marvelled for them all.

"All right, up, up, we're only two thirds there." Nina started the rest of the climb.

A few feet from the ruins, Kathy's knee cracked again and she veered, her face scrunched in severe discomfort. "Three strikes, I'm out, folks. Off you go. I'm all right here." She perched on a large stone outcropping, as if she belonged there, and propped her knee up where she could rub it. "To quote the master of hurting songs, *'Pick me up on your way down.'*"

"Are you sure, Mom? I could stay here with you." Kathy rolled up the leg of her jeans, and Joy gently touched her mother's knee, where there was already a deep blue bruise forming.

"Not bloody likely, and blame me for the rest of your life for never sitting on the top of Arthur's Seat? Get going, or do I have to get mad?"

"I'm going, I'm going. Come on, Cherise. We don't want her on our case, do we?"

"Are you sure, Kathy?"

"Get." Kathy growled convincingly.

They had no sooner turned the first full bend than Kathy groaned just as deeply. "Shit, they're going to have to hire a helicopter to get me out of here."

Her good foot was resting on something solid, almost hidden in the tall grass. A carved rock, with a dip in the centre, right below the standing stone. Kathy hopped down to investigate, her pain subsiding for the moment. It looked like one of those old pagan shrines, a healing spring, the real water of life. Kathy brought the burbling moisture to her lips, then bent to the business of splashing the medicinal waters on her knee.

The three of them struggled to the top, the wind blowing their breath back, almost hurling them off the ridge. Below, Edinburgh and much of Scotland unfolded before them. You really could see forever, or until the fog closed in over the ocean, and overland, perhaps all the way to Glasgow and to the border lands.

Joy dropped to a cross-legged crouch on the thin grasses. Cherise sprawled beside her. Nina was pacing over the summit, her arms spread wide as if she were contemplating flight.

"You know what I'm learning about most on this trip, Auntie?"

"What's that?"

"Adults can be kind of fun."

Cherise slung her arm around Joy and pulled her shoulder close. "And I'm learning a new respect for mothering."

"I can be a real brat, I know," Joy said.

"And don't forget beauty," Nina called from a few feet away, her voice carried farther in the wind. "You've learned about beauty, don't you think?" She loped from vantage point to vantage point.

"I think they call that grace, Nina."

"Sure, grace is beauty in action. Or is beauty grace in action? I really do love high places." Nina began to perform, quoting a passage from *All's Well That Ends Well,* her voice scattered by the wind to the four directions, although her audience of two could hear every word:

Our remedies oft in ourselves do lie,
Which we ascribe to heaven. The fated sky
Gives us free scope; only doth backward pull
Our slow designs when we ourselves are dull.
What power is it which mounts my love so high?
The mightiest space in fortune nature brings
To join like likes, and kiss like native things.

Peering down the mountainside before them, Cherise could see Kathy far below, kneeling beside a standing stone, spreading or smoothing something into the shadowing grasses. "And I'm learning a new respect for mothers," Cherise murmured. It may have been a trick of the light, her shortness of breath, or maybe a reflection from the gorse, but to Cherise's eyes Kathy had an aura glowing all around her, illuminating and golden as the sun.

Stories for Joy

JOY'S VOICE SOFTENS TO NOT-QUITE-WHEEDLE. "The girls want to go to the music festival next weekend. Can I borrow the tent, Mom?"

Kathy puts down her fork and rests her elbows on the table. "What music festival? Where? You're camping? Who's going? Who's driving?"

"The one in the valley and we're still figuring all that out, Mom, but I'll let you know later, okay? Just, can I go?" Joy swirls the last of her spaghetti around her fork and waves the end strands like a pendulum over her plate. "Mom?"

"Shit, Joy, I need more information. Let me think about it."

"Everyone is going. It's not very far."

"Maybe I should come with you."

"No, Mom, please no." Joy is emphatic. "Come on, Mom, you're avoiding my question. Will you let me go to the music festival?"

"Let me think about that. Right. So as I was saying, I'm walking down the sandy beach and what do I see? A pair of mirrored eyes looking out at me. He's leaning out of the car window, a beat up Ford with no handles on the doors and a windshield cracked to blue prisms on the passenger side, as if someone had put the boots to it." Kathy pauses to pick up her knitting, the thing she does now that she doesn't smoke after supper.

Joy stands to clear the dishes with that how-do-I-get-out-of-here-faster look on her face. "Mom, the girls are expecting me in half an hour."

"Right. And we were not looking for trouble, my cousin and I, just hoping for it." Kathy says. "The kind of trouble we could whisper and giggle about after lights out." *The kind of trouble that makes mothers fret about how fast their little girls grow up,* Kathy thought.

"Mom," Joy's eyes roll back, "that is so last summer."

Kathy grins. "I know. Anyway, I don't even see his eyes, he's leaning out and 'hello girls' and we march on, our thongs flapping furiously. I start to turn around, and my cousin grabs me, pulls me along so we're out of there, and the car follows us as far as it can, to where the road veers off to the bush again."

"Thongs, Mom? Thongs are underwear. I believe you mean flip flops." Joy flings herself on a chair in resignation.

"Okay, flip flops. I'd never felt such a strong attraction to anyone before, and I conspired to find a way to see him again."

"So? So what?" Joy is fifteen now herself, and has heard this story a dozen times, maybe more, "like what are you trying to tell me?"

"A different thing each time, girlie. This time about knowing."

"Knowing what?" She cuts off the *what* so it sounds dangerously like a curse, but Kathy's tough-skinned.

"My mother always warned me I'd get my reward for being such a trial." Kathy has not yet said such a thing to Joy. So far no need. Joy's been very easy, very straightforward, and very open with her mother. "Except I wasn't a trial, of course. I always knew what I was doing, except when I didn't, in which case I trusted my instincts, and it's this knowing, this deeper knowledge I'm trying to tell you about."

Joy is not for listening, she's for action, and clearly aching, in a way Kathy finds all too familiar, just pushing for a fight. So she can take the phone and close herself in the hall closet with it, and explain to her friends how she suffers. It's part of growing up.

When Joy was five Kathy would hold her little girl, and Joy would say "tell me a story now, mom, the one about the dancers" and her sage sweet head would nestle on Kathy's collar bone, small hands wrapped around Kathy's hard right arm, her ear by her mother's heart. Kathy would lower her voice, so only Joy could hear, and the story changed every time. Often Joy would offer corrections. "No, that's not what he said, no, that's when it started to rain, and they went in the trees, Mom, don't you remember?"

Kathy does remember, but also knows when it's time to shut up. "Okay, let's do this another time."

"Right. I'm going out for a while." Still, from the doorway, "Bye Mom, love you."

Kathy can't seem to stop herself with the Mom stuff. "Call if you're going to be later than twelve."

Joy doesn't grace her with an answer, jounces out the door, her dark hair a river of reflected light in the entrance, her young woman body wrapped tight in blue jeans and white cotton. She is achingly beautiful. The door closes on Kathy and the waiting hours.

Kathy addresses the clock on the wall. "I can do no right, she knows everything already, or at least thinks she does. Comes by that naturally."

It's been twenty years since Kathy went to a music festival, when she was nearly twenty. Older than Joy, but younger too, somehow.

Thinking about it isn't a *no.* It does buy some time. This parenting thing is so tough, Kathy thinks. At least I'm not as clueless as my poor mother. Everything Kathy did was a threat to a decent lifestyle, even the music she listened to. At least Kathy and Joy didn't differ in their musical tastes.

There are some things Kathy's mother did not know about. It must have been easier for her to say no. At least it seemed to come automatically: *No, absolutely not.*

Kathy's mother had said *no* to the movie theatre, the pool hall, even the dance pavilion, although Kathy did sneak there, sometimes, with her cousin. A girl has to live a little.

Most of what Kathy wanted to do was harmless. Just play. A vigorous, lusty dance, a short-lived bloom, a burst of fragrance, of spectacle, an opening to something larger, much larger than the smoky bar, the cabaret floor sticky with beer.

Of course the dance moved from the public floor

to the parked car, the abandoned green room, the makeshift bed in the basement. That was part of it, naturally, the closest she got to celebration, the few moments when Kathy felt totally loved, absolutely loveable, and a far cry from this virginal living room, this suburban yard, this formal bedded garden with its single poplar tree.

Kathy never thought she'd live past thirty. Now she's having to deal with the life-giving force again, through the maturing, the blossoming of her daughter, when for years sex for Kathy consisted of labia unfolding for only her own hands, the hands of irregular lovers, the occasional touch of the midnight penis when child and work and the obligations are all tucked away and play is a weary dance.

And of course the girl will get hurt. Joy is out looking for romance, the opiate of the masses, the societal control that blocks community love, the true-hearted love of everyone. Is it a mother's job to protect her daughter from experiencing this hurt? Is it a mother's role to always say "No"?

When once upon a time, when she was not much older than Joy, Kathy enjoyed making eyes with the lead singer, bumping and grinding for the bass, shaking her breasts at the drummer. Falling in love with the mandolin.

It was the minor key, the vibrato, the throaty sorrow of the mandolin that she loved. The way it spoke about some parts of her she didn't even know, her history, maybe her parents' history. Mandolins know suffering, humble people, life on the land. And the mandolin players, men with quick, certain fingers and eyes you can squeeze your soul into.

There are parts of this story she has not yet shared with Joy. A part of Kathy's life before she was a mother. Before she was tied to a man. Before she was tied to Joy's dad. Before she was tied to anyone.

Everybody deserves a break now and then, and Janine, Kathy's good buddy, had a gleam in her eye and a music festival in mind. She wanted some adventure, and some company. And though Kathy loved her like a sister, sister she was not. Janine was a wild flower, an opportunist and free.

They take the weekend off when they should have been working. And they hop into J's beater with a canvas tent and a sleeping bag. Yahoo.

It's easy to convince the aging heavy at the gate that they are part of one of the featured bands. Kathy lets J do the talking and slips in a couple of subtle winks. The best parties are in the performers' campground. Kathy and J do not plan to sleep. Cat naps at most, since coupling bodies are everywhere. The music emanates from every campfire – little need to blanket a spot near the main stage.

Kathy's eyes gleam in the firelight, watching hands move over the strings, deep in the angst of the song. She closes her eyes and softly, shyly first, soon bolder, she sways, and that's her voice too, an instrument of the night. She harmonizes, wails, by morning, after the first bottle of tequila and half a pack of Drum, growls. It feels so right.

Like a cigarette would right now, Kathy thinks, tucking away the knitting. Do I really want this for my girl? It was so easy then. Would I have been able to guide myself if someone hadn't been there, pulling the hand brakes? Does a mother always have to say no? Should I always say no?

The first morning, Kathy and Janine are in the sellers' stalls, trying on Afghani coats in the scorching July sun over their bare, sun-burnt shoulders, and just as Kathy shrugs the coat off, he's watching, just happens to be nearby, and it's the look of sexual surprise, as if he thinks she's bare under the wool of those goats, his naked wonder that attracts her. Her gut's doing somersaults, cartwheels, and she knows it's mutual.

His dancing mandolin feet walk disembodied directly into Kathy's path, and he asks if she'd like to go for a stroll, just like that, and she says *why not?*

In the shade of the nearby bluff, the whisper of leaves in the almost mid-day stillness, the silence in the midst of things, he is Pan of the woods, lord of the hard-on, rough and tumble, squeezing, biting her breasts, touching her as if she were a goddess as her body cracks open for him, for the sky. There must have been mosquitoes, thistles, but she didn't notice. His face is hair shaded, and smoothed in complete and innocent pleasure, as her stomach and breasts slide, sweat-moist, over his belly, his chest, her necklace banging softly against him, the ankh that is the sign of eternity. The sighing of leaves. Isn't it only natural to want this again? The sharing, shouldn't it have been forever?

But forever is not the nature of men and women. Like picking apples, try a different kind every day, see which one is to your taste. Most of them have their good aspects. Kathy was too busy that summer trying out the many and varied to settle for any one. Maybe it was that she didn't know any better, maybe that choosing and settling was too scary.

Of course, as it turned out, she's always been alone. *So I'm happy to live in a frigging cocoon and encourage my daughter to live in one too? A family tradition?* Kathy settles on the back step, wishing she had some smoke to blow at the mosquitoes. There are regrets, lovers knocking softly, but the hinges are rusty.

Mid-morning the winding campground path explodes with awakening bodies, puffy-eyed, en route to washrooms and the lake. It's a good time to find people. "Hey!" Kathy, bare shouldered, swings her hair, loose and golden, over her back, so it spins in a momentary halo. "I missed you last night."

The mandolin man, sweet smiling, quick fingered, with the kind of energy she might try to hold down, bounces, dizzies her with his sudden changes. "Where were *you? I* was backstage, doing music things, you know. Getting ready for our gig. I'm working here, you know. At least some of the time." He touches the place where the side of her neck meets her shoulders.

"I ran into this biker type from down south. We sat up and watched the stars."

"Sure, watched the stars. It did rain."

"It rained?" Busted.

""Yeah, your tent leaked. I slept there last night."

"Oh."

"So, what're you doing later? Like, can I book an appointment?"

"Sure, I think I have space for you," and this with the smile she thinks is impish, the one that has never failed. "How about midnight."

"Ah, the witching hour."

Her tent isn't hers alone. Watching him walk away, she realizes she'd better talk with Janine. Like, just what was he doing in their tent all night? But J is nowhere to be found. And Kathy's stash of Comfort is gone; empty; the bottle's on its side in the campfire's ashes. There is nothing in the tent, not even a blanket. Wet clothing flaps from the anchor lines and tent poles, from the branches of the poplar trees.

It must have rained.

Kathy needs a swim, a good clean up, and she has a hunch she'll find Janine at the shower house, if she really does want to talk to her, so she grabs a damp towel and walks to the beach front, a mile or so down the lake. The bells dangling from her rope belt tinkle joyfully against her legs with each step, and ultimately twist to her belly, tangled in the flow of her gauzy skirt.

As she walks by one campsite, cooler-strewn, a guy in a ball cap comments to his friend, "Now there's a real hippie."

Kathy glances around, wanting to see too, but there is only her, and she bites the inside of her cheeks for as long as she can, until the laughter bursts from her, around the next corner of the tent village path, the well-worn dust trail leading to the beach.

At the far end there's a promontory, a stone erection large enough to leave a shadow in the mid-morning water. Below it a man, buck-naked, wading gingerly, the water now just above his knees. Kathy walks carefully in that direction, tugging at her belt.

Kathy finally locates Janine, back at the car. J is peering at herself awkwardly in the rear view mirror, trying to put in her contact lenses. She has make-up and brushes all over the front seat. "Having a good time, girl?"

"Kathy, you wouldn't believe what happened!"

Kathy settles herself cross-legged on the grass beside the open car door. "Okay, try me."

"This guy came by last night, this musician, some old friend of yours, and tonight we're going dancing! I forget his name, Brian or something. You know. The mandolin player with the band from Vancouver."

"Dancing, umm. Have fun, kid." Kathy smiles beatifically, and it isn't until she has pulled down her sleeping bag and climbed into the tent that she allows herself the luxury of a tear or two. The sleeping bag smelled of him.

Surrendering the night to the insects, Kathy watches the in-your-face glow of the street light moon on the poplar leaves, from the quilty safety of her bed. Even now she trembles at the aftermath of this folk festival, this celebration where music was the through-line and making love the unquestioned motive. No, love was the unquestioned motive. How could she be so ungenerous, so unkind, so critical of the mercurial woman she was, the one who was not afraid to dance alone?

Which is what Kathy did, after her nap. Yet she was not alone. Many others, uncoupled, and in a kind of ecstasy, some drug induced, but most dancing out of the deep joy of the true-hearted.

Whatever the hell 'true hearted' *means. Only it was right, that's what it was.* Kathy turns away from the bedside alarm clock. It is almost midnight.

Kathy weeps as she dances, the night wind blowing tears into cool rivulets across her face. Janine and Brian find her there, and fold her into their arms. Holding hands they move together until the music ends, and arm over shoulder over arm, they sway back to the tent. Oh, enfolded in love.

So do I tell my daughter that? That it *doesn't matter whose body or what body, gender, or age, that it's all celebration. I can't do that. The sharing, the Eucharist, the most sensual night of my life, and I'm too much of a prude to talk about it. I never dreamt I'd grow up into such a spiritless hypocrite.* Kathy swings her legs over the bed's edge. Some thinking demands movement.

The memory of her body's generosity, its act of giving, of living – there was nothing cheap or tawdry or sleazy about it. Once she got over her little fit of jealousy, went beyond that, it was all good.

Kathy's mother said she'd always been alone, as if she were proud of it, as if that's what she always wanted, and she wanted Kathy to be like her too. Part of Kathy envied her that solid, pristine, almost defiant aloneness. But her mother sure didn't have much fun on the way. *I've tasted being part of something. Part of the dance.*

ONCE JANINE PULLS THE TENT ZIPPER DOWN, the three of them just fall together, like puppies, licking and kissing and nudging each other. They take off each other's clothes and roll into something more like the snake ball Kathy saw once at the farm, all limbs and bodies and faces, in a frenzied tangle. The only time Kathy ever touched another woman that way, but then it wasn't another woman, it was Janine. And Brian. Or both of them. Everything melding into giving. Into beauty.

WHEN KATHY IMAGINES WHAT SHE CAN TELL Joy, it's not the specifics, which the girl might very well be curious about, but the totality of the experience Kathy wants her to understand. Although she hasn't practiced it in her life, complete sharing is possible. What you try to hold with you is the memory, not the people.

Kathy sits cross-legged on the floor, looking through her old vinyl albums. *It's not just physical. Skin against skin is part of it, like that child's game, hand over hand over hand. We need that. I do.* But it's not just a sound, it's a song, an evocation, all the power of sound and tone and memory combined. Kathy knows it's never been a beauty contest, or a capabilities competition. It is about giving. Dance.

THE NEXT MORNING, WHEN THE INTENSE SUN discouraged snuggling, Kathy was the first to roll out of the tent, after jigging and wiggling into her rain-dampened clothes. And before the new day the dancers are spreading their arms like wings, and their hips are moving to the beat of remembered music, and she is in Janine's arms and in Brian's and their eyes are more knowing, full of light. The leaves catch the sunlight, as the tree branches swivel to the ever-present wind.

IT'S GOOD TO GO THIS WAY AGAIN. I'VE BEEN *apologizing for years at how desperate I was for love. But I was right to live in the sweetness. I have been wrong to regret.*

The front door opens cautiously. Joy, Kathy's near-grown daughter, dances into the living room, ear-phone deaf.

Kathy stands over the turntable, drops the needle. "True-hearted," she calls in greeting. She swirls, laughing, and Joy stares at her quizzically for a moment, then dances with Kathy to her own private orchestra, which Kathy can't hear over

Dada dada dada duh
Dada dad dada dah dah dah
The trembling mandolin.

Correction Line

IF YOU GO IN A STRAIGHT LINE TOWARDS THE horizon long enough, you can get seriously off track. In fact, the only way to go straight on a planet full of curves is to curve yourself. Or make periodic adjustments.

Kathy knew the curve of the correction line was nearby. She also knew there should be two lanes on this thin-membrane road, the highway to her parents' farm.

It was a classic April Fool's – a freak blizzard. The afternoon had been perfectly clear as she left the city. The heavy snowfall at first decorated, then distracted, and now distressed her as she tried to see the few feet ahead, as far as the headlights reached, to where the two beams now converged on what she could only hope was the centre of the road. She was pavement-blinded by the dense snowfall, the sodden thick blanket of white over everything. When she pulled over, creeping, waiting to feel the passenger-side wheels drop over the pavement edge, she kept her headlights on – dim or bright didn't matter – hoping someone coming would see her in time to stop. Later this precipitation would all freeze and make progress even more treacherous. For now, she slowed gradually, and when the wheels stopped, slapped her little car into neutral, leaned her head on the top of the steering wheel and wept.

Joy, her seventeen year old daughter, sprawled next to her, oblivious to this outburst of emotion, headphones on, CD whirring, passenger seat pushed back to nearly reclining. Eyes closed, mouth open a bit. Likely sleeping. Even in her late teens, the kid still fell asleep after ten minutes in a moving vehicle. If she did wake up, it didn't matter. Kathy was past being strong. She was confused, confounded, and yes, on the run, for now, from her own home.

From the shadowy face in the basement window as she did her laundry. From the candy bars left under the windshield wiper of her car in the morning. From the phone calls without voices, just ragged breathing into the receiver. Into her ear.

At first she thought the stalker might be Cherise, Joy's dad's former girlfriend, who may have had reason to be jealous of Kathy's relationship with Joy, being somewhat conflicted on the issue of parenthood. But Cherise could see Joy whenever she wanted to, so that would just be too bizarre.

And if Ron wanted to date again, to be part of Joy's immediate family, he would just call, wouldn't he? Not skulk around like some peeping tom. That wasn't his style. Then she thought it might be Adam, this really creepy guy she'd dated until she figured out he was more interested in Joy than in her. But Adam was years ago. Besides, this was a weird mix of snoopiness and benevolence.

Kathy even got Anna to find her a protective rattle-stone, which she then carried in her shirt pocket for weeks. Her friend Anna, one of the women Kathy worked with in the house-painting trade, had seen trouble coming all along. She possessed a sharp business head, a direct benefit from her previous excursions into entrepreneurship and the sex trade. Kathy was making a living for herself and her little girl house painting, taking night classes at the university, coming into the classroom after a long day's work spattered with paint, smelling of turpentine. In January, she landed a job teaching palaeontology. That was when the weirdness started.

During the second month of the winter semester, the anonymous tormentor was getting bolder, moving up from the relatively benign but weird gifts and the amorphous breathing on the phone. Kathy was finding envelopes in her mailbox with pages of junk from the Internet. Not porn, but disturbing relationship commentary, stuff about possession and revenge, mostly written by spurned men. Messages from her stalker. Then the voice mail, with portions of songs, some sweet, others with lyrics a tad on the scary side, the 'in my bed or dead' kind of thing. Caller ID blocked. Her phone at work was shared, no message function, and the calls the department receptionist let through were heavily screened now, after the first few.

The phone company suggested taking out an unlisted home number, which she did. Still the mail and the phone messages. Joy was the first one home, the one to find these things there, and she was getting really freaked.

"Never give a client your home address," Anna had said when Kathy started tutoring at home. Kathy guessed she'd learned that the hard way, but surely this was different, these students weren't bar scum or lounge pick-ups, or horny businessmen on the make. They were young people who really were only interested in what she could teach them, or at the worst, in a bit of brown nosing for the next term paper or exam. And, as a sessional she had to time-share her campus office with a resentful and unco-operative colleague. Besides, most of her students were ten or fifteen years younger than her, for Christ's sakes. Just kids. Only a few years older than Joy. "Exactly," Anna said, and Kathy's cheeks were flooded with the blushing she showed when anyone tried to tell her what to do.

Besides, only three students requested extra tutoring. Angie needed a bit of confidence-boosting. She was heading for the master's program. And they were becoming friends. Justin loved to argue, but hated to do papers. He was clever, charming, and so damn lazy. She met with him half a dozen times, hoping to incite ambition. His big doe eyes and nervous energy reminded her of Joy's father. And today, Ray, sweet-tempered and easy going. He had the smarts but not the organizational ability, and somehow he'd gotten to university without learning how to write an essay.

She had given him some reference documents to review, and then suggested they meet at her kitchen table to go over his most recent paper.

Because of them, Joy and Kathy were now trying to drive through a freak blizzard which showed no signs of letting up. Kathy's rusty Rabbit shuddered in a sudden gust. She pushed herself from the steering wheel, dry-eyed again, and rummaged in her jacket pockets for a tissue.

A set of headlights appeared out of the dense snowfall behind them and in a moment, a white car, a white Charger, for Christ's sakes, passed them, moving very slowly. The car was lovely, slightly the worse for wear, with wet snow stuck to the sides and the wipers pushing two half moons like dark eyes into the windshield.

It pulled up in front of her, and stopped, the motor throbbing. Needs a new muffler, Kathy thought, ignoring her heart in panic mode.

Joy woke up. "Where are we?"

"Far enough out of town that it's too late to turn back."

"About halfway, then." For the kid, it was always halfway, until the farm was almost in sight. Halfway seemed safest, seemed closest to turning back. Joy always accepted that. Trusted her.

Someone was opening the door, stepping out of the white car up ahead. Shit. Best defense is a good offense. Kathy opened her door too. Wiped her cheeks and stretched her legs out onto the wet frost-boiled pavement.

"Hi, need a hand here?" Young. Male.

"Nah, just taking a break," Kathy said. "Rotten weather."

"Yeah, it was fine when I left town."

"Yeah. That a Charger?" Kathy pointed with a nod at the car.

"Ummhum." He was exhibiting traditional prairie modesty.

"It's a beauty. I thought they stopped making those twenty years ago."

"About that. I fixed her up myself," he said.

He was close enough to eyeball now, a clean-cut guy in a ball cap, some auto-parts shop logo on the peak. Sheep-lined denim jacket over well-worn jeans, strong looking hands, eyes the blue of the prairie sky just a few inches above the horizon. He was checking out her old VW, went so far as to gently wipe the slush off her headlights. "GTI, eh? How far you going in this weather?"

"Another hour or so north west, just the other side of the dam." Was that too much information?

"I'm heading almost to Loreburn, but you can follow my lights until the turn-off."

Kathy was not one to follow anyone or even to take advice. But she had to nod with him when he said, "Better'n sitting out here waiting to get hit."

"Or iced in."

"No ice yet, but I wouldn't want to be out here tonight." He walked backwards to his car. "Take care, then," he said and reached for the driver's side door handle.

Right. She ran her sleeve up and down her driver's side windshield and climbed back into her Rabbit.

"Who was that?" Joy was wide awake now.

"Some guy we're going to follow."

"He's cute."

Kathy checked her daughter's face. She was serious.

"What could you see anyway?"

"Enough." Joy pulled her car blanket over her shoulder, leaned back into the seat again.

Kathy followed the tail lights. The guy was going fast, but he was heavier and higher; no doubt he could see more than she could and if he left the road, she would have time to stop.

The road started to curve, making an adjustment in the grid system that ruled the roads in this part of the world. The snow hit the window intensely, exquisitely for a few moments, and she almost lost him.

Trust a stranger. Well, it wasn't a risk, really. Not this time. Her doors were locked. She had her foot on the gas. And Joy liked him. A lapse or two in judgment can really shake your faith in even the good ones.

"What the…!" Kathy braked hard.

"Mom, what's happening?"

The car in front of them was skidding, fishtailing, and swishing a spray of wet cloud between them.

"Must have hit some gravel on the side, or a break in the pavement."

They called it pavement out of habit, but the thinly oiled surface was more deadly than mud this time of year. Blocks of road broke off with the thaw, revealing washout holes beneath, some big enough to bury a wheel to the axle. Any one of the pieces of broken surface rough enough to ruin an oil pan or a gas tank, even in his bigger car.

"He doesn't know what he's doing, Mom. Why are we following him?"

"Because he's bigger, he's got better lights, because I'm too tired to break the trail."

"Oh, I wish you would let me drive."

Kathy glanced over in sympathy. "It only seems as if it would be easier when you're in control, sweetie."

Her knight in the shiny Charger was back in control of his car. He blinked a high/low beam as if to say *I'm okay* or *Watch out* or *Back off, you're too close* or all three.

Kathy eased her foot from the gas pedal and felt the jig in the back wheels. "Oh, that was it – ice. Already. Shit. Joy, call the Highway Hotline."

Joy pulled out her cell, her second most prized possession, a lovely curving palm-sized phone, encased in soft pink plastic. Kathy knew the number by heart, and Joy's face, once she'd keyed in, listening, told her everything else she needed to know. "It gets worse, right?"

"Oh yeah. Travel discouraged south half of the province, roads closed everywhere north of the city. Visibility zero. Ice."

"All right, enough. When this guy turns off, we'll just sit tight until it melts."

"Mom, I'm hungry. And I've got to pee."

Sure as sleep, about an hour down the road, this girl's body always needed a nature break. And although they both were seasoned ditch users, today it would not be pleasant to expose one's buttocks to the wind.

Ordinarily, they'd be at the farm by now. Ordinarily they'd be in Grandma's kitchen, drinking coffee and eating gingersnaps and watching the snow fly by the window.

COULD IT ONLY HAVE BEEN THAT MORNING?

Ray had just nicely sat down at the kitchen table, term paper in front of him. Kathy was bringing them each a cup of black coffee in the earthenware mugs she'd found at the farmers' market, when the pounding at the door began.

"Someone's going to smash through if I don't open that soon." Kathy tried to get a look at the step through the porch window, but whoever was attacking her door was beyond her sightlines. Not the kind of knocking anyone opens up for.

"Okay, Okay, what can I do for you?" Kathy yelled over the pounding, through the sturdy porch door.

"Open up, you fucking bitch!"

Open up you fucking bitch? Kathy did not recognize the voice at first. And no one called her a bitch. She backed out of the porch, closed and dead bolted the entrance. By this time Ray stood beside her.

"You get guests like this often?" he asked,

Joy ran down the stairs that led to the front door. "What's going on, Mom?"

"Call 911, girl. Now."

And that's why they're out here in this weather.

The Charger's left signal blinked. "Okay, we're on our own, baby."

The white knight turned slowly off the main road and came to a full stop. Kathy gradually stopped as well. The highway disappeared, an ominous white tunnel up ahead. He walked back to her car, slipping a bit. Kathy rolled down her window.

"Look, why don't you wait this out at my place. I'm just a mile up the road."

It was logical. It was the decent thing to offer. It was part of the rules of the road. In weather like this, people help each other out. They do. He peered into the car, as if he could sense Kathy's reservations, her fear.

"Look, to tell the truth, I've got to get home to check on my herd. I've got a couple heifers due anytime and if one of them calves today, I could really use an extra set of hands." After years in the painting trade, Kathy was obviously fit for hard work. "I bet it's been a while since you've been around during calving season."

Oof. Sucker punch. A soft spot. Wasn't that a better reason to be on this highway in the first place? Because it was spring? Because there was new and healthy life out there? Because somewhere under the snow the stream was flowing and the grass was starting to come to life in the pasture and because the calves would be sniffing her hand and spooking and kicking into the warm air. The tomato plants would just be sprouting on the windowsills and the last of the ice-water snow banks would be trickling their load into the valley and the dugout. Because the geese were going north, so was she.

Joy leaned across the seat. "Hi."

He almost blushed. Joy had that effect on young men. He nodded at her shyly and turned back to Kathy. "If you ladies like, you could certainly wait in the house."

Kathy glanced at Joy. No danger signs here. Well, no unhealthy ones. She grinned.

"Could do. It's been a long time since I did any midwifery with cattle."

"Not much has changed, is my guess. I'm Martin. Took over the spread from my dad, Don Clarke, when he and Mom retired. Trying to go to university in town too."

Ah shit, kid, why couldn't you just be a simple farm boy. I've had my fill of students for a while.

"I'm Kathy. This is my daughter Joy. We'll follow you."

THE ALL-WEATHER DOOR OF KATHY'S HOUSE was hollow and they could hear it splinter. The intruder kicked it into shreds and was working on the main door.

"Who are you? What's going on? I think you have the wrong house." Kathy kept her voice as calm and reasonable as possible. And then she connected all the dots: the phone calls, the weird mail, the gifts and then the voice. It was her student, Justin.

The inside door was solid wood, but the frame would not hold long.

"Justin, is that you?"

He was lunging at the inside door, breathing heavily.

"Who've you got in there, you bitch?"

Mild-mannered Ray pulled his jacket off and threw it over the banister. The biceps of his well-developed arms displayed an impressive array of tattoos.

"Let me at that weird fuck."

The pounding and kicking started again.

"You know him?"

"Of course. Everyone knows crazy Justin, the spaz kid. He's in love with you. Everyone knows that, too."

"Everyone except me."

"Yeah – get out of the way." Ray didn't seem surprised by this turn of events, seemed almost expectant. Or at least eager to flex his fists.

The doorframe collapsed with a sudden crack. Justin punched the door open.

"Joy, stay upstairs!" Kathy stepped towards the stairway in spite of herself.

Justin waded through the ruined door frame, his face twisted with purple rage.

"You bitch." Vocabulary had never been Justin's strong point.

Kathy felt the adrenalin rush of a teacher, a mother, and a homeowner on the defensive. She waved both hands before her in the universal signal for settling disputes. "All right, Justin, calm down. I don't know what you think is going on here, or why you think you have any right to break into my home, but we've called the cops, and it's just me and Ray working on an essay here."

"That's not what he said to me." Justin stepped forward, seized her wrists too tightly and pulled her abruptly towards Ray.

Ray stood a few feet down the hall, in the entrance to the kitchen, taking on some martial arts stance.

"Oh God," Kathy groaned, "I'm too old for this. For Christ's sake, Ray, back off. I don't want you guys fighting in here. And Justin, let go of me right now."

Justin swung Kathy around and let go. She flew against the wall by the stairs, cracking her elbow, knocking a painting from the wall, and scrambled up in time to see Ray land his first punch, the only one he landed before the police were at the door, or what was left of the door. Justin was swinging open fisted at Ray, and then at the first officer, who easily pinned Justin's arms.

"Fucking bitch, fucking bitch," Justin screamed as they dragged him out of the house, twisting to stare at Kathy, wild-eyed.

"Settle down. Ray, out of here," Kathy said. Ray obeyed. Kathy glanced around, assessing damage. "Joy, you okay?"

"Too weird," Joy said from the foot of the stairs. "Mom, are you okay?"

Kathy shrugged, slung her arm over her daughter's shoulders and they stepped through the devastated porch.

Ray was bouncing like a boxer in the front yard as he talked to the first officer, his voice choppy, his arms waving, animated.

"Once your partner's done talking with him, he can tell Ray, there, his presence here is neither required or desired," Kathy said to the second officer, when he returned to the house after cuffing Justin, pushing the young man's head down, shoving him, still struggling, into the back seat of the police car. "And thanks. That was a fast response."

The officer shrugged. "We were in the neighbourhood." He pulled a notepad and pen from his pocket and prepared to take notes.

Of course Joy ripped into Martin's house as soon as possible. "Can I use your bathroom?" she called without waiting for an answer.

"Upstairs," he called after her. Mark's house was a modest 40s style two story, not too different from the one Kathy had grown up in.

"You'll have to excuse the mess." he said.

Kathy lived in chaos by comparison. She collapsed on a kitchen chair.

Joy whipped downstairs. "Can I use the phone? My cell's out of juice." She had her hand on the black wall phone before he could answer. "I'm calling Grandma, okay Mom?"

"I've got to check on my animals," Martin said. He pulled on a sturdy pair of barn boots and headed directly back out.

When he did not return, Kathy and Joy rather shyly braved the last of the year's blizzards to stand by the corral fence, peer through the poles. In the eerie glow of the yard light Martin paced behind a panicking heifer. He was waving his herdsman cane at an overly curious Hereford-cross bull. The bull was young and not huge as bulls go, but easily big enough to trample Martin into the sodden manure with one thoughtless lunge.

Martin waved at them and then pointed to the wooden barn door twenty yards behind him. Joy clambered over the fence before Kathy could give a word of advice, nimbly leaping between frozen piles of cow snow, bound to open the barn door. Kathy climbed over the pole fence more slowly and moved indirectly towards Martin. The dark spot at his feet, as she'd suspected, was a newborn, still wet, and on its side, too weak to stand up yet. The smell of the after-birth made the young bull aggressive and Martin was trying to keep the terrified new mother and the silly bull from trampling the calf.

The kid should have the bulls separated from the herd this time of year, she thought. She drew up behind Martin as quietly as possible. "If we move the calf, will she follow?"

"We've got to get it out of this snow anyway."

Kathy nodded. "Here, I can do it." Although it looked tiny, the calf weighed forty pounds, was limp, and awkward to carry, slippery and bloody. Kathy couldn't see the uneven ground, and fell twice on the way to the door, wincing as her knees hit frozen lumps of manure.

Joy swung the barn door wide open.

"Go on, get back there," Martin was yelling, not far behind her. She heard the cane hit home twice.

"Stand back and be ready to close the door quick, Joy," Kathy said.

The barn was dark and close and dry, smelling of hay and cow shit. Kathy managed to heave the calf, still uncooperative, to an out-of-the-way corner, and move aside in time to evade the push of the frantic mother. Martin knocked the bull's nose once more before Joy pushed the door shut. Martin waved Kathy and Joy aside and in a low voice, began to soothe the cow.

"Thanks. I knew you would be the kind of people I could trust around animals."

"Thanks. We just knew you would be the kind of person we could trust in a snowstorm."

And that was how Kathy and Joy ended up seated on a square bale in the corner of the lean-to barn, whispering excitedly as Martin lifted the exhausted calf to its feet, the new mama murmuring encouragement, the whites of her eyes rarely showing now, as she settled into her role.

After the police left, the front step seemed like the only safe place to sit. "What's with that guy?" Joy was very tense, her voice quavering.

"With both those guys." Kathy was rubbing her raw wrists with soothing cream. *"If you love something set it free/If it comes back it's yours/If it doesn't, it never was."*

"What?"

"A poster I had when I was about your age. Always thought it was kind of stupid."

"Sure," Joy said. "How about, *If you love someone,*

tell them. If they don't love you, leave them alone. If they do, be happy."

"Sounds healthy to me, kid. Anyway, we're not dealing with love here. We're dealing with some sort of controlling thing. Ah, more on the nutbar side of controlling."

"Obsession."

"Okay. Whatever that means. Some steroid, testosterone guy thing. Like this wasn't about me or you at all."

Joy seemed to be staring, unfocused, across the street and into the neighbour's picture window. "Sometimes, Mom, people like people who don't like them back, or love people who can't love them back. Like Dad."

"Your dad loves you!" Kathy answered automatically, emphatically.

Joy's eyes were clouding over. Kathy hugged her hard. "*I* love you, kid."

IT WAS UNLIKELY THAT JUSTIN WOULD BE HELD in custody long. Kathy called Anna, who arrived within the half hour to inspect the damage, smudge the entrance and porch with sweetgrass, and arrange for a crew from Women in Trades for the doors and frames by early evening.

"Even so, Anna, we can't stay here tonight."

"Go on." Anna patted her head, something she had taken to lately, ever since Joy had announced to them all that she was taller than her mom. "Go on, Little Mom; take a drive in the country. I've got everything under control here."

"Oh Anna, I love you."

"Sure, no problem," Anna said.

The spring storm settled at nightfall, leaving polished sheets of ice between thin wet drifts as they stumbled into the farmhouse, having made sure the calf had fed and that the mother would accept and not step on her little one.

"It'll melt by morning. There's room for you, if you want to stay over," Martin said.

Kathy smiled. "May I use your phone?" The folks back home would be relieved to know they were someplace safe for the night.

Martin made a pot of tea and heated up bowls of stew while Joy and Kathy dug in the car for a change of clothes. Kathy's jacket and jeans were a sodden smear of shit and blood and afterbirth goo. A comforting smell, somehow.

Joy, of course, was able to sleep, curled up on Martin's couch with her car blanket. The fresh air and the steamy barn had exhausted her, or at least given her a need for some alone time to think about birth and life, and all the gory details. Kathy was now more awake than she'd been in years. Martin did not seem tired at all. He regaled her with tale upon birthing tale, well into the night.

April second, the sun was as intense as the prairie spring. By noon, no one would know there had been a blizzard. For now, at dawn, after checking Mama and baby with Martin once more, Kathy and Joy drove into the white blanket, the tires easily cutting through the skin of last night's ice to solid ground. Martin's farm had been a slight detour but, as Kathy hit the road, she felt as though she was finally on the right track.

She had wanted to say something warm to Martin today, post-blizzard, post-trauma, a man who was what he appeared to be after a long line of disconnected men, including Joy's dad, who was never coming back to them. Major adjustment. Joy called, "Thanks for the loan of the couch," as she climbed into the passenger seat. Kathy wanted to say something warm, but stumbled, couldn't, just waved as they backed out of the yard and turned onto the highway.

Her car hummed, hugged the curved road of the correction line, heading straight to the horizon.

Credits

"Kaleidoscopes" (under the title "Rainbow Show") was previously published in the anthology *Sky High* (Coteau Books). "Women Waiting" (under the title "Peacock Blues") was previously published in *Grain*.

An excerpt from "Stag Line" was previously published in the anthology *Listening With the Ear of the Heart* (St Peter's Press).

Acknowledgements

Thanks and a big hug to Byrna Barclay, Pat Krause, Dave Margoshes and Robert Currie, and also to Barbara Kahan, for your constant faith in my writing and your consistent and insistent critiques. Without Byrna's generous push and Dave's outright bullying, these stories might not have ever made it off of my desk. Thanks to Sandra Birdsell for being a great mentor, and to Edna Alford for your expert advice on the writing and on the place. A tip of the hat to the Poets' Coterie – Kim Morrissey, Bill Klebeck, Craig Grant, Allan Barr, Lorne Kulak, Susan Andrews Grace and Charlie Taylor – for your never-flagging friendship, and for forgiving me for writing non-poetry. Thank you, Douglas Glover, for your sage advice and guidance. And thanks to J. Jill Robinson for the editing adventure, Nik Burton for your calm in the face of every storm. This book was thirty years in the making. It's been fun being on this road with you, my friends.

About the Author

Brenda Niskala's novella *Of All the Ways to Die* was published in 2009; her short stories have appeared in several anthologies and literary journals. Her poetry has been published in chap-books, the co-authored *Open 24 Hours*, and collected in *Ambergris Moon*. *For the Love of Strangers* is her first book of short fiction.

Brenda has taught Creative Writing for the University of Regina Extension Department, the Festival of Words and the Sage Hill Writing Experience Teen Camp. She has read her work to audiences across Canada, in Finland and England. Saskatchewan born and raised, she currently makes her home in Regina.